I0771056

AÏDES THE UNSEEN

HEATHER LONG

For the ones who remember —
the truth beneath the tale,
the woman behind the warning,
the love behind the ruin.
May we always find new ways to tell old stories—
and still make them sing.

FOREWORD

Dear Reader,

Thank you for picking up *Aïdes The Unseen*—my reimagining of the myth of Hades and Persephone. If you've known me for any length of time, it probably won't surprise you to hear that I've long been captivated by Greek mythology. There's something timeless in those old stories—their grandeur, their grit, and above all, their humanity. They may wear the faces of gods and monsters, but at their core, these myths are always about us: our frailty, our flaws, our longings, and our love.

This particular tale... it consumed me.

Hades and Persephone have always stood apart in my mind—not just for the darkness and desire, but for the ambiguity, the duality, the *questions* that remain unanswered. Is it abduction or awakening? Power or partnership? Love or longing? Or all of it, tangled together like vines creeping toward sunlight and shadow alike?

When I finally sat down to write this, I thought I'd struggle to find the voice. Instead, the story poured out of me—lush, lyrical, and insistent as if a gift from the muses themselves. As if they had been waiting for me. As if the tale wanted to be told, and I was only the vessel. The language came with it—flowery in places, perhaps, poetic even—but it felt right. It felt *theirs*.

So now, I invite you to join me. Pull up a chair. Settle in. Let the fire crackle low, and the world fall away for a while.

This is a story of love and loss, of descent and return, of two souls—god and goddess, shadow and spring—finding each other over and over again across time, against fate.

And if you find echoes of your own heart in theirs, then I've done what I came here to do.

With all my love and myth-loving heart,

xoxo

Heather

PART ONE

THE BEGINNING

CHAPTER

ONE

KORE

I had always known that the world was wide. Broad enough to cradle storms and lullabies and vast enough to bloom with secrets I hadn't yet learned the shape of. That day, however, the wind held something different in its hands. Not just the scent of jasmine or the pollen-drunk murmur of bees. No, something else pulsed beneath the wildflowers and honeyed sun: a tremble, as though the earth itself had paused to breathe in.

Bare feet brushing over moss and budding crocus, I wandered from the meadows past the sun-stung edges of the forest where ivy whispered gossip to the trees. The path curved into a golden clearing where the veil between realms was soft. So soft that the air shimmered faintly, like it remembered some forgotten god had passed this way before.

Below the hill lay a mortal village. I often watched from afar: children racing with wild hair and wooden toys, old women carding wool and singing lullabies that echoed with fragments of forgotten rites. Today, a festival. Ribbons streaming from tall poles, pastries cooling on woven mats, laughter like a choir of bells.

But it was not they who held my gaze.

No. It was the stranger standing where the shadow met the sun.

I saw him before he saw me, and, even then, *I felt him.* The way the warmth recoiled around him. It wasn't fear or anger, but reverence. As if even light knew not to touch him too quickly.

He stood by the edge of the trees, dressed in simple black, his presence impossibly still in a world that moved constantly. He did not belong here. Not among laughing children and honeycakes.

Yet, he didn't look out of place.

He was quiet *power.* The kind that didn't have to speak to be obeyed.

His gaze was turned toward the humans below, unreadable. Though the sun shone bright and golden on the hillside, around him the light thinned, just slightly, like it couldn't quite reach him.

I stepped closer. The grass cushioned my feet, blooming slightly in my wake, trailing violets and small dandelions. He noticed, whether the movement or the change, I couldn't say. His head turned just a fraction, as though he'd caught the scent of something he couldn't name but could not ignore.

I stopped two paces away, heart foolish and fluttering.

"Hello," I said, sun in my voice. "You're not from around here."

His eyes met mine. They were impossibly dark, not cruel or cold, but ancient. Like they had seen the end of stars and not flinched.

He studied me. His silence was not awkward but dense, deliberate. Finally, he answered: "No."

I smiled. "You don't say much, do you?"

He looked back toward the mortals. "I do, when I'm somewhere I belong."

I tilted my head, teasing. "Do you belong here, then?"

A pause. Then, softly: "No. But you do."

He said it like it was a fact carved into the bones of the world.

I came to stand beside him, both of us watching the humans below. Their joy was loud, warm, oblivious. None of them looked toward us.

"They don't see us," I said, mostly to myself.

"I'm shielding them," he replied. "It's... easier for them. Mortals have never done well under the gaze of gods."

I turned to face him fully. "You care if they're afraid?"

His jaw twitched, but not with annoyance. "I care about the weight of fear. It binds too tightly. I don't come here to burden."

"What *do* you come for?"

He hesitated. Then, "I heard laughter, and I was curious."

I laughed, soft and light as a petal falling. "So the god of the Underworld follows laughter into the sun."

His expression didn't change, but there was something, a shift, subtle as the way shadows lengthen in late afternoon.

"I'm not what they call me," he murmured, and there was an edge beneath the words. "I don't steal souls. I don't hunger for death. I keep what is lost. I remember what the world forgets."

My heart ached, not from pity, but from recognition.

"I'm Kori," I said. "Kore, if you want the name my

mother uses when she's angry or proud. Goddess of spring. Joy in bloom. Life with a heartbeat."

He looked at me, and something in his gaze softened. Like he hadn't expected the world to smile at him and mean it.

"*Aïdes*," he said, the name folding in on itself like dusk wrapping over twilight. "Some call me Hades."

I offered my hand. It glowed faintly in the places where my fingertips brushed sunlight. "Well, Aïdes," I said, voice playful, "since you've come all this way for laughter, you might as well stay and enjoy it properly."

He looked at my hand like it was a secret too beautiful to trust. Then slowly, almost reverently, he took it.

Our fingers met, opposites in every sense. Heat and cold. Bloom and decay. But not fighting.

Fitting.

Around us, the light didn't retreat, nor did it dominate. It shifted, dappled, folding around us as if it had no choice but to find a way for both of us to exist in the same breath.

When I looked up at him, really looked, I saw not death, not shadow, and not the dread king painted by trembling myths.

I saw the man who walked into the sun without a crown, seeking only the sound of joy.

And I wondered—*dangerously, deliciously*—what would happen if he ever looked at me like I was joy itself.

The humans laughed and danced below, unaware that the seasons had shifted in a way no equinox could measure.

Spring had touched shadow.

Twilight softened the world.

It always did. That liminal hour when everything—colors, thoughts, even time—felt more fluid. Where shadows stretched long and slow across the grass, and the sky flushed like it was shy to let go of the day.

I didn't leave.

Neither did he.

We wandered, not down to the village, but sideways through the meadows, past the murmuring creek that still remembered my childhood footsteps. The mortal songs drifted faintly through the air, distant and golden, but here, it was only us. Stillness wrapped around us, not awkward, not heavy.

Comfortable. *Curious.*

"I didn't expect you to walk," I said after a while. "I thought Death rode chariots made of bone and fire."

He glanced at me. That ghost of a smile tugged at the corner of his mouth again, as if it had long since forgotten how to fully bloom. "That's what they say. You'd be amazed how much humans invent about me. The truth is more... ordinary."

"Ordinary?" I raised a brow. "You don't feel ordinary."

He looked ahead, into the softening mist that edged the trees. "Power isn't the same as presence."

A thoughtful silence followed.

"I'm not used to being seen," he added, voice quieter now. More *intimate.* "Most mortals only sense me when they're dying. Or mourning. And gods... well, most avoid me entirely. Unless they want something."

I turned to face him, walking backwards with a smile that curled like a vine around a fencepost. "Well, I don't want anything."

"Don't you?" he asked.

I stopped.

There was no accusation in his tone. Just a careful curiosity. A question asked by someone who'd spent eternity offering silence instead of demand.

"I came because I felt something," I admitted. "Something strange. Like a thread pulled tight through the roots."

"That was me," he said, matter-of-fact. "Or part of me. I wasn't trying to call you."

"Maybe not," I said softly, "but something called."

He paused, then gestured toward a fallen tree near the water's edge. We sat, and the moment he settled beside me, the grass stopped growing. I noticed the stillness around him immediately, the absence of life, not destructive but... *final.* Like a book gently closed.

"You're quiet for someone so full of noise," he murmured after a long while.

"Noise?" I laughed. "You mean joy?"

"I mean *light.* It dances off you."

I flushed. Gods didn't usually blush. But it wasn't his words so much as it was the way he said them. As if he didn't know how to make things beautiful, but couldn't help noticing when they were.

I shifted closer. "Is it hard?" I asked. "Being the place everything ends?"

He didn't answer immediately. The creek babbled nearby, catching the light like it wanted to show off for me.

"It's lonely," he said. "But not because it's dark. Because it's... misread. Misnamed."

"What would you name yourself, if you could choose?"

He turned his head, eyes meeting mine under the breathless hush of dusk. "Keeper. Not taker. Guardian. Not god."

A silence stretched between us. This time, I didn't fill it with laughter.

"I don't think I'm what they say I am, either," I whispered. "They think I'm just the bloom. The newness. But no one asks what I become after the flowers wilt."

He looked at me for a long time, really looked.

"You keep growing," he said. "That's what you do."

"I wither too," I replied. "Everything that grows must. Even joy."

He didn't flinch. "Then maybe we're not so different."

Our hands rested beside each other on the fallen tree. Not touching. But close enough that I could feel the pull, the *tension* between warmth and cool, bloom and stone.

"I should go," I said, though I didn't stand.

"I won't stop you."

But he didn't want me to go. I could feel that truth, low and quiet in the earth between us.

"I'll come back," I said.

"You shouldn't promise gods things," he warned, but there was no real threat in it. Just a sadness that felt older than temples.

"I'm not promising a god," I said, my voice like the hush before a kiss. "I'm promising *you*."

Then, for just a breath, he leaned closer, his hand brushing mine.

Just that.

But it felt like the whole world inhaled.

A crackle in the thread between us, a spark not of fire but of *recognition*. The moment before the seed breaks open beneath the soil. Quiet. Sacred. Irrevocable.

Night came gently. The first stars rose like offerings.

Somewhere in the space between what we were and what we might become, I smiled.

So did he.

It had been days. Sunrises and sunsets blurring together as time marched on, unyielding.

The petals on the almond trees had opened and fallen, the crocus had faded to saffron threads, and the bees had started their slow waltz toward the lavender fields. Spring moved, always; it didn't stop for anyone. Not even me.

Yet I found myself... *waiting.*

For a shadow at the edge of a sunbeam. For silence to feel like *him.*

I told no one.

Not my mother, who would have noticed the way my laughter had turned quiet around the edges. Not the other sprites and nymphs who danced in groves and painted the sky with birdsong, because they wouldn't have understood. This was mine.

He was mine.

Was he only a passing curiosity? A pull, not a promise.

I wasn't sure. It wouldn't explain the way the light leaned differently now. The way I found myself walking the paths he'd walked before. Listening for footsteps no one else could hear.

Then one dusk, when the air tasted like endings, I found him waiting beneath the yew trees.

He said nothing at first.

I didn't need him to.

"Is it time?" I asked.

He studied me. Eyes the color of what the world hides —deep, endless, aching.

"It's never time," he said quietly. "But I'll show you, if you want to see."

Anticipation threaded through my veins and I nodded. "I do."

He didn't ask *why*. That was one of the things I liked about him, he didn't try to name what I didn't offer. He only held space for it.

He held out his hand. I took it.

It was cooler than mine, yet it didn't feel like death. It felt like stillness. Like the hush between heartbeats. Like something waiting to become.

The world shifted.

No thunder. No shattering sky. Just the softest blink, and then, the forest was gone.

We stood at the threshold of a vast cavern, its entrance hidden behind a waterfall of mist and falling stars. The air changed first. Heavier, not oppressive, but solemn. Holy, in a strange and unspoken way.

"This is the path down," he said. "There are faster ways. But I thought you might want to... *see*."

Oh, I did. I really, really did. I smiled at him. "Show me *everything*."

The descent was long, but not painful. Every step felt like shedding light, sound, even breath. Spring still clung to me in flecks of pollen and warmth, but it grew quieter the deeper we went. Not dimmer. Just *calmer*.

There were no torches. No need. The cavern lit itself with a gentle light that pulsed from the walls. It was subtle, like the last glow of sunset before it disappears.

He showed me the Meadow of Echoes first.

"This is where the names go," he said.

Not souls. Not people. *Names.*

Sure enough, I saw them: threads of glowing script floating through the mist, some curling into one another, some fading gently as though exhaled. They shimmered and whispered and sometimes cried out, not in pain, but in longing.

"The world forgets," Aïdes said, watching them. "I don't."

I touched one. It trembled and hummed my own name back to me. It felt like holding an old lullaby. The whispering stroke of Kore teased me.

We moved on.

"The Vigil Hall," he murmured before leading me through a chamber of stone statues. They weren't carved, rather they had *formed*. As if the memories themselves had sculpted the statues. Each figure stood in stillness, not mourning, but waiting. Some with tears carved into their cheeks. Others with laughter half caught in stone. None forgotten.

"They chose to stay," he said. "To remember. Or to be remembered."

"Are they trapped?" I asked.

"No," he answered. "Just... *resting*. Some wait for the ones they loved. Others just wanted to matter somewhere."

Still, he led me deeper.

I don't know how long we walked. Time folded strangely here, more a dream you forget in pieces as you wake. Light had no source. Air had no direction. It was a realm of pulse and pause. I began to understand why mortals feared death. Not because it was cruel, but because it was unknowable.

We moved in silence, but not the hollow kind. It was the hush of snowfall in the woods. Aïdes did not explain every place we passed. He only spoke when I lingered or when I reached for meaning he was willing to give.

We came to the Hollow of Wings.

The chamber opened wide and round, a great black

dome overhead that shimmered with movement. I thought they were spirits at first. Then I realized they were birds. Pale, translucent, gliding in endless, soundless circles. Souls, perhaps, untethered from form. Unnamed. Unburdened.

"Do they wait for rebirth?" I asked.

"No," he said. "They wait for the will to want it."

There was something breathtaking in that. The idea that even in death, choice remained. I didn't speak again until we left the soundless fluttering behind.

Next came the Grove of the First Grief.

It looked like a forest petrified in mourning. The trees were tall and black-barked, their silver leaves dripping not with dew, but tears—liquid sorrow, suspended. I reached out to one tree, curious, and the moment my fingers met the bark, I felt it.

Grief. Not mine. Someone else's. A flood of sorrow so raw and unspoken it pulled the breath from my chest. I gasped, but didn't pull away.

"You don't have to take it," Aïdes said quietly. "You only need to witness."

I nodded, but I kept my hand there and thought of all the things we push down just to keep walking.

Then the Garden of Forgotten Joys.

I recognized it before he spoke the name. Even in shadow, it bloomed. Violets, honeysuckle, hyacinth. Flowers that shouldn't have thrived here. The air was thick with sweetness, but not cloying. Laughter hung like light between petals, laughter that didn't belong to me, and yet I felt it in my chest.

"These are joys no one was allowed to have," he said. "Dreams unfulfilled. Love unspoken. Lives that never made room for happiness."

Tears pricked my eyes from the ache of *almost*. I let the petals brush my fingertips and thought: *I could stay here forever.* But I didn't.

The path twisted, and we reached the Furnace of Oaths.

A stark chamber. Stone walls scorched black, though no flame touched them now. In the center, fire danced without heat, but there was no mistaking the existence here. It was a flame that knew.

"What burns here?" I asked.

"Promises. Lies. Words that can't be taken back."

I looked into the fire and saw pieces of myself—truths I wasn't ready to speak, truths I wasn't ready to accept. I stepped back. My hand brushed Aïdes' sleeve, and I didn't apologize.

He took me to the Mirrorway.

A narrow corridor lined with mirrors, each one taller than a man and framed in obsidian. I looked into the first and saw myself—not as I was, but as I *could have been.* Laughing in a garden. Crownless. Unchanged.

The second showed me as I am, aware, shadowed, and a little lonely. That image humbled me. The third seemed to be what I might become if I stayed too long here.

"You shouldn't look too deeply," Aïdes warned. "Some forget which reflection is theirs."

Still, I touched the glass. My own eyes stared back at me. I wasn't sure which version they belonged to.

We passed next into the Chamber of Quiet Sleep.

Beds—hundreds, thousands—lined the vast room, each one shaped from smoke and soft stone, cradled in fog. Souls lay sleeping, not restless, but complete.

"They don't wake?" I whispered.

"Not unless they choose to," he said. "Some lives are too full of ache. This is their peace."

I wanted to kneel. To bless them. But it didn't feel right. This was *his* sanctum. His mercy. Not mine.

And then, the River of Once.

It was narrow, more a stream than a river, winding through the rock like a silver thread. The water shimmered strangely, as if it remembered light but hadn't seen it in a long time.

"What flows here?" I asked.

"Memories," he said. "Ones willingly surrendered. Touch it, and you'll remember something you didn't know you'd forgotten. But only once. Then it's gone."

I knelt beside it. Let one finger trail through the current.

A memory bloomed: my mother's hands in my hair, humming a song I hadn't thought of in centuries. The warmth of it broke me open. Then it was gone.

I didn't cry. But I pressed my hand to my chest for a long time afterward.

At last, we reached the quietest place of all: the Passage of the Unnamed.

No grandeur. Just a long, narrow hall filled with endless rows of candles, flickering softly. Each flame was a soul who'd never been named aloud. Children lost before their first breath. The murdered. The forgotten. The unseen.

I stopped walking. Lit a single candle. I didn't know for whom.

Maybe it didn't matter.

Aïdes knelt beside one flame that had guttered to almost nothing. He cupped his hand around it until it steadied. He didn't say a word. That was his offering.

Mine was silence, too. Eventually, we reached the final chamber.

There was no grandeur to it.

No throne. No crown. No fire.

Just a garden.

Underground.

It shouldn't have been possible, but it was. Pale blossoms, white as bone, bloomed from black soil. Vines curled up stone pillars. Water, dark and clear, dripped from stalactites into a small, moonlit pool.

"I made this," he said simply.

I turned to him, breath caught somewhere in my throat. "For yourself?"

A slow nod. "Even death needs beauty."

I knelt beside a flower and let it brush my fingertips. It didn't bloom brighter in my presence. It didn't need to. It was already whole.

"I think I understand now," I said.

He knelt beside me. "Do you?"

I turned to him. The space between us was no longer an emptiness. It was an invitation.

"I thought I was the goddess of beginnings," I said. "But beginnings mean nothing without endings. We're... halves, aren't we?"

His gaze darkened, not with anger, but something almost too tender to look at directly.

"Not halves," he said, his voice low. "Mirrors."

The word settled in my chest like a seed.

I don't know how long we stayed in that garden. Long enough that even the silence seemed to grow petals. And when we finally rose, he led me gently, quietly, back toward the world above.

At the threshold, where twilight once again bled into spring, he paused.

"This is where I leave you."

I turned, startled. "You're not coming with me?"

"I don't belong there."

"What if I want you to?"

He looked at me then like I was the last secret left in the world.

"I would come," he said, simply. "But not as a god. As a guest."

I hesitated.

He saw it. He felt it.

"You don't have to decide now," he said. "You can go. You can grow. This doesn't have to be a beginning."

"But it already is," I whispered.

He smiled.

Not the ghost of one.

A real one.

Small. Quiet. Beautiful.

I stepped back into the sunlight, and the world rushed to meet me. Warmth, birdsong, life blooming at my feet.

And yet...

I turned, but the cavern was already gone. A hollow in the earth, filled with echoes and roots. *He* was gone.

The question hung like dusk on my lips. Would I see him again?

A part of me wanted to go back to the hollow, to see if the cavern would open for me once more. Before I could act on it, though, I felt it. Felt *her*.

A soft thread, taut and golden, pulling at the edge of my being.

Kore.

My mother's voice, no louder than a breath, but filled with warning.

I swallowed the garden whole in my silence. Hid every shadow-laced memory like a pressed flower inside my ribs.

I didn't answer her.

Not yet.

CHAPTER
TWO

KORE

When I stepped out of the wood, the land around me bloomed, releasing a breath held too long.

My mother was already walking the fields, her feet bare, her arms open. Vines coiled toward her like children rushing to greet her. She didn't call for me, not aloud. She never did. But her joy rose in the barley and the wheat, in the fruit trees waking too fast, in the gardens bursting out of their own roots.

I stepped back into that abundance with the certainty of someone slipping into an old garment. Everything fit, but something felt different. Tighter, maybe. A little too warm at the collar.

She met me with open arms. "Kore," she said, soft as summer wind. "Kore."

I let her hold me. I even smiled. She smelled of grain and sunlight, as she always had, and her hands were stained golden from the fig harvest. But I kept my eyes low. I didn't want her looking too closely.

"You're thinner," she said, brushing a curl from my forehead. "Did you sleep at all?"

"Time felt strange," I answered, which was not quite a lie. She hummed and didn't press, but the pause lingered between us like mist refusing to burn off.

We worked together for a time. The new season needed tending. She walked with the ease of someone returning to herself, her laughter like wind across ripe fields. Wherever she touched, the crops grew fuller, bloomed stronger. I followed beside her, quiet, careful. I was not less than I had been. Still, I had learned something of silence. This silence, once known, had become a companion.

I thought she might ask about where I'd been and about whom I'd met. But she didn't. Not directly. Instead, she said things like, "Your color's different," or, "You used to hum more."

I nodded. I smiled. I bent to gather the wheat.

Because this was not the time to tell her anything she wasn't asking. Not when the humans were coming with their offerings.

They brought bread still warm from their ovens. Grapes laid in woven baskets. Pears from early trees. Even jars of honey, tucked between sprigs of mint and thyme. Children carried small bowls of beans and garden squash, shy in their giving, while their mothers whispered prayers into the wind.

"To the Mother of All," they said. "To the Bringer of Harvest."

They didn't look at me. I didn't expect that either. Instead, I stayed by her side as they piled up the harvest's generosity. The drinking and revelry would last into the night. Dionysus would appear before too long. Mother would share the bounty with him.

Still as the humans continued to come, I weaved the wheat stalks absently. At first, I thought I was making a wreath, but it was too small. Eventually, my mother looked at the creation in my hands with pure delight.

"For me?" The question held the shimmer of love and surprise.

"Of course," I answered her, because they were the only words that would satisfy. She dipped her head so I could place the crown woven from golden wheat upon her head. She positively glowed, the warmth radiated from her and spilled over onto the celebrants.

It was a good sign that the first harvest was so plentiful.

A very good sign.

As the sun dipped low, the fields did not quiet. They pulsed.

The golden hour spilled out into something looser, warmer. Children fell asleep curled beneath fig trees, their mothers swaying in time to reed pipes and hand drums. Men passed amphorae between them, laughing with wet eyes. A group had gathered to dance—barefoot, flushed, pulling each other into spirals until the dust rose in clouds and clung to their skin like pollen.

I stayed at the edge, half in the shadows of the olive grove. My hands were sticky with crushed apricot. My mouth tasted of honeyed wine. The warmth didn't bother me, not even as the air thickened with sweat and sweetness.

Then Hermes appeared beside me, as he so often did, not arriving so much as just simply being *there*.

"Missed you earlier," he said, biting into a pear he

hadn't held a moment ago. "Did you come with the season or just behind it?"

"With it," I said. "More or less."

"Time's slippery like that." He chewed thoughtfully. "Everything's late and early, depending who's watching."

He said it casually, but his eyes flicked toward mine. I didn't answer the unspoken question hanging in the air. I just looked out at the dancers.

A new rhythm had taken hold of the music. Lower, dirtier. Feet stomped harder. Someone laughed too loud and stumbled into the firelight. Lovers pulled each other into the long grass with little ceremony, no pretense. The sounds of coupling joined the beat, moaning, panting, the rustle of limbs and breath tangled together.

"Ah," Hermes said, licking juice from his fingers. "There it is."

"What?"

"Fertility," he said. "In all its forms."

Then came Dionysus.

You always knew when he was close. The air ripened, wine-heavy, soft-edged. He walked in crowned with ivy, his eyes alight, his skin glowing like he'd never been anything but full of joy. The mortals rushed to greet him, no fear in their bodies, only delight and fever.

They poured wine over into their goblets, onto the ground, and into each other's mouths. Someone brought out a tambourine. Another woman stripped naked, wreathed herself in poppies, and began to chant.

"He's been invited," Hermes said, nodding toward the makeshift stage they'd built from crates and woven rugs. "There's a play."

The actors stumbled into place as the sun gave up its last breath and slid behind the hills. Torches flared. The people cheered. This was no tragedy, not tonight. It was bawdy, vulgar, ecstatic. A tale of drunken gods and seduced mortals, of mistaken identities and divine mischief. Dionysus laughed the loudest, throwing a handful of figs at one of the actors mid-line.

Hermes leaned toward me, his breath cool despite the heat all around. "You should try laughing more."

"I do," I said. "When no one's watching."

"Ah," he mused. "One of those laughs."

I looked at the stage again. Dionysus had taken a seat on a wine barrel, surrounded by girls who didn't care whose god he was, only that he was beautiful and alive. He let them touch him. He kissed one on the mouth and pulled her into his lap without missing a beat of the clapping.

My mother was gone by then. Back among the wheat, maybe. She might have already returned to her temple where the offerings waited in neat rows—loaves and fruit and tokens carved from wood. She had accepted the mortals' reverence. She had blessed them. She would rest well without pulling me with her, a true sign of her contentment with the day's harvest.

But I remained in the dark, beside Hermes, watching the mortals dance themselves raw.

"They think it's all for her," I murmured.

"Isn't it?" he asked.

I turned the pit of a plum over in my hand. "Part of it."

He grinned. "You're learning."

The play ended in a tangle of laughter and limbs, with one actor passed out and another pretending to give birth to a goat.

The crowd roared their approval. Dionysus stood, raised his cup, and toasted no one in particular. Then the first bonfire was lit.

It caught like it had been waiting—dry pinewood snapping, sparks rushing upward like spirits returning to the sky. More fires followed, dotted across the field like constellations turned inside out.

That's when they came.

The dryads slipped from the olive trees, pale green and willowy, their eyes wide and gleaming. Nymphs danced barefoot from the riverbanks, wet hair glistening. A few sprites buzzed in on wings too small for their bodies, but full of laughter, flower-faced and bright. The mortals barely paused, too deep in their revelry to question the guests who shimmered slightly when they moved. Tonight, the veil was thin. That was enough.

One dryad took a young farmer's hand and pulled him into the ring of dancers. A water nymph stole a girl's necklace and fled giggling, only to be chased into the reeds. The celebration had begun to tip toward the wild, the sacred, the dangerous.

Then the music changed.

It started with a single string, plucked just once—perfect, clear, sunshot. Then a second note followed, then a cascade like water poured over marble. The revelers stilled as he stepped into the firelight, golden as the dawn, a lyre in his arms.

Apollo.

He wore a crown of laurel and arrogance, and he walked like the ground loved him. His smile cut through the night like a blade of polished bronze.

"Ah," Hermes muttered beside me. "The god of subtle entrances."

Apollo didn't look at him. He looked at *me*.

"Kore," he said, and my name in his mouth was softer

than I'd expected. "You glow with the season, and still, everything bends toward you."

I didn't move.

He strummed once more. "Let me offer you a song," he said. "No riddles. No prophecy. Just music."

Hermes scoffed under his breath. "So, a lie, then."

Apollo glanced sideways. "Must you always be the mosquito at the feast?"

"I live to irritate," Hermes said with a shrug. "It's one of my more honest traits."

Apollo turned back to me, his voice a little lower. "Spring is always yours, but even the sun would turn in its course to warm your feet."

I met his gaze. His beauty was absolute, crafted and distant. He was poetry without the flaw that makes it human. It was not the kind of beauty I wanted anymore.

"I'm already warm," I said.

He faltered for half a beat. Then he smiled, gracious in his retreat. "Then let the rest listen." And he began to play.

The mortals circled close again, caught in the melody, their eyes reflecting firelight and longing. Lovers leaned together. One nymph wept. Even the fig trees seemed to lean in, heavy with fruit and listening.

Beside me, Hermes sat on a flat stone, swirling a fig leaf in a half-empty cup of wine. "He really doesn't do well with *no*," he said.

I watched Apollo's hands on the strings, the light in his hair, the perfection of his face. Nothing within me stirred.

"No," I said softly. "He doesn't."

I kept the rest of my thoughts a secret. Apollo was not the one I missed.

The mead was thick and golden, laced with crushed petals and herbs that numbed the tongue and warmed the throat. Hermes refilled my cup without asking. His own was already empty. He drank like someone who never worried about the cost.

"Do you see her?" he said, nodding toward a mortal girl wrapped in violet-dyed linen, weaving through the dancers with the grace of a hunted deer. "She's run from three suitors tonight. One was a blacksmith with hands like tree bark. Another was a poet who tried to win her with a poem he definitely stole from Hesiod. The third—ah, that one's a mystery. She whispered his name to a tree and then bit the bark until it bled."

I raised an eyebrow. "And you know this how?"

"I'm terribly observant," he said, grinning. "Also, the tree told me."

The libations made me warm enough to laugh, a soft thing. The world shimmered around us: smoke from the fires curling upward in blue spirals, the nymphs gliding like mist between the dancers, and the sky above smeared with stars.

"Now, that boy," Hermes went on, pointing with his cup, "thinks he's descended from Poseidon. He's not. But he's convinced a girl from the coast he can breathe underwater. He's never seen the sea."

"And that one?" I asked, tipping my chin toward a reed-thin man with a crooked nose and three lovers hanging on him.

"Oh, that's one of mine," Hermes said smugly. "Born with his fingers crossed. He'll sell his grandmother for a good joke and a better lie."

Apollo's music threaded through it all, light, aching, full of restrained beauty. It wound around the revelers like ivy, pulling them in, making their joy seem deeper than it was. I could feel his attention drifting toward me again, delicate and constant. He was playing for everyone, but his thoughts were not communal. They tickled at me like a breeze behind my ear.

Why don't you look at me?

Because I know what you want, and I will not give it. The cup in my hand was nearly empty when I felt a shift—not in the music, not in the revelry, but in the air around us. It was the way space clears before a quiet truth enters the room.

Hephaestus came without torchlight or flourish. No ivy crown or perfume of divine roses. Just the smell of forge smoke, oil, and iron. His steps were uneven, slow, and honest. He moved through the dancers like someone used to not being seen.

But I saw him.

He glanced my way, once, and then looked away quickly. As if it had been a mistake.

I moved aside on the low stone bench without speaking, patting the space between Hermes and me. He hesitated. Then sat, careful and quiet, his broad hands resting on his knees.

"Evening," Hermes said. "You're late."

"I was working," Hephaestus said, his voice low and rough like stones settling in a riverbed. "Didn't realize the night had started."

"Time's a liar," Hermes said cheerfully. "But the mead's still good."

Hephaestus nodded. I poured him a cup.

We sat like that for a while—the three of us. The beautiful music carried on. The fires crackled. Laughter rose and fell like wind in wheat. Somewhere behind us, someone screamed in pleasure or madness or both.

Hephaestus sipped his honeyed drink slowly.

"You've been missed," I said softly.

He didn't look at me. "Most people don't notice when I'm gone."

"I do."

The words surprised even me.

Hermes said nothing, but I could feel his smile. Not mocking. Just pleased.

The forge god gave a quiet grunt, the closest thing to gratitude I think he could manage. His shoulder brushed mine slightly. It was solid. Real. Not golden or glowing. Just comfortable and steady.

I liked it more than I expected.

The mead dulled the edges of the firelight. Or maybe the fire itself had softened, grown contemplative like the music.

Hephaestus sat beside me, not fidgeting, not trying to charm. Just being. It was a rare kind of comfort, divine, but undemanding.

"You don't come to these often," I said, watching the play of gold on his forearms. They were marked with burns and soot, rings of dark where the forge kissed him too closely.

He shrugged, a quiet roll of thick shoulders. "They're not built for me."

"Maybe they should be."

He huffed. "You're kind."

"No," I said, meeting his gaze. "I'm observant." At the echo of his earlier words, Hermes grinned.

The god of the forge, however, gave me a look like he was testing whether to believe that. Then, after a long moment, he said, "I like the quiet in your voice. Most gods talk like they're echoing their own names."

"Even you?"

"Especially me," he said, smiling faintly. "When I was younger."

I glanced across the field. Apollo was still playing, but slower now. His music curved in on itself, introspective. Dionysus had vanished somewhere into the dark with a trail of followers. The revelry had dipped into that strange lull that comes before either sleep or something sharper.

"I used to think quiet was emptiness," I said. "But now I think it just needs time to settle."

"That sounds like something Hades would say," Hermes chimed in from his spot, spinning an olive pit between two fingers. At my glance, he winked, all teeth. "Don't worry. I'm only listening with half an ear."

Hephaestus chuckled once—a dry, warm sound—and leaned forward to stoke the fire in front of us with the end of his hammer, which he'd tucked at his side like most people would carry a satchel.

"I've never seen you outside of spring," he said.

"This is what they want me to be," I answered. "Bright. Blooming. Harmless." Spring would come soon, this was the harvest. In the misty dawn of another sunrise or two, it would be my time again.

"Are you not?" The soot-streaked man studied me.

I didn't answer. The peace between us felt too good to disturb it with the troubling direction of my thoughts. Then the fire nearest us flared too high, too fast. Hermes straightened. Hephaestus turned his head.

The drums had stopped. A ripple passed through the field, one of those shifts that lives in instinct, not sight. Even the dryads paused.

I smelled metal before I saw him, all iron and blood, leather and heat. Ares stepped from the smoke like a storm made flesh. No armor. Just skin. Just strength. He scanned the crowd, choosing where to start.

Conversations died in his wake.

He didn't smile. He didn't acknowledge anyone. His eyes passed over Hermes, skipped Apollo, paused—briefly—on me. Then lingered on Hephaestus. The hush wasn't reverent. It was braced. Hephaestus didn't flinch. He sat tall, hands still folded around his cup.

Hermes gave a low whistle. "Well. Now it's a party."

I looked to Hephaestus. "Will there be trouble?"

He didn't answer. Just stared into the fire and said, "That depends on who he came for."

I rose to greet him because not doing so would've felt like a challenge.

"Ares," I said, folding my hands before me. "The revel burns brighter now."

He stopped just shy of the fire's glow, his chest rising slow and deliberate. His eyes were the color of polished war bronze, and when they locked on mine, I felt them not just on my skin—but beneath it.

"Kore," he said, not smiling. "You wear spring like a veil. Does it ever feel like armor?"

I didn't answer. Not with words. I let the stillness in me speak.

He turned his gaze then, slowly, toward the silent god of the forge sitting next to me.The air drew tighter, as though the night itself had taken a breath it didn't want to release.

Hephaestus didn't stand. He didn't move. He just looked up at the god of war with something that wasn't fear but wasn't peace either. A kind of resigned steadiness, like a mountain knowing the storm has come.

To his credit, the god of messengers, thieves, and

cunning didn't vanish or interrupt. Not yet. But I could feel his presence lean slightly forward, his grin sharpened into readiness.

"I came to see what you've been forging," Ares said to Hephaestus, voice quiet, dangerous in its ease. "You've been underground too long. Makes a man forget the sun or beauty—or softness."

"I remember them," Hephaestus replied, low and even. "I just know better than to worship them."

A flicker passed through Ares' jaw. Not quite anger. Something older. He took a step closer, and the fire between them hissed.

Hermes muttered, "Gods save us, someone give them both something to punch."

I moved between them, not directly or foolishly, just enough to draw Ares' eyes back to me. "You didn't come for the play."

"I don't enjoy theater," he murmured, his voice softer now. "But I do enjoy watching people wear masks." His eyes traced my face as if he could see something hidden under the surface. I held his gaze. I would not step back.

Then, with a flicker of mischief or, more likely, madness, Hermes clapped his hands and declared, "Who wants figs? I've got a basket of indecently ripe ones, and I'm not afraid to bribe a war god with dessert."

It worked.

The tension cracked, just a hairline fracture, but it was enough. Some of the breath came back into the firelight, into the crowd nearby. Ares blinked, then looked to Hermes with the faintest snort of amusement.

"Keep him leashed," he said, nodding toward Hephaestus. "Or I will." Then he turned back to me, and his smile appeared—slow, unsettling, a blade dipped in honey. "I hope the turning doesn't soften you too much, Kore," he said. "You're too lovely to be broken. But beauty doesn't stop blades, does it?" He took one step closer, close enough that I could smell blood and myrrh, and bent his head just slightly toward mine. "Call me if the forge ever grows too cold."

Then he was gone. No flourish, no flare. Just absence, swift and sudden, like a weapon withdrawn.

I exhaled, not realizing until then that I'd been holding the air in my lungs like a shield.

Hermes handed me a fig, solemnly.

"God of war," he said, "still doesn't know how to read a room."

Hephaestus hadn't moved.

"Are you well?" I asked.

"Yes, I always am," he said, voice even, but the edge in it was hammered sharp.

We sat again, the three of us. The fire crackled. The music had stuttered to silence. But the night, it seemed, had remembered what else it could become.

The fires burned low behind me. Laughter echoed faintly, already fading.

I walked toward the temple, where offerings would sleep in baskets by the altar, and the marble would still be warm from the day's sun. The air had cooled, touched with dew and a hush that felt almost sacred.

Hermes strolled beside me, hands in his sleeves, humming something tuneless.

"You don't have to follow me," I said softly.

"Who said I'm following?" he replied. "I'm just walking. Coincidentally in the same direction."

I glanced at him, and he gave me that half-grin—easy, quicksilver. But he didn't press. For once, his silence felt like a kindness. The path wound through olive trees, silver leaves fluttering like coins overhead. Crickets sang. A moth passed close to my face, its wings the color of ash.

"Did you enjoy yourself?" Hermes asked, finally.

I considered the question. "I watched. I listened. I was part of it, and not," I said. "Like a statue someone dressed in flowers." It was how I often felt.

"Sounds familiar," he said, tilting his head toward the moon. "You can always tell the real gods from the ones that like to perform being gods."

I smiled faintly. "What about you?"

"I perform so well I forget who I am most days," he said, with a wink. "But you? You're starting to know. That's the difference."

I let his words settle, dust floating on water.

The night had been so many things, ripe with joy and danger, full of beauty and threats wrapped in silk and honey. Apollo's music still echoed in my bones. Ares' voice still lingered at the back of my neck. Hephaestus' warmth sat beside my own, like coals that hadn't quite gone out.

And yet... none of them held me.

I was Kore, maiden of spring, daughter of the harvest. But the girl who returned from the dark was not the same one who had entered it. I had stood between revel and war. I had not broken.

The temple rose ahead, white and still in the night. My mother's being pulsed inside it, steady, vast, undeniable.

Hermes stopped walking.

"You're not coming in?"

He shook his head. "Too many expectations in there."

I nodded. "Thank you, then."

"For what?"

"For walking *near* me," I said.

He laughed, soft and genuine. "Anytime." He vanished like breath from a mirror.

I climbed the last few steps alone, the stone cool beneath my feet.

Inside, the offerings waited: bread braided with herbs, apples and squash, jars of honey, bowls of beans and barley. All for her. For Demeter.

Mother.

The turning of the harvest meant soon it would be time for planting again. I wondered—not for the first time—when they would start leaving offerings for me. Did I even want them to do that?

CHAPTER

THREE

The planting season always began with rain.

Not the kind that storms or threatens, but rather softens the skin of the world. It was petal-warm and silver-laced, quiet as a lullaby hummed into earth. It soaked into the soil without apology, waking seeds from their hush, urging roots to remember their shape. The air smelled green, the way only spring could: alive, becoming, more *soon* than *now*.

I liked the rain best in these first weeks. It made everything feel new again.

Already, the lambs were finding their legs, tumbling soft and wide-eyed through pastures spangled with clover. The sprites had begun weaving blooms into their hair—narcissus, crocus, snowdrop—giggling as they danced between puddles and bees. Even the trees seemed eager, lifting newborn buds toward the clouds like little offerings. The whole world shimmered with wanting.

This was my season. I loved it all.

The ache of new life. The dirt under my nails. The push and pull of sprout against stone. I wandered barefoot through fields not yet tamed, my fingers trailing over stalks just beginning to green. Everything I touched bloomed a little brighter, just enough to know I had passed through. Just enough to be loved.

My mother was meant to meet me here. She always did. This was our domain in tandem. She who made things *grow*, and I who made them *feel* it.

But today, I was alone.

She had been gone since the morning, summoned by some divine council or another. The type where tempers frayed and seasons bent if egos weren't soothed. She hadn't said when she'd return.

I didn't mind, not at first.

I liked being alone here, especially in the rain. There were no rules in solitude, no need to be *perfectly light*, perfectly joyful, perfectly Kore. The land loved me even when I was quiet.

Even when I wandered to the farthest field, where the lavender hadn't risen yet and the sky broke open in silver threads.

Even when I tilted my face to the rain and closed my eyes.

It was then I felt it.

A tremor, not rippling through the earth, but through something deeper. The kind of shift you couldn't see, only *sense*. A weight. A knowing. A certainty.

I opened my eyes.

He was there far across the field, near the edge where the flowers ended and the forest began. Standing still as a cairn, clothed in shadow and rain, he gazed at me as if he'd been watching since before I knew to look.

He did not move.

Neither did I.

The rain curved around him, just slightly. Not enough to flee, but enough to *recognize*. Like the drops knew they were falling through something older than sky. Something older than spring.

Aïdes.

Not summoned. Not expected. Not even entirely real yet. Just... appearing, like memory, like myth.

We had not seen each other since the garden below.

Twenty-three sunrises had passed, and I had almost convinced myself he had returned to forgetfulness. That I had imagined the hush in his voice when he called me mirror.

Yet, now, here, in the rain-soaked harmony of planting season, he stood again.

He did not call out. There was no need.

My feet moved before my mind did, slow steps across the damp field. The clover leaned toward me as I passed, but even they were quieter now.

Still, he didn't move while I continued to walk.

When I reached the edge of the field, close enough to see the water beading in the hollow of his throat, he finally spoke, quiet, almost hesitant.

"You're alone."

A statement. A question.

"My mother was called away," I said, voice calm, though my pulse leapt like a colt.

A pause. Rain slid off his shoulders as if this world was truly reluctant to touch him. "They usually wait for her."

"They?"

"The ones who come looking for you."

Who came looking for me? It took a moment for me to

grasp his meaning. The other divine who would come to call. Many of them waited for Mother. Not all, but most.

I tilted my head. "Are you one of them?"

He didn't answer right away. Then, very softly: "No."

Silence.

Not awkward. Not cold. But charged.

He looked like he belonged to a different season entirely. He might not be made of sun or fresh dew, more the whisper that followed the last fallen leaf, but here he was. In my season. In *my* world.

"You shouldn't be here," I said, not unkindly. More because I liked that he was here whether he *should* be or not. "This is the time of beginning."

"I know." His shadow-kissed eyes flicked to the field, where new shoots curled toward light. "That's why I came."

He looked back at me then. His expression wasn't cruel, or claiming, or even particularly bold.

It was *curious*.

Had he come to see what grew without him? Did he know how beautiful it was in the first throes of spring?

"You're different," he said after a moment.

I shrugged. "I'm always changing. That's what growing means." Mother didn't care for it. More often, she preferred that I endured as she did, ever the same, unyielding to time or experience. That it was not my nature baffled her. Often, it was easier to just pretend.

For her, anyway.

I grew tired of trying to be what I wasn't.

"I don't change," he said. "But I notice more. Since you."

My breath caught. I didn't step closer. Not yet. Instead, I let the rain fall between us like a veil. Like a question.

"What do you want, Aïdes?" I asked, more curious at his presence than anything else. Not afraid.

He tilted his head slightly. A raven might have done the same. "To see you. As you are. Not below. Not in memory. *Now.*"

Something in me wanted to bloom at that. At the same time, something else within me wanted to flee. The competing reactions threatened to strangle me. Instead, I said, "What if my mother returns?"

He stepped forward, just once. The earth stilled beneath him. Not died—*stilled*. A reverence. "Then she will find me here." His voice held no fear.

Just acceptance. My mother didn't frighten him. Nor make him wary. So many avoided her wrath, for her temper was legendary. I was one of them. Aïdes, though? He just waited for me, utterly serene. Pleasure sparked inside of me. The rain fell heavier, more like a shield around us now, rather than a barrier between.

Still, I stayed.

Why? While I didn't need a reason beyond, I wanted to stay, I recognized it was so much more. I had planted my seeds, the underworld had come to watch them grow. At my continued silence, he took a step forward and I met him halfway. The rain didn't stop, but cloaked us as though it wanted to walk with us. Without a word, I turned and began to walk. Not away, not ahead, but *with* him.

We moved through the wet fields in silence, our footsteps light against the softening earth. The new shoots didn't recoil at his nearness, just bowed slightly, as if they knew he was not their end, only their witness.

I led him first to the grove where the almond trees had begun to flower again. They were always first, their hurry much like my own. Their petals clung like blush to the branches, so delicate they looked like breath.

"This is where I first learned joy," I said softly. "Not

because of the trees. Though, they are truly lovely. No, I learned joy because I once saw a fawn take its first steps here."

He glanced at me, then back to the trees. "Did it stay?"

"No. It ran. Not because it was afraid, but because it could run." Stumbling feet, gangly legs, and a nose that quivered, yet there was something inescapably beautiful in the way it threw itself at whatever came next.

He nodded, as though he understood.

Next, the orchard. The bees were still quiet this early in the season and the rain would keep them dormant for a bit, but the blossoms were beginning, pale pink and white, soft as sighs.

"They say spring smells sweet," I said. "But it's not sweetness, really. It's hunger. The hunger of things just beginning. The world stretching back toward life."

He paused near one of the trees, laying a hand, *carefully*, I'd say almost reluctantly, against the bark. "It welcomes you."

"It's mine," I said. "I don't rule it. I *am* it."

The wind shifted, carrying the faint scent of hyacinth from farther down the path.

"Do you miss it?" I asked.

"Miss what?"

"Life. The sun. The way things bloom."

He was quiet a long time. Then: "I miss not knowing. Not having to remember everything that comes after."

We walked a little farther. He didn't hurry. Neither did I. I took the time to turn over his words, to examine them and try to understand.

I brought him to the knoll where the wildflowers always broke first. It was the most innocent of places, an accidental altar, scattered in crocus and columbine. Sprites often played here, but today it was empty. Maybe they sensed him. Maybe they made space.

"This is where I come when I don't want to be a goddess," I admitted. "Where I can pretend I'm just a girl who loves flowers."

He glanced around. "I don't think you're pretending."

I blinked at that. "You don't?"

"No. I think the world just hasn't learned to make room for both."

I looked at him then, really looked. For a moment, he wasn't the shadow who waited in silence or the keeper of sorrows. He was a man in the rain, learning the shape of spring for the first time. Then, because he was, I took him to the last place.

A grove tucked behind the hills, where the moss was thick and warm and the water from the high creek tumbled into a small, laughing pool. The goats came here sometimes. So did the sprites, when they wanted to be alone but not *lonely*.

"This is my favorite," I said, sitting down on a rock veined with old quartz. "No temples. No offerings. Just *existing*."

He sat beside me, careful not to touch.

Still, I felt him. The gravity of him. Like a low drumbeat, steady beneath the skin.

"I thought your world would be louder," he said quietly. "More singing. More laughter."

"It *is*, usually," I said with a small smile. The night of the harvest festival it had been booming. "But sometimes I need it quiet. Joy doesn't always shout."

He looked at the pool, where raindrops stitched silver rings across the surface.

"I don't know if I can belong here," he murmured.

His voice carried a melody that was both soft and somber, the calm of twilight descending over a forgotten shore. The depth of it, an ancient cadence, wrapped each word he spoke. Even the air leaned in to listen.

"You don't have to," I replied. "You're not a seed."

His gaze flicked to mine. "What am I, then?"

I tilted my head, thoughtful. "The pause between seasons. The shadow that lets light mean something."

He looked away then, but I saw it, the way his mouth curled, just barely.

"You say things like they've always been true." The dark velvet timber of his voice held a melancholic warmth that beckoned to me.

"Maybe they have," I whispered. None of it felt like a lie. "They just needed someone to say them."

For a breath, a moment that felt too full to be brief, we simply sat. The rain, the moss, the serenity of blooming things.

Then, slowly, *deliberately*, he turned his hand palm-up on the rock between us.

Not touching.

Just there.

Invitation, not command.

With care, I laid my hand over his. His skin was smooth, cool, and yet there was heat. The contact itself was quiet, infinitely gentle and almost kind.

He curved his fingers around my hand, the grip barely there but unmistakable. I blew out a long breath, relief spilling through me for what, I had no idea. Yet the connection, it echoed.

We had just agreed without words. In the distance, the first daffodils opened.

For a long time, we didn't move. The rain slowed, soft as a caress.

His hand beneath mine was still, cool and steady, like a river stone in shade. Not demanding. Not reaching. Simply *there*. Allowing. Trusting.

The quiet between us swelled, full of unnamed things. Wonder. Recognition. Something that had nothing to do with fate, and everything to do with the way stillness sometimes seemed like belonging.

Eventually, he stirred. While he didn't shift away, he gave the barest motion, enough to ask *are you ready?*

I was.

We stood.

The moss recorded our footprints. This time, when we walked, it was side by side. No path, no plan. Just the rhythm of two steps—mine light, his soundless—moving through a world that bloomed and watched.

He didn't ask where we were going. I didn't tell him. The wild knew.

We passed through the whispering grove, where the birches whispered rumors to the wind. Their silver bark gleamed wet from rain, and the sprites hidden in their boughs peeked out, curious. I felt their eyes. Felt the way the forest tried to place him in its memory.

It didn't, but it didn't reject him either. Instead, it waited. Maybe it was as curious as I was.

At a low ridge where the ground was soft with clover, I paused and knelt, brushing my fingers across the pale green. The scent of damp petals and earth filled the air.

Aïdes crouched beside me, watching. "You're not just spring," he said quietly.

I looked at him, brow lifted. "No?"

"You're hope."

A laugh caught in my throat. Not mockery. Surprise. "Is that what I look like to you?"

He shook his head. "It's not how you look. It's how things look *at* you."

Surprised, I went motionless. Even as I tasted his words, I knew he *meant* them. More, it was what he saw.

Not the petals and painted joy others praised, but the stretch beneath it. The stretch that made it beautiful. *Hope is only hope when it has something to lose.*

I sat back on my heels. "What do you see when you look at yourself?"

He didn't answer me immediately. If anything, he seemed to weigh his answer. Then: "A question. A boundary. The end of what things dare to imagine."

My chest ached with the urge to undo something I didn't know how to name. I didn't even know why, but the *need* burrowed deep.

"Then maybe that's why you're drawn to me," I said, as much searching for an answer as I was trying to offer one. "Not because I'm light. But because I *reach*."

He looked at me like he was seeing the world remade.

Not brighter.

Just possible.

Eventually, I rose and he followed me to stand. We kept walking, slow and unhurried. I showed him the lambs nestled under the thornbushes, their soft wool damp but warm. I pointed out the first blush of elderberry on the vine, the green tips of fennel pushing through mud. Every new thing, every small start, *I gave it to him.*

I rather doubted he needed any of it, but I *wanted* him to have it. We paused at a broken stone altar, this one long abandoned and overgrown with lichen. Ivy coiled through its cracks, and a wren had made her home in the hollowed center.

"No one remembers who it was built for," I said.

"But the bird remembers," he murmured.

I turned to him, caught off guard.

He met my eyes, gentle and sure. "She chose this place. Made it hers. That's what matters."

That was the moment I realized a truth so quietly devastating, it wrenched my heart: *he doesn't ask to be chosen*. Not because he didn't want to be, but because he didn't believe he could be.

So I stretched—not physically, not yet, but with something deeper. A tether, invisible and warm, reaching across the inches between us.

"You could stay," I said, voice hushed as wind in reeds.

His breath caught. I'd surprised him. Then, just as gently, he asked, "And what would I become here?"

I turned, facing him fully. The rain had stopped, but his hair still glistened with it, dark and gleaming. His face was quiet stone, but his eyes—his eyes were asking for so much more than I dared name.

"You wouldn't become," I said. "You'd *be*. Isn't that enough?"

His gaze searched mine, a man setting out for a shoreline he never thought he'd reach. For one long moment, he said nothing.

Then just before his mouth could shape a reply—

I felt it.

A pull at the edge of my spine. A shift in the light. A tension in the air that belonged only to *her*.

Demeter.

My mother.

She had felt the thread. Perhaps not the full weave of what had passed between us, but enough. Too much.

I retreated a step. Of course, he noticed, though he didn't ask.

He only said, voice lower than before, "I should go."

Lost Mysteries help me—

I didn't want him to leave. Not yet.

"Not like this," I whispered. "Please."

He hesitated. Then, slowly, almost reluctantly, he reached out. Not to grasp—but to trace a curl of hair that had fallen across my shoulder.

His finger stilled a breath above it. Never touching, but hovering right there on the edge of wonder. My heart raced even as I held my breath almost desperate for the contact.

Then he dropped his hand.

"I'll find you again," he said. "If you want me to."

I nodded. The words wouldn't come. Not yet.

So, I gave him something else instead.

I leaned forward and pressed my hand to his chest, over his heart. "I want you to remember what it feels like," I said, "when someone looks at you and doesn't flinch."

He stared at me, and in his eyes, I saw it all:

The garden.

The daffodils.

The stillness that bloomed even underground.

Then, with a breath like the hush before twilight, he vanished.

My world felt colder for his absence.

I turned toward the path home.

Mother would be waiting.

There was no escaping the ineffable truth. Spring had already begun to shift.

Part of me—part of *Mother*—knew it.

The path to her temple wound upward through the green hills, still damp from rain.

I walked slowly.

The hem of my dress clung to my ankles, streaked with mud and crushed petals. Every step was gentle, careful, as if I could somehow keep what had just happened inside me. I was about as successful as carrying water cupped between trembling hands.

The wind had changed, and so had I. The grove thinned as I climbed. Cypress gave way to olive, then to the wide-boughed fig trees my mother favored. Their roots ran deep —through time, through soil, through the memory of every harvest that had ever fed a mortal mouth.

I passed under their shade and felt a hum beneath the ground.

Not that I needed the warning, I'd recognized another truth. Mother was already waiting.

The clearing opened ahead, wide and sun-dappled, though the sky still hung heavy with cloud. My mother stood in the center, her back to me. A thyrsus of ripe barley rested across her shoulders, and her golden hair was braided with early wheat.

She did not turn.

"Kore," she said softly, though the wind should have stolen the word.

I stopped at the edge of the clearing. The grass shivered beneath my feet, unsure whether to grow or shrink back.

"Mother," I said, voice even.

She turned. Her eyes found mine, and the breeze paused. Not harsh. Not yet. Just still—like the space between lightning and thunder.

I braced.

Demeter did not storm. She crossed the clearing slowly,

gaze searching, not my body, but my *being*. The way the earth around me pulsed a little differently. The way the light clung to my edges.

She stopped two paces away.

"You've been somewhere," she said.

Not a question.

I didn't reply. Not with words. That was enough.

She exhaled, the sound too soft to be a sigh, too weighted to be nothing.

"I felt it," she said. "Before I even stepped above the roots. Something shifted."

The silence stretched long and thin between us.

At last, I said, "I was only walking."

She looked at me then—really looked. Not as a mother. Not even as a goddess. But as a woman who had lost before, and refused to lose again.

"Kore," she said, and this time her voice cracked on the name, "I *know* the difference between footsteps in the rain and footsteps in the dark."

A pause.

I swallowed, and said the truth: "I didn't mean to meet him."

She flinched like I'd struck her. Demeter turned away, pressing her fingers to her temple as if trying to hold her shape. "The Underworld," she whispered. "Even its breath on you—*how could you let it touch you?*"

I sighed. "He didn't take. He only stayed."

Demeter whirled back, eyes flashing gold. "That's how it begins. With presence. With politeness. Then the silence grows around you until you forget what the sun felt like before you stepped into shadow."

I stood my ground. "You think I'm still a seedling. I'm not."

Her face twisted, sadness and fury tangled. "No. You're a bud. And every bud is vulnerable. He *knows* that."

"Mother, he didn't ask for anything."

"That's worse!" Her voice rose, thunder hiding just behind it. "You don't understand how gods like him love. They don't beg. They *wait*. And you—" Her voice broke again. "You're *mine*, Kore. You are the bloom. The promise. You don't belong underground."

"Mother," I said, voice low and steady, "I'm here and I didn't feel buried. Not with him."

She went still. A wind passed through the clearing, lifting the scent of lavender and wet bark. My mother didn't speak. But I saw it—the storm rolling behind her eyes. Not rage.

Fear.

"I lost before," she said, quieter than I'd ever heard her. "Not to death. But to time. To silence. Now I see the same silence in you."

"I'm not gone," I whispered. Why didn't she hear me?

"But you're not all here, either."

I stepped forward. My hands stayed at my sides, but I met her gaze, unflinching. "Maybe I'm not meant to be *only* here. You said I was spring. Spring *moves*. It *changes*. It *goes*."

Her shoulders sagged. For the first time in my memory, Demeter—the great, golden mother—looked tired.

"I made this world soft for you," she said. "I rooted joy into its bones, so you'd never have to ache the way I did."

"But I do ache," I replied. "Because you taught me to feel. Because you taught me to love the world, and now I love *all* of it. Even the parts you fear."

She looked at me as if finally seeing the shape of a woman where a child once stood. "I won't forbid you," she said at last.

I blinked. She wouldn't?

"I should," she added. "But I won't. Because I see it now. You've already begun to reach toward him."

I didn't answer that. I couldn't. Not... yet. Was she really not angry with me? She stepped close again, and this time, her hand did touch my cheek. Gentle. Steady. But there was grief in it. The emotion threatened to undo me.

"But promise me one thing," she said.

"What?"

"If the shadows ever ask you to forget your name—*don't*. No matter how warm they become. No matter how gentle the dark feels. You are Kore. You are the spring. You belong to me. You belong to yourself. You belong *here*."

I pressed my hand over hers. This I could do.

"I promise."

CHAPTER
FOUR

The rain still clung to me when I returned to the shadows.

Not that it mattered. I carried her scent now—of almond blossoms and damp moss, of something young and unguarded that had no business clinging to a thing like me.

She had offered me her world.

Not with garlands or gold, but by *walking beside me.* That was worse, in a way. Gentler. More dangerous. I've never feared blades. But I have always feared beauty, especially hers, as it wasn't rooted in the superficial but in kindness.

She didn't know what she was doing.

Or maybe she did.

That's what unsettled me most.

They watched her. The others.

They arrived cloaked in laughter, in sun-touched ambition, with garlands in their hands and conquest in their

51

eyes. Beautiful, powerful, gilded with the blessings of Olympus. Gods who sung, shone, and *deserved* her.

They waited for her mother, of course. Played the game. Offered tribute. Spoke of legacy and harvest and the joining of great lines. All the same lines.

But *she* didn't look at them the way she looked at me.

She *sought* me.

I should not have taken pride in that. But I did.

I waited at the margins—always at the margins. I watched her from the edge of things. Where the season faltered. Where green faded to gray.

Not because I meant to haunt her.

Because I didn't know how to stop returning.

She walked with me. Took my hand. Not to bind. Not to claim.

But to *see* me.

Even when I said nothing, even when I stood still as stone, she filled the silence with *recognition*.

When I touched the bark of her trees, I feared they would wither.

They didn't.

They bent.

They *welcomed*.

The underworld didn't welcome. It claimed, consumed. It forgot warmth. But her world—her world leaned toward me like I was not an ending.

Just... something *outside* the cycle. Something necessary.

I didn't belong there. I knew that.

But when she smiled, quietly, shyly, like something unfolding for the first time, I began to think that maybe it didn't matter.

Maybe it never mattered.

I saw how they spoke to her.

Apollo with his poetry and Helios with his glow. Hermes with his clever tongue, all charm and movement. Even Ares, brutal in his want, tried to cloak it in gallant silence.

They all saw a bloom.

They wanted the season.

But I knew the *soil*.

I knew what she hid.

I knew what it *cost* her to bloom, again and again.

They didn't know the girl who curled into moss when no one was looking. Who questioned her shape, her power, her path. Who knelt at broken altars and asked nothing of the gods. Of Gaia.

But I did.

Because of that, I couldn't be what they were.

I couldn't ask for her.

Only wait.

SHE TOLD me I was the pause between seasons. A shadow that made the light mean something.

No one has ever called me anything without fear in their voice. Not even the other immortals. They might speak of balance, of necessity—but in the end, I was the gate they refused to look behind.

Except her.

She sat in silence and offered no promises. Just *presence*.

I would take that over worship. Over prayer. Over anything. Because it was real. It was hers.

When I stepped forward, she met me halfway.

Could she understand what that did to a being like me?

We were not built for halves. We took. We dominated. We held dominion over law, death, sky. Even love. But not her. She gave me only what I dared hold.

Somehow, that was more than I'd ever had. I couldn't stay away from her. Day after day, season after season, I returned to watch her, certain that it would be enough. It wasn't.

How could it be? I hated how I remembered her now. The way her hand felt over mine, warm, living, trusting. The way the rain softened around her like the world was listening. The way she looked at me like I wasn't a mistake.

I hated that I knew it wouldn't—couldn't—last.

Demeter had felt the thread. Her power was old, older than most remembered. It guarded her daughter like a wall woven from root and wrath.

She would come.

She would take her.

Not because she was cruel. No. She would take her because she *knew what I was*. She was right to fear it, fear me. I vanished because I had to. Not for safety. For *mercy*. If I stayed, I would not have left. If she asked, I would have stayed beneath the almond blossoms until the last star died.

But she didn't ask.

I didn't *want* her to ask.

I wanted her to choose.

She won't—not yet.

She was spring.

Spring always left.

I would wait at the edges. In the hush. In the pause before the first dew. Hope was not my nature, but it was *hers*.

And Gaia help me—I would follow her *anywhere she dared bloom.*

Even into the light.

THE WHEAT HAD TURNED GOLD. That was how I knew it was safe to come. Safe enough, anyway. She wouldn't be alone —no goddess is truly alone at the height of her power—but her mother was gone from the fields. I felt Demeter's absence in the soil. The hush wasn't fear. It was... *watching.*

Still, I stepped lightly. Harvest was a holy thing, and I'd never been welcome at holy things. Not unless they ended. This was a celebration of *what endured.*

The ground did not shy from me. It did not bow, either. It simply *allowed* me to pass. I think, perhaps, because she had walked beside me once before. That blessing lingered longer than I deserved.

I found her near the granaries, barefoot and brushing chaff from her fingers. She wore no crown. That unsettled me more than it should have. She always wore a crown near the equinox. A circlet of barley and gold, vines and woven laurel. Power and harvest made visible.

Today she had pulled her hair back with a ribbon, and her dress was wrinkled, and she looked—Gaia save me— *young.*

Not fragile. Not weak. Just *still becoming.* Yet she turned to me as though she had known I was coming long before I did. "Aïdes," she said simply, with a smile that didn't try to be anything but true. "You waited."

"As long as I could," I admitted. My voice came rougher than I meant it to. Drier. Like something disused. "You... look well."

"I am." She turned back to her work, plucking a bent stalk from the sheaf beside her. "You came while she's gone again."

"Yes." There was no point denying it.

She dusted her hands against her skirt, eyes flicking to mine. "You don't have to."

A pause. A long one.

"I do," I said, quietly. "Because she will not meet me in peace. And I will not come to you through war."

Her eyes softened, but she shook her head. "She hasn't forbidden me from seeing you."

That stopped me. Not because it pleased me. Because it *terrified* me. "She hasn't?" I asked, carefully, as if the words were still dangerous in the air.

"No." Kore looked toward the fields, where the stalks bent in the wind, sunlit and full. "She knows. She feels the thread. But she hasn't spoken of you. Not in warning. Not in anger. Nothing."

I stepped closer, the silence between us tightening like a drawn bow. "That's not permission. That's restraint. *Tension.* She's waiting."

"She trusts me," she said, but I could hear the question beneath it. Like she didn't know if she believed it.

"No," I said, too fast. Too firm. "She fears what you might choose."

That made her still. Not angry. Not sad. Just... thoughtful.

"She has reason to fear," I added, softer now. "I am not part of this world. I am not meant to be part of *you.*"

"You keep saying that," she replied, still not looking at me. "As if meaning has already been written."

"Hasn't it?"

She turned then, slow and sure. "Then why do you keep showing up to rewrite it?"

That hit harder than I wanted it to. I didn't have an answer for her. Not one I trusted.

We walked, not toward the trees this time, but through the fields themselves. The grain brushed our thighs. The wind rustled overhead. In the distance, I could hear songs —harvest songs, rising in rhythm with scythes and laughter.

It was a season I had never touched. Not truly.

Ripe things made me nervous. They are one breath from rot. One shadow from surrender. I know that moment too well. I live there.

"I don't belong here," I said, quieter than I meant to.

Kore glanced at me, a secret smile teasing over her lips. "Then why do you keep coming back?"

"I don't come for *here*."

Her smile grew like that of a blossom in spring. "No. You come for me."

I said nothing. I didn't have to. She led me to the edge of the granary grove where the plums hung low and bruised with ripeness. The air was heavy with sweetness—*almost too sweet.* The kind that turned the stomach if you lingered too long.

"This is where things tip," she said softly, her hand trailing across the bark. "Where everything starts to ache from fullness. Where life begins to bend toward ending."

I looked at her then. Her throat. Her hands. The way the shadows clung to the hollows of her collarbone, deeper than they had in spring. "You feel it too," I said.

She nodded. "I always do. The world knows. It just doesn't want to say it out loud yet."

A silence fell between us again. But this one wasn't

empty. It was *thick* with knowing. With the grief that came with knowing and longing.

I reached for her hand. Not suddenly. Just gently, like I was returning something I had borrowed. She let me take it. She always did. At that moment, the most horrifying thought struck me: *She might choose me.*

Not because I claimed her.

But because she wanted to. Because *she trusted me.* She saw what I didn't show anyone else. And that—*blessed Gaia have you forsaken me?*—was what frightened me most.

I didn't deserve it. If I *took* it, I made it real. If I lost it... lost her, it would destroy me. I held her hand and said nothing for a long time.

Until at last, I whispered, "I don't want you to regret it." She looked up at me. Steady. Clear-eyed. No blush. No girlish shimmer. Just truth.

"Then don't give me a reason to."

The wind changed then. A warning. A ripple through the ripe stalks. A shift in the gold. Her mother wasn't *here.* The world remembered her. She wasn't here. Yet. Still, Kore didn't step away from me. She let me hold her hand.

The harvest would come. So would endings. For now— she stayed. I waited. Again.

THEY LIT the fires as the last of the sun fell.

Piles of wheat stalks and dried laurel, cracked olive wood and old garlands, each fed to the flame in offering of hunger and joy. The smoke curled skyward like a promise no one meant to keep. Gold flickered against the dark. Below it, they danced.

She danced.

I shouldn't have come. I always did. Each spring and harvest since we met. I cannot stay away.

This time, I wore a different face. Not fully glamoured—just *dimmed*. Enough shadow to be mistaken for one of the lesser spirits. A forgotten demigod. A handsome ghost. No one would look too closely.

Not tonight.

The wine had already been poured heavily. Dionysus was in rare form, half-dressed and howling laughter from atop a barrel, his cup perpetually overflowing. Mortals pressed around him like bees, caught in the sweetness of his madness.

Hermes darted through the crowd with winged glee, flicking grapes into mouths and stealing kisses from anyone bold enough to meet his eye. He tugged on Kore's hand like a child one moment and spun her like lightning the next.

She was *radiant*. Not serene. Not quiet. Wild.

Her hair was tangled with olive leaves, skin lit by fire-light, and her eyes bright and fierce. No longer only maiden or bloom. She was the essence of abundance, the heavens made visible upon the earth. Her laugh danced like a flame set loose—reckless, warm, and alive.

I was nothing in the face of it. Just a shadow at the edge of gold.

Watching.

Wanting.

She hadn't seen me yet. Not fully. But I felt her—how her joy twisted every time her eyes skimmed the edges of the firelight. Looking. Expecting something more than wine. More than the revel. Looking for me.

I tried to stay away. I told myself I would only watch. That was a lie, and I thought I knew it before I even crossed into the grove.

Because even masked, even veiled in glamour and smoke—I found her.

She stood at the center of the spiral now, surrounded by godlings and dryads and laughing mortals. They threw grain and petals into the sky, wove flowers into hair already slick with sweat. The drums were thunder. The pipes were a storm.

When she turned, her gaze locked with mine. She *knew*. Immediately. Despite the mask. Despite the crowd. Despite everything.

I stilled. But she didn't. She walked toward me like nothing else existed. Like the other gods didn't gawk and satyrs didn't whisper and Dionysus didn't raise one amused, drunken eyebrow.

She just walked.

Then stopped, close enough to smell like crushed thyme and smoke, and said, "I was wondering when you'd come."

I swallowed hard. "I shouldn't have."

"But you did." Her voice was softer now, edged in something older than the harvest. Something that knew the feel of endings and chose them anyway. "Why do you hide?"

"Because this isn't my world."

Her mouth curled. "Yet you're here. Again."

The circle of dancers grew looser now, more chaotic. Heat pressed in from every side, human and divine bodies blurring in wine and flame. Laughter like birdsong. Skin like gold.

A pulse of something hedonistic, thick and ancient. The kind of joy that forgot itself. She turned and looked at the madness around us.

"They won't remember half of this come morning," she said. "They'll wake with mouths like ash and bruises they don't remember getting. But tonight?" She looked back at me. "Tonight is *mine*." Then, softly, like she whispered to something fragile: "Don't leave without me this time."

My heart stilled.

"Kore—"

"Take me with you," she said. Not begging. *Asking.* Choosing. "Please."

I wanted to say no. For her. For the world. For the aching, golden weight of what she meant to so many. But she was looking at me with open hands, not chained wrists. No fear. No illusion.

Just firelight and ash and hope.

And I—I had always loved beautiful things most in the moment before they fell. So I nodded.

Just once.

Enough.

Around us, the gods laughed.

Dionysus caught my eye and raised his cup in unspoken toast, a slow grin blooming like bruised fruit. He *knew*. Of course, he knew. The lush enjoyed the drunken revelry whether it was sex or brawling. Better if it were both.

Hermes stilled beside a nymph mid-laugh, watching me with narrowed eyes and a tilt of his head. His tongue paused, just for a second, just enough to *notice*. No one moved to stop us. Not yet. She took my hand. Again.

But this time, it wasn't the gentle touch of a girl unsure of the line she was crossing. This was a *claiming*.

I let her.

As we slipped from the edge of the circle, between bonfires and thickets and drunk, gleaming mortals, I felt the turn in the world.

Harvest always ends. The grain is cut. The bounty taken. The field emptied. For the first time, however, something was *being taken with me.*

Not by force. Not by fate. By choice. By *her*.

Kore.

No longer only spring. No longer only seed.

She was the girl who danced in firelight then found me in shadow, and asked to go where no living thing goes willingly.

And I—I was no longer the god who waited. I was the god who *took*. Because *she asked me to*. And by Gaia's sacred breasts, I could not refuse.

The fires faded behind us. Laughter dimmed to echoes. The songs bled into the dark. Even the wine-heavy wind seemed unwilling to follow, trailing off like a dream that knew it was ending.

We walked in silence through the olive groves, past the stones the gods no longer named. Her hand in mine was warm. Sure. She did not stumble.

I knew where I was going. She did not ask. She just came.

Not with haste. Not with fear. Just the steady rhythm of her breath beside me. Her hair caught moonlight. Her footsteps did not pause. Not once.

We reached the cave just before dawn. The light behind us had lightened the sky to gray. Ahead, the mouth of the earth yawned open revealing a doorway. Old as bone. Older than gods.

It knew me. It bowed.

The stone shifted subtly, breathless, like a creature waking from a long slumber. The arch deepened. Shadows widened. The air turned still.

Welcoming. Not to her. To *me*. Yet, I stepped forward alone and released her hand. The moment I did, the chill returned. It slid up my spine and across my shoulders. I stood just past the threshold, wrapped again in the weight of where I belonged.

The underworld knew me.

But it did not yet know *her*.

I turned.

She stood a few paces away, watching me, haloed by fading starlight. Behind her, the last breath of night curved around her like a veil. Her ribbon had come loose. One tendril of hair curled against her cheek.

She didn't speak at first, just looked at the threshold, at me, and at the choice before her.

Then—softly, lightly—*teasingly*. "Well. This isn't exactly the triumphal arch of Olympus."

I blinked.

She smiled. "Bit of moss. Some fog. Very dramatic, though. A shadowed welcome worthy of legend."

A laugh caught in my throat. A real one.

She stepped closer. "Do you bring *everyone* through here?" she asked. "Or am I getting a special tour?"

I didn't speak. I only lifted my hand. Not reaching for her. Just offering. Open. Waiting.

Her smile softened. The mischief in her eyes didn't fade, but something else joined it now—something quieter. Deeper. Determination. Without looking back, she crossed the threshold.

She didn't flinch. Didn't hesitate.

The earth shifted beneath her, not rejecting, not resisting—just adjusting. Accepting.

Welcoming.

Like it knew, even if it didn't yet understand.

Her fingers brushed mine, then closed fully. No trembling. She said nothing. She didn't need to. Her hand was in mine again.

I—

I was undone.

We walked deeper.

The world behind us sealed itself in silence. The cave narrowed. Grew colder. Faint bioluminescence shimmered from unseen stone—like stars scattered under skin.

Still, she did not slow, nor speak.

Not until we reached the place where the cave widened, opening into the mouth of the descent proper. The true path. The sacred path. The one that winds through silence and memory and the bones of forgotten things.

Here, the Underworld waited. Here, she turned to me. "So," she murmured, voice low and steady, "this is what happens when you choose the shadow."

I nodded, the breath catching in my throat.

She studied my face, as if committing every line of it to memory. As if she already knew what it meant. Then, slowly, deliberately, she rose on her toes, one hand still in mine, the other at my collar, and kissed me.

It wasn't wild. It wasn't frantic. It was deep.

Certain.

The kind of kiss that wrote a promise in the marrow.

She kissed me like she already belonged.

Like she had always known where she was going.

And I—I kissed her like time had bent around us, like the stars had waited lifetimes for this collision.

When we pulled apart, the doorway behind us no longer existed. The path was sealed. The world we left behind was gone. Only what we chose remained. Only *her*. Only *me*.

And the silence that welcomed us home.

CHAPTER

FIVE

She crossed the threshold and my world bent around her presence.

The Underworld was not made for light, but she did not bring it the way mortals do. No fire. No brightness. She softened the dark instead and made it *breathe*. Not invaded, not claimed. Just *filled*.

Like roots claiming a forgotten place, not to break it, but to make it *true* again.

She walked beside me down the winding path of the underdeep. No fear. No second glance. Even the spirits stilled at her passing.

She touched nothing. Yet everything leaned toward her. *I* leaned toward her.

We reached the first hollow, one of the hidden courts near the Lethe, and I paused, waiting to see if she would ask. She didn't. She only looked around, her eyes thoughtful, absorbing the space.

Then she said, "It's quieter than I imagined."

"Most things are," I said, "once you stop fearing them."

She looked at me then—truly looked—and I saw it again, the shift in her eyes. The knowing. The hunger.

"You don't fear me," I said.

"No," she murmured. "Does that bother you?"

"It humbles me."

She blinked. Once. Slowly. "Show me more."

I took her through the asphodel fields, now gray with the memory of sunless days, and the black gardens I'd planted before memory. My palace stood beyond them—long and low, not golden like Olympus, but veined with obsidian and moonlight.

She walked its halls like she had always belonged.

Even the walls whispered a quiet welcome for her.

When we reached the inner chambers, she paused near the great bronze doors carved with vines and serpents and wings.

"Your throne?" she asked, voice soft and gentle like the hush of morning light breaking over the horizon.

I shook my head. "Not tonight."

She smiled faintly, brushing a finger along the cool metal. "Good. I don't feel like kneeling."

Something in me shattered—*gloriously.* That night, I did not summon wine. I did not light a hundred lamps. I did not drape her in jewels. She did not need them.

I offered her a room with velvet-dark walls and a view of the silver river. She barely glanced at it. She followed *me* instead. Into my chamber. My sanctuary.

She stood near the hearth, barely burning, more shadow than flame, and let me look at her. Like she *knew.* Like she *wanted* me to.

Her voice was low. "You've never asked me to stay."

"I don't need to."

"Why?"

I stepped close, close enough to feel the warmth of her skin, the promise of breath between us.

"Because you already have."

When I touched her, it was not with the hunger of conquest. It was with *wonder*.

I brushed a knuckle along her cheek, soft and deliberate. I slid a hand to her waist like she was a myth I had once read and never dared to speak aloud. My touch was careful, the awe in my core devastating.

She leaned in. Not yielding. *Offering*.

"Say it," she whispered.

I did.

"I want you."

Then, again, as I let my mouth trace the curve of her shoulder—

"I want you."

When I laid her beneath me, the hollows of the world sighed like stone made warm. It wasn't frantic. It was *inevitable*.

We moved like the tide pulling against the sky, old and sure and rhythmic. Her mouth opened to me. Her breath shuddered against my throat, then I marked her not with bruises but *belonging*.

She arched.

I stilled.

"More," she whispered.

And I gave her everything.

Later, her head rested against my chest, and my arm curved around her bare waist like instinct. The fire was almost out. Still, neither of us slept.

Outside the chamber, soft paws padded across polished stone. A low whine. Then a *snort*.

She lifted her head.

"What is that?"

"Kerebos," I said.

Sure enough, the pup, a mass of too-large paws, over-sized fangs, and fur like midnight silk, trotted in. Only one head for now, still growing, but the promise of three burned in his eyes.

He looked up at her and gave a pleased little *huff.*

Then promptly laid down by the bed like he'd always been there.

She laughed, warm and real and open.

"You never told me you had a dog."

I let my hand trace her spine. "He's more than that. He guards the gates. He knows who belongs."

She glanced down at the curled form beside the bed. "He seems to think I do."

"He's not wrong."

∿

THEY CAME, of course.

On the third day.

First, Hermes.

He didn't knock. He *appeared,* a ripple of winged impatience and shifting silver.

I was already at the gates.

Kerebos snarled before I spoke.

"She isn't yours to retrieve."

Hermes narrowed his eyes. "Zeus will not let this stand."

"She crossed freely."

"She's *Demeter's* daughter."

"She is *herself.* That is the name she answers to now."

He hesitated. Then, smiling, clever, dangerous, he said, "You're in love with her."

I didn't deny it. I didn't *have* to. I simply said, "Tell your king that she is *not gone.* She is not a *prize.* She is *becoming.* And if they cannot bear it, they can rot."

Hermes vanished. But he did not cross the boundary. No one could. Not while I guarded it. Not while *she stayed.*

Back in the chamber, she stood by the window, wrapped in one of my robes, hair falling loose around her shoulders. Her eyes met mine as I entered.

"They're coming, aren't they?" she asked.

"They tried."

Her mouth curled, amused. "And?"

"They failed."

She turned fully to me then. Bare feet. Bare throat. Crownless and free. No longer maiden. No longer only Kore.

"I don't want to leave," she said.

"Then stay."

"I *am* staying."

Then she crossed the space between us. When she gripped my face and kissed me again, not like our first kiss, not like invitation, but *confirmation,* I knew.

The world above would mourn its spring.

Down here, in the hush between endings, something *new* had taken root. It would bloom.

We didn't sleep. Not for long, not deeply. Not the way gods sleep when the world moves without them. Kore stirred beside me, warm and alive and *so utterly present,* and the hush of the Underworld shifted with her every breath. As if even the darkness listened now.

Her fingers skimmed my ribs, idle, curious. Her leg slid across mine. She moved like someone still drunk on joy— not dazed or dulled, but *open.*

She pressed a kiss to my chest, then another, slower, just above my heart. I watched her in the lowlight, eyes half-lidded, not daring to speak.

"You don't talk much," she murmured.

"I wasn't made for it."

She looked up at me then, a smile tugging wickedly at the corner of her mouth. "You were made for something." Before I could answer, she moved.

Great mother.

She straddled me, slow and smooth, a shift of silken skin and certainty. My hands gripped her hips, but lightly, *always lightly.* If I held too tight I might shatter the moment.

"Let me see what else you were made for," she whispered.

What followed might not be considered sacred to others. Yet, there was holiness in it.

She rode me like the season rides wind, all wild and graceful. Her laughter filled me as I kissed her, as I clutched at her, as I came apart beneath her. She bent down, hands pressed to my chest, hair falling around our faces like dusk, and the sounds she made, low, unguarded, *nearly feral*, broke me open.

When it was done—when I was undone—she curled beside me, head on my shoulder, and the room swelled with a strange, bright ache I did not know how to name.

It felt like *living.*

Later, she dressed in a different robe, perfect for the silk of her skin to wander into the long hall. The Underworld draped her in shadows shot through with midnight blues. I followed, content to watch the way she touched the edges of this world. She didn't change it, not once did she even attempt to change it, but she sought to know it.

That's when Kerebos barreled into her again.

Still just the single head, soft ears, oversized paws, more energy than grace, but full of joy. She squealed when he leapt, catching her around the waist with too much enthusiasm. They tumbled to the floor in a knot of fur and laughter.

"Kerebos!" I called, half-chiding.

She just waved a hand, face flushed with laughter. "No, no—it's fine. He's perfect."

She wrestled him playfully, pushing his head away only for him to lick her cheek. She shoved him back again with mock dignity, robes rumpled, hair wild, eyes gleaming.

"You're raising a monster," she said, breathless, "and I adore him."

"He likes you," I said.

She looked up at me, radiant and disheveled. "*You* like me."

"I worship you."

She stood then, tugging me toward the hearth with mischief still sparking in her grin. "Then let's see how well you play."

That night we played in every way.

In the warm pools beneath the palace, she coaxed me into the water and tugged me under. In the shadowed chambers of the west wing, we chased each other barefoot and half-clothed, laughing like fools until I caught her against the wall and made her gasp my name.

She bit my shoulder. Left marks. Dared me to leave some of my own.

I did.

When I pressed her down onto the silken bed once more, she wrapped her legs around my waist and whispered, "Make it thunder."

I did that too.

Despite our joy, the world beneath—and above—never slept.

I felt the pull deep beneath the palace. The shifting of bone and memory, the stirrings of the ancient quiet. A matter older than gods. Something I was bound to answer.

I sat up, breath still unsteady, and reached for my tunic.

Her hand caught my wrist. "I'll go with you."

"It's not—"

She tilted her head, solemn now. "Don't say it's not for me. You brought me into your world. Don't close the doors again."

I searched her face. She meant it. She *wanted* to walk the deep places. Not as a guest. As a partner. I nodded.

She rose beside me. We descended together, through halls no soul walks willingly. Down where the Styx runs thick and black, and the air sings of endings no one speaks aloud.

Kore did not tremble. She walked at my side, the hem of her robe trailing shadow and silver dust. Even the spirits that haunt the deepest roots parted for her. Not in fear.

In *recognition.*

She touched no souls. Asked no names. But I watched the way her eyes softened at their silence. She belonged here, not as death. As *mercy.*

We reached the chamber of the still throne, where the First Sleep waits, older than Olympus, deeper than Tartarus.

I laid my hand on the black stone, felt the pulse of it pass through me. A question. A weight. I answered.

Beside me, Kore stood still. Listening. Accepting. And then—

A ripple. A sound too clean, too precise. Someone else had entered the realm.

Kerebos barked once from high above. A warning.

Then a flicker of wings. Not Hermes. Too heavy. A scent of copper. Bronze. Laurel and challenge.

Ares.

Of *course.*

He never came for peace.

But I only turned to Kore. "Shall I deal with him?"

She arched a brow, the edge of a smirk at her lips. "No," she said. "I'll deal with him." When she climbed the steps back toward the gate, her spine straight, her eyes bright with fire and frost, I felt it again. She was no longer just the girl who danced in the fields or even the goddess who kissed me in shadow. She was a *queen.*

Mine.

She had no fear of War. She ascended ahead of me. Each step she took, the realm shifted. The river slowed. The walls of obsidian turned inward, waiting. Even the ever-burning braziers dimmed, not extinguished, not afraid, but as if squinting to see her better. Not spring. Not maiden.

Kore.

Crowned now by something I had not placed upon her.

A corona of dusk, neither fire nor thorn, but woven from the void between starlight and soil. Shadows curled like smoke above her head, wreathing her temples, not bound but *born.* As if the underworld had simply decided: *This is who we answer to now.*

And I, god of all that ends, lord of silence and decay, stood behind her, speechless.

I would have forged her a crown myself. I would have built it from bone and onyx, poured the night sky into its setting, bent knee before her and offered it without a word. But she had not waited for it.

She had taken the throne of her own will. That,

perhaps, was the first moment I understood that she was not mine. She was *herself*.

And the world would answer to that.

Ares arrived in thunder and scent—iron and sweat and scorched laurel. No subtlety. He burst through the gate with all the grace of a siege weapon.

He was expecting me.

What he was *not* expecting was *her*.

Kore turned slowly, not startled. Just... aware. Measured. She was dressed still in my black, but it clung to her like ink to flame. Her hair wild, her eyes molten. The crown above her barely visible—but undeniable. I'd followed merely to enjoy the view and as a reminder should War seek to damage what was mine.

Ares stopped dead. His helmet flickered with the light of the brazier behind him. His mouth parted. He was not used to beauty that refused to burn itself soft for him.

"You," he said, voice low with confusion and something sharper. "You are not—what I thought you'd be."

"No," she agreed. "I'm not."

He took a step closer, and I stepped forward without thinking, hand on the pommel of a blade I hadn't summoned in centuries.

But Kore lifted a hand. Not to *me*.

To him. Not to welcome. To *warn*.

Ares paused again. His head tilted, and he smiled, slow and predatory.

"Power looks good on you," he said. "Are you keeping him company? Or something more?"

I didn't speak. She didn't need me to.

"I'm not *kept*," she said, voice smooth as oil on steel. "Nor am I yours to measure."

Ares gave a low laugh, admiring her now, not with leering mockery, but with a warlord's greed.

"You remind me of someone," he said, circling slightly, careless of how Kerebos growled low at his flank. "Athena, maybe. But warmer. Wilder."

Then, fool that he was, he reached for her hand. Just to touch it. Just to see. Power lashed out—*not mine.*

Kore's.

It bloomed from her palm like a bloom of dusk-touched flame, like soil cracking to reveal something unnameable beneath. It didn't strike him down, it *warned*. A curl of shadow, a snap of wind, a sudden pressure in the air like a coming storm.

Ares pulled back sharply. But his eyes lit. "You're dangerous," he murmured, low and nearly reverent.

She smiled then, all teeth. "I have to be. I live with ghosts."

Gaia help me, I *loved* her in that moment more than any eternity could hold.

Ares turned to me, finally. Still grinning. Still tempted. "She's going to draw attention," he said. "More than me. More than her mother. They'll come."

"I know."

"Do you care?"

I met his gaze with all the weight of every grave, every silence, every ending the world had ever known. "Let them."

When Ares left, reluctant, intrigued, *aching* for battle, I turned to her again. She stood in the echo of what she had summoned, the remnants of power still spiraling like wind around her hair and throat. "I didn't know I could do that," she said softly.

"You didn't take power," I murmured, crossing the

space between us. "You *are* power. You were only waiting for the world to stop pretending otherwise."

Her eyes lifted to mine. "Do you still want me like this?"

"I want you *more*," I said. When I pulled her close, this time it was not to consume or to protect. It was to *honor*.

The shadow crown on her brow may not have been made by my hand, but I would die a thousand times to defend it. Time bled. Not forward. Not back. Simply... away.

In the realm beneath the world's heartbeat, it lost meaning, as it always had. Centuries might pass in a breath, or a night might stretch so long the stars above forgot how to turn. But it was not time I marked.

It was *her*.

Kore.

Except, no.

Not anymore.

Even I had stopped thinking of her by that name. Not aloud, not even in thought. That name had belonged to spring. To a girl with soil under her nails and sunlight on her cheeks.

She was still that—she would *always* be that. But she was *more*.

She had been more the moment she took her first step through the door I'd left open. When she strode into the dark with her crown of starlit shadow, unafraid. When she looked at death and didn't flinch.

I didn't need to give her another name. Names were the weapons of gods. Tools. Chains, sometimes. If she had wanted one, if she had asked for it, I would've carved it into the stone bones of the world.

Instead, I called her nothing but *mine* and never once did I mean possession. I meant *presence*. I meant *belonging*.

Not because I claimed her. Because she stayed. Because she *chose.*

The Underworld changed around her. Walls that had stood still since the river first began to run now breathed anew. The air held a softness in the quiet hours, a strange, warm hush. Not grief.

Something gentler.

Rooms long forgotten bloomed with moss and pale flame, not bright enough to banish the dark—but enough to ease it. The spirits came closer to her each passing day. Even the Furies, once sharp as razors, softened in her presence, blinking like wolves at a firelit threshold.

She never tried to fix them.

She simply *saw* them.

And I—

I saw her. I basked in her nearness, drank in all that she shared. I watched the realm shift to greet her not as queen, not as consort, but as *equal.*

She sang to Kerebos when she thought I wasn't listening, scratching the velvet between his ears and humming lullabies in no language I knew. She wandered the deeper halls with bare feet and a soft laugh that made even the sleeping bones stir. She did not flee from silence. She filled it.

We did not bind one another. There were no chains. No vows carved in stone. She could have left a hundred times, and I would have let her.

But she never did.

The longer she stayed, the more I understood a new kind of power. Devotion. Freely given. Fierce. Unflinching. Not the kind that demanded kneeling. The kind that *stood beside you.*

One night, after the river stilled and even Kerebos had

curled into sleep, she turned to me in the silver hush of our chambers. We were wrapped in one another, our limbs a tangle of ease, not want.

"I'm not Kore anymore," she said softly.

"No," I agreed.

"But I'm not entirely someone else, either."

I traced the edge of her jaw. "You don't have to name it. You *are* it."

Her lips quirked into a smile. "You're not going to give me some dark title? Queen of Ashes? Lady of the Lost?"

I shook my head. "You were never lost."

She leaned into me then, voice quiet, but certain. "If they come for me…"

I stiffened.

"They will," she continued, before I could speak. "One of them will try again. Not to persuade. To take. Because I'm no longer in the sun. Because I'm not so easy to smile over and forget."

"You think they'll try to cleave you from me."

Her gaze lifted. Unafraid. Unapologetic. "No. I think they'll try to *bind* me."

My throat burned with the fury of it. "They'll find I burn too."

She laid her hand over my heart. "That's not why I stay."

"I know," I said. "But it is why I fight."

It didn't take long. The next came with no noise. No scent of smoke. No iron tang of war. This one came like a breeze you didn't know was there until your breath was gone. A god of beauty. Of persuasion. Of *desire*. A god who *never asked*.

Only *took*.

I felt him first—long before he crossed the gate. Even

the spirits paused. The air shimmered with illusion, with soft heat and the hint of roses that never grew here. A glamour meant to charm.

I stepped into the hall as the threshold flared gold. A slender figure appeared at its center. Not a warrior or brute.

An artist of unraveling.

A god who knew how to pull the strings of devotion until they snapped—and re-tie them around his own wrist. He smiled when he saw her. Not at me.

Her.

In that moment, I understood that I would need *all* my power. Not because I feared he'd win her. No, I had no fear of him in that. However, if he tried to *touch* what was freely hers, I would bring the whole realm down to stop him.

She stood, radiant and calm, shadow blooming behind her. Not a girl. Not a maiden. Not a victim. Just—*herself.* More than Kore. More than spring. Just more.

I was already reaching for my blade. The scent of him came first. Not sulfur, not blood, not divine fire. Jasmine and ripe peach. Myrrh. The faintest copper of open skin. Pleasure masquerading as peace. A seduction in every inhalation.

I did not need to hear his name. Only one god carried that scent into death and expected to be welcome. *Eros.*

Not the winged child painted on the pottery of mortals. Not the laughing imp who flitted through lovers' chambers with arrows and whimsy. No. That was his charm.

His *lie.*

The true Eros, born of shadow and night, first flame of hunger in a godless void, stood just beyond the archway of the throne hall. Cloaked in something finer than silk, his body ageless, his face a study in perfection so measured it could only be cruel. His eyes were not warm.

They were *weaponized*.

When he saw her—my queen, my flame, my fierce spring turned sovereign—his smile bloomed like a slow bruise.

"Kore," he said.

She did not flinch.

Blessed Gaia, *how I loved her* for it.

"I was told," Eros continued, voice like molten amber, "that you had been *stolen*. Taken beneath the earth by the Lord of Silence. I came to retrieve you. To offer you light again." A pause. "But I see now... you do not appear lost."

Her smile was small, polite. Not warm. "I was never lost," she said evenly.

He tilted his head, stepping inside without permission. "No? Then what name shall I use for you now?"

"She needs no new name from *you*," I said, stepping forward.

Eros turned his eyes on me for the first time, assessing, unbothered. "Ah. The shade who thinks himself a king."

"I do not think," I warned, voice low. "I *know*. And she is not yours to address, let alone retrieve."

He offered a small laugh, sweet and honeyed as poison. "Are you so certain? I have undone stronger bindings than yours with a glance."

At that, her eyes narrowed. "There are no bindings here."

Eros stilled. I watched him. He was used to desire. He could drown cities with it. Spark wars in mortal veins.

What he saw in her, what he could *not* touch, was choice.

It baffled him.

He stepped closer. "You were made to be adored," he said softly. "To be worshipped. What are you doing buried in rot and bone, when you could be sung to from every peak? Painted on the backs of temples?"

She didn't answer. She didn't need to. Instead, she descended the steps of the dais with slow, deliberate grace. Her crown of shadow flared above her, not because I willed it, but because *she* did. "Why do you assume I am buried?" she asked.

Eros frowned slightly.

"Because you live in shadow," he said.

"I *am* shadow," she corrected. "I am also soil. Root. Bloom. Rot. You would have me on marble, pinned and perfect. But down here—I *grow*."

Then she stepped beside me, not behind. Not beneath. Not in need of defense. But as flame walks beside ash. As power walks beside stillness.

Eros' eyes flicked between us, his honeyed smile souring. "You could be loved more," he said, voice like a knife drawn behind a silk curtain.

"I am loved freely," she replied, lifting her chin. "Can you say the same?"

For the first time since he arrived, Eros was silent. He turned his attention back to me, the charm now gone. "You'll regret keeping her here," he said, voice gone flint.

"I regret nothing," I said. "But you may regret staying."

Power gathered beneath my skin, not fire, not rage, but the endless gravity of *no*. The immovable weight of *mine*, not as a claim, but as a shield. If he reached for her, the walls would fall. The river would rise. The dead themselves would answer.

Wisely, he didn't.

He watched us both—her with hunger, me with cold calculation—and stepped back.

"One day," he said, eyes on her, "you may want more

than devotion. You may want *adoration*. When that day comes, call my name."

She smiled. It was almost pitying. "When I want arti-fice," she said gently, "I'll look to you." With that, she turned her back on him.

I watched her go. She did not waver. She *never had*.

In that moment, I knew, I understood. There would be others. Gods who could not abide her being *free*. Being *chosen*. Being *more*.

I would never chain her. Love, if it was true, stood ready to fight. I would fight the whole pantheon, if I must.

Because she was not just spring. Not just Kore.

She was the dark before dawn. The bloom that breaks through stone. She was *the* queen who walked into shadow and made it bloom.

CHAPTER

SIX

It began as a whisper. Not words. Not wind. But *numbers*. More than usual. Too many.

Souls streamed down the rivers, not in a trickle or tide, but a flood. Slipping past Charon's skiff before he could speak their names. Sliding into the gates not from war, not from plague, but from hunger. The dead did not lie.

The whisper I heard in the shuffle of their feet was a single, terrifying truth. Starvation. The kind that takes not with fire or fury, but pitiless cruelty. Fields unbroken by plow. Trees heavy with ice. Children, too tired to cry.

I felt it like a crack beneath the stone of my chest. The Underworld had always made room for the dead. But this? This was *too soon*.

Too many.

I called the shades to stillness and summoned the records, but even before they reached my hands, two gods stood at my threshold.

Not warriors.

Not lords.

Not threats.

But beggars.

Small gods, usually proud enough to ignore the underworld entirely. Now, desperate. One brought an offering of barley, scorched and spoiled. The other, a woven crown of hay long since gone dry.

"They come to you," one said, kneeling, "because *she* will not listen."

"Demeter?"

They nodded. "She does not walk the earth. She does not hear us. She has become ice and rootless rage."

"And the mortals—?"

"Perish," said the other. "Even those who pray to her."

My blood was still. Cold. Yet, I knew what must come next. I found her in the gardens near the Phlegethon, the river of fire, her hands dusted with silver ash. Her laughter drifted soft as pollen.

Kerebos lay beside her, tail thumping as she teased him with a carved bit of bone, not cruel, never cruel, but light. There was peace here, in her. For her, the storm had passed and left the world washed new.

But she was not alone.

Hephaestus stood beside her, stooped and massive, his arms crossed, soot marking the creases of his beard. No flame curled in his forge-broken hands, only concern. Of all the gods I expected to come calling, he was not among them.

But my queen, my root-deep wildfire, spoke to him as if he were an old friend. He answered her in kind, voice low and roughened by smoke, with words I'd never heard him offer anyone.

Gentleness.

"Even the mountains weep ice now," he was saying, gesturing with one thick hand. "My forges dimmed last week. The iron grows brittle. My fire doesn't hold."

She tilted her head, a furrow between her brows. "And Olympus?"

"Divided. Poseidon blames the frost, says the sea is strangled. Apollo hides behind riddles, and Hera…" He shook his head. "Her silence is colder than the rest."

I stepped forward, and Hephaestus inclined his head to me, not with deference, but respect.

"Lord of the Dead," he greeted. "You've felt it, then."

"I have."

She stood between us now, her shadow long behind her, her crown a soft gleam of darkness woven through with root and flicker.

"The world above suffers," she said. "And my mother does not move."

"She moves," Hephaestus corrected gently. "But only *against*. She's closed the seasons. Frozen the cycle. Even the animals fall in the woods. There is no food. No growth. She will not listen to any god."

My queen's expression did not waver. But I saw the edge of ache in her jaw. "She knows I've stayed."

"She knows," I said.

"And this is her answer." Not a question. A truth.

Of course, that was when Hermes arrived. A crackle in the air, a rush of sudden breath. He appeared like he always did, with a half grin, half threat, eyes sharper than most gave him credit for. "Ah," he said, glancing between us. "The hearth is warm down here. Cozy."

"Hermes," I said evenly. "Come to collect more pleas?"

He waved one hand. "No. Come to deliver one." A pause. His face sobered. "From Olympus."

Her shoulders stiffened.

"From Zeus."

Of course it would come to this.

"Let me guess," she said. "He wants the world to turn again."

Hermes gave a grim smile. "He wants all of you. Now. Olympus convenes."

I stepped between her and the god of messengers before I realized I had. "She is no longer his to summon."

The messenger looked past me. "To be fair, my lord, she's never belonged to any of us. And that's the problem."

My hands curled at my sides. Then she laid hers atop mine. Cool. Steady.

"I'll go," she said.

"Heartsong—"

She met my gaze.

"I'll go, beloved," she said again. "Because if I do not speak for myself, they'll try to speak *over* me."

Her voice held the weight of frost and flame. Not defiance.

Authority.

She wasn't walking into Olympus to be taken back. She was walking in to *take her place.* The gods had no idea what was coming.

Olympus never changed.

It reeked of power too long stagnant, of gold piled like rot, of laughter that broke like brittle bone when examined too closely. The air was thick with ambrosia and arrogance. They built palaces here, high above the world they forgot to tend. Yet when it burned, they demanded *answers.*

They could never have expected *her* to come wearing a crown of shadow and a mouth full of spring.

We stepped onto the marble causeway carved from cloud and stone, and the whole of the court turned as one. Even here, in the highest seat of heaven, she drew the sun.

Olympus itself welcomed her, whispering her name, but she did not answer to Kore. Not anymore. She stood not behind me, not beneath me, but beside me.

I, who had ruled unseen since time began, remained awed by the gravity she carried in that moment.

Zeus surged from his throne like a wave made of storm-cloud and wounded pride.

"Aïdes," he thundered, robes crackling with false sky. "Return the girl and let us put this madness to rest."

Beside him, Poseidon grunted, trident in hand. "The earth is dying. Is that not enough for your cold heart, brother? Must all the seas freeze before you see reason?"

I did not flinch.

"Firstly," I said, voice level as the stone beneath the world, "you do not command me. We are equals. You've worn your title so long, you've mistaken it for divinity."

Zeus' nostrils flared, but I pressed on.

"Secondly..." I turned my head, just slightly, to her. "My queen is not something to be *returned*. She is not a *thing* at all."

She met my eyes and smiled. It undid me all over again.

Still, I continued, "She goes where she chooses. And I —" I stepped forward, letting the weight of my vow fill the golden hall. "—*I will always choose her.*"

That was when the goddesses descended.

"This is folly." Athena, sharp-eyed and steel-voiced, emerged from behind her father's throne. "You speak of love like it outweighs wisdom. Do you not see the cost? The world shudders beneath your passion."

Artemis folded her arms, brows knit. "Passion, perhaps," she said coolly. "But I see no chains. I see a woman who walked into the dark on her own terms." A nod. "That, at least, is something sacred."

"She allowed herself to be *soiled*," Athena said flatly. "She has abandoned her nature."

My heart, unshaken, tilted her head. "Or perhaps I've *fulfilled* it."

That drew a ripple through the court. *Hera*—silent and severe on her high throne—lifted her eyes. Yet it was Aphrodite who finally stepped forward, hips swaying, mouth curled in a smile that didn't quite reach her eyes.

"Well," she purred, "I must say... you wear devotion *deliciously*, dear." A pause. "Even Ares can't stop looking at you." She turned her head, golden curls catching the fire-light. "Isn't that right, my love?"

Ares, still leaning in the shadows like a lion denied its pounce, offered no denial. His eyes burned.

But my queen... *she did not look away.*

"If you desire me," she said to him, calm and unbothered, "then desire what I *am*. Not what you remember. And know that you will not touch what belongs to *no one but myself*."

Ares blinked. Then grinned—wolfish and wanting. But he said nothing more. Because even he knew, this was not a girl trembling in the spring bloom.

This was a *queen* who had fed the roots of herself to the dark, and come back crowned in it.

Zeus raised his voice again, desperate now. "You endanger the *balance!* You sever the seasons!"

To that, *she* spoke. Low, clear, devastating. "Then

perhaps the balance was never mine to hold alone." She turned her gaze on the gathered host. "You demand I return to the field. You speak of crops and famine, but when have any of you knelt in a field and *sowed*? When have you wept for the dead, whose names aren't etched in temple stone?"

Silence.

Not even Hera interrupted.

Hermes muttered, "Well, that's a fair point," before being elbowed by Hephaestus.

And then, *she* stepped close, and slipped her hand into mine. "There will be no more summoning," she said, voice soft but final. "No more pleading for my return. No more stories of abduction."

I stared at her, heart aching in ways I had no name for. She looked to the gods.

"I am not Kore anymore," she said. "And I never truly was. That name was chosen *for* me. Maiden. Bloom. Innocence."

She lifted her chin, crown gleaming with root and coal.

"I am *Persephone* now. I am what you cannot bind. And what I choose... is *him*."

My name never passed her lips. She didn't need to speak it. The word was in her eyes. In the way she stepped closer, not for protection, but for *companionship*.

In the stunned silence that followed, all I could hear was the pulse of eternity stretching out, hers, mine, *ours*.

Zeus growled. Poseidon turned away. Athena looked thoughtful. Artemis, almost proud. As for Aphrodite? She simply smiled. Hera's reaction surprised me more than any other. She nodded her head, not in approval or acquiescence, but acceptance and acknowledgement. One queen to another.

Then the Queen of the Dead turned from Olympus. And

I—God of Silence, of Ends, of Shadow—followed her. Not to lead. Not to claim. But to walk with her, wherever she went.

The world had watched her rise, and now, it would have to reckon with the goddess she had become.

All about had just begun to hush when the true storm broke.

Demeter came not as a goddess, but as *grief incarnate*. Beside her, cloaked in ash and smoke, Hecate moved like an omen with eyes that saw too much.

They did not announce themselves. They did not need to. The air grew heavy, thick with the scent of wilted wheat and soil long denied the kiss of rain. The sky above Olympus, eternal and golden, *dimmed*.

From the shadow of the marble, Demeter emerged. Gaunt. Weathered. Once the earth made flesh—now a mother made ruin. Her gaze fell first on her daughter. Then her mouth parted with the sound of something breaking inside.

"*Kore.*"

The name was both a plea and an accusation. Persephone, no longer the maiden, no longer the girl who needed her mother to shape her name, stood tall. "You don't get to call me that," she said, not unkindly. "Not anymore."

Demeter's lips trembled. Her fingers clenched around the hilt of her sickle. "You... you are not this. You are *spring*, child. You are *green and bloom and breath*. Not this—" Her eyes snapped to me, venom rising like frost. "—this *thing of rot!*"

She lunged.

I moved before I thought, the Underworld coiling

around my fists, shadows surging to meet her, but Persephone stepped between us.

"*Enough.*" Her voice stopped us both.

Demeter reeled back as if struck.

"You blame him?" Persephone said, fire licking the edges of her. "You blame *him* when it was *I* who chose. I went. I *walked* into his world."

"You... were taken," Demeter hissed, almost desperate.

"I *kept my promise*," Persephone said. "He did not take me. He *waited*. And I *went*."

All of Olympus seemed to suck in a shocked breath. Hecate's eyes glimmered, watching not like a judge, but like a witness. A guardian.

"So that's it, then?" Demeter's mouth curled, and then came the blade—not her sickle, but the sharper edge of her tongue as she whispered, "You've left me. Abandoned your mother for a lover made of shadow. Does this mean—" Her voice broke, *cracked.* "—does this mean your love for me has *died?*"

Persephone flinched. The words struck deeper than any weapon I could summon. In that moment, I wanted to strike *Demeter*. Not for rage. But for the wound she carved *knowingly* into her daughter's heart.

My beautiful queen did not cry. She *breathed*. One sharp breath. One tremble in her jaw. "I have never stopped loving you," she said. "But must I be *cut in two* to prove it?"

Demeter opened her mouth, but Persephone surged forward, voice rising now—still beautiful, still fierce. "Am I not allowed to *change*? To grow into something you didn't plant in me? I loved you then. I love you now. But that love does not *erase* the rest of me. I am not your spring to harvest, Mother. I am not your crown to place. I am *mine.*"

The hall echoed with all that was unspoken. Not even the wind dared stir.

"I love you," she said again, softer now, "but I love him, too. You don't get to call that betrayal."

Her mother's face twisted, grief and pride and confusion in equal measure. Her hands trembled, but her power had ebbed. The frost she'd carried, the blight she'd cast, began to crack at the edges. Still Hecate stood behind her, a veiled presence at her back, eyes unreadable.

My queen stepped toward me. Her mother watched. As if every step was a nail in the coffin of the child she once knew.

Persephone said one last thing. "I am not what you lost, Mother. I am what you helped create. I am *so much more than what you dreamed*. Can you not be happy for me?"

Demeter didn't speak again. She turned and this time... she wept. The gods said nothing as the earth goddess left, her sorrow trailing like roots torn from the soil.

And I—*Aïdes*—God of the Underworld, keeper of silence, watched the only soul who had ever chosen me lift her chin beneath the weight of divine judgment and not falter. Later, I would hold Persephone. Later, I would press my hand to the place where her mother's words had struck and try, without magic, to make it whole.

But for now, I stood beside my queen as Olympus finally *saw her* and trembled.

Olympus, already reeling from the storm Persephone had unleashed, fell into stunned quiet when Thanatos and Hypnos, twin gods who rarely left the veil between wakefulness and death, stepped forward together.

Their steps made no sound.

Their presence drew mist and memory like trailing cloaks behind them, one wreathed in the hush of eternal sleep, the other veiled in the finality of ends. Though neither were given to meddling, they approached the thrones of the high gods with solemn purpose.

It was Thanatos who spoke first, voice like steel cooled in quiet water.

"She cannot be severed," he said, nodding once toward Persephone. "Not from us. Not from below. The moment she took the Underworld into herself... it *changed* her."

"She is no longer just Kore," Hypnos finished, his voice soft, warm, almost melodic. "She cannot become her again. Not fully."

The Olympians stirred. Even Zeus seemed momentarily quieted by the eerie grace of the brothers.

"She is now the pulse between breath and silence," Thanatos continued. "Between the bloom and the fall. She walks where no other goddess has ever dared, above *and* below."

"She brings life to death and death to life," said Hypnos. "But the world... the world above still needs her. As much as the one below now sings in her presence."

Persephone's fingers brushed mine. She didn't speak. Not yet.

The twin gods turned to her, and this time Hypnos drew closer than the rest had dared come. "Goddess of Two Worlds," he said, eyes glimmering as if dreaming. "You cannot be divided. But you may *choose*."

Persephone's brow furrowed.

"You may choose," Hypnos said again, gently, "when to rise. When to descend. When to unfurl your spring among mortals, and when to bring solace to the dead."

"And when she rises, the earth shall warm," Thanatos said, his voice resonating with quiet finality. "Demeter will see to the harvest, Dionysus will celebrate, and life will know joy again."

"Then when she returns," Hypnos continued, "the Underworld shall not mourn. For she brings *light*, not its absence. She is needed above and she is loved *below*."

Then silence. A moment suspended between possibility and fate. The gods waited. All of Olympus balanced on the edge of a single heartbeat.

Persephone turned her face to me. *Only* me. Her voice, when it came, was quiet but unwavering. "Can you accept that, Aïdes? That I will leave you—to bring spring, to soothe her pain? That I will walk from your arms and your realm for a time?"

Gaia's tears.

I felt it like a wound, clean, deep, and righteous. Yet, I saw the way she looked at me. The flame behind her eyes. The love that refused to be shadowed. If I said no, she would stay. She would burn the world to do it.

But she would grieve, and I could not bear to be the hand that dimmed her. So I bowed my head, doing as I swore in my being I would do, and chose her. "Yes," I promised. Even if it cost me the sun. Even if the hollow left in her absence might one day unmake me. "Because," I added, "your heart is worth more than mine."

Her lips parted. She looked as if she might fall into me, and I was already gone to her, devotion thick in every breath I took. "I will always return," she said, softly. "Not because I'm bound. But because I *choose* to."

Then she turned to the gods.

"To all of you, I am *Persephone* now. Do not call me Kore. I am not yours to command, or barter, or mourn." She raised her hand, and the very air shimmered with shadow and sunlight twined together. "I *choose* to walk both paths. I will bring spring when it is time. I will return to shadow when the harvest sleeps. Not because you demand it. But because I *will it.*"

The gods could only bear witness. The pact did not come from Zeus. His anger over the fact burned in the air. No, this pact came from Persephone.

Then it was sealed, not by decree, but by the echo of every heartbeat that had ever straddled the space between sorrow and joy.

Persephone turned to me once more and took my hand in hers. She smiled. Not as the maiden. Not even as the queen. But as *herself.* Whole. Unbreakable.

Eternal.

And so it was…

Persephone, goddess of the turning year, split her time as no other deity had before her—half in shadow, half in bloom. When she rose, she walked the fields in bare feet, bringing warmth to sleeping roots and laughter to the skies. The mortals danced, the animals birthed young, and Demeter—though never as she once was—tilled the earth in silent reverence.

When she descended, she ruled the Underworld with neither mercy nor cruelty, but grace. The dead whispered prayers to her name, and even the shades found gentler dreams. I walked beside her not as master or captor, but as beloved.

And thus the world spun on.

A cycle, a song.

Spring and fall.

Life and death.

Until one day—

She did not rise.

And she did not descend.

The flowers bloomed late.

The dead stirred without peace.

Demeter cried out to the wind, and I scoured every corner of my realm.

But my queen was gone. Not taken. Not lost.

Gone.

No gate opened for her. No footprints pressed the earth. No scent lingered in the air.

So, as the poets would one day write:

There came a year when spring never came, and the dead waited longer than death required.

And no god, nor mother, nor king of the Underworld could call her forth.

For Kore did not rise, and Persephone did not descend.

And the world held its breath in mourning for the goddess who had chosen both—and vanished into neither.

And I—I have searched every shadow. Every silence, and I will never stop.

For even should the sun burn black and time unravel, I remain—

Aïdes, the unseen. The god who waits.

PART TWO

THE PRESENT

CHAPTER

SEVEN

I'd always had a thing for beginnings.

First days. First blooms. First cups of coffee in a new neighborhood where the pigeons don't recognize you yet. There's a kind of hum in those moments, low and soft. It reminded me of a violin tuning under your skin.

I chased that feeling. Maybe too often according to some people.

I'd moved cities three times in the last four years. Changed my name once—not legally, just enough to feel different. I told my friends it was a branding decision. Artists can get away with things like that.

So now I was Irina Bloom.

It *fit*.

I worked at the Greenhouse Annex in Lower Manhattan, a museum–laboratory hybrid that smelled like soil and ozone. I curated interactive botanical art. Living installations that reacted to movement, breath, skin temperature.

Nature met tech in a gentle combination. The kind of work that made people slow down.

Today, a new exhibit opened: *Future Flora*. Our *first* day... My latest piece, *Regrowth*, was a half-sculpture, half-plant that responded to a person's presence. If it liked you, the flowers bloomed. If it didn't... they stayed shut like secrets. It was the product of so many hours of research and work. I couldn't wait to see *Regrowth's* reactions. It was all I could think about.

I wasn't expecting *him*.

He came in around noon. Tall, sharply dressed, the kind of dark that absorbed light instead of reflecting it. Everything about him looked... intentional. From the black dress shirt to the matte watch on his wrist. He didn't have the distracted posture of a tourist or the bored stance of a funder. He stood still. Like he was waiting for something.

The moment he stepped near *Regrowth*, the petals tensed. I caught it from across the room—barely perceptible, but enough. The plant recoiled. That had never happened before.

I walked over, curious. "She's not usually shy."

He turned his head slowly. His eyes met mine. Pale gray. Cold, but not unkind. The rest of him was dark, from his raven hair to his sun-kissed skin that seemed edged in bronze. If someone wanted to transform him into a statue, he'd be—perfect.

"Maybe she's not shy," he said in the softest of elegant British accents that proved both tempting and hypnotic. "Maybe she's just aware."

"Of what?"

He studied me like he could read the answer in my eyes. "Things that don't belong here."

I laughed, unsure what was making me nervous, him or his words. "You don't strike me as a nature guy."

"I'm not," he replied. "But I know how to respect what's alive." Something about the way he said it made the air around us shiver. Not awkward or electric. Just—*brimming with possibility.*

He left without giving his name. No card. No pretense. Then again, I hadn't really asked him for his name, had I?

After he left, I stood there a while longer, watching *Regrowth* uncurl her petals again. Slowly, cautiously. Like she'd been holding her breath.

I reached out and brushed the stem with my fingers. "You okay?"

The plant didn't answer, obviously. But there was a shift—just the faintest lean of green toward me. Familiar. Like a cat brushing past your ankle without looking at you.

I took that as a yes.

It wasn't until I checked the visitor log later that I saw it scribbled in careful block letters.

Graven Skotos - Thanatek Industries.

Thanatek. The company was trying to buy up natural death like it was intellectual property. They dealt in digital memorials, grief engines, and predictive mortality models. And now, apparently, plant partnerships?

I should've rolled my eyes and moved on. But when I Googled him later in my office, not much came up.

No LinkedIn. No profile photos. No interviews. Just one blurry image from an old tech symposium, and his eyes. Watching from the edge of the crowd, not quite focused on anything that made sense.

My time to focus on him was fleeting as my afternoon filled up fast. A class of college students came through for a tour, led by Dr. Lane from NYU's urban ecology department. He was in his late fifties, soft-spoken and always smelled faintly of cedar. I didn't know whether it was his soap or something older, something earned.

He greeted me with a nod. "Ms. Bloom."

"Doctor."

"Your installation is stirring some very gentle arguments in the back row. Well done."

He always spoke in that same dry, faintly amused tone. Oftentimes, I felt like he knew something that I didn't.

"Tell them to come talk to her," I said, gesturing at *Regrowth*. "She plays favorites."

He gave a rare smile. "Don't we all?"

The students scattered through the exhibit. A few waved their hands near the plants, whispering and laughing when they moved. One girl whispered something to *Regrowth* like a secret. The petals twitched, and the girl jumped back, delighted.

I loved that part of my job. The reactions. The feeling that the world was more alive than most people gave it credit for. It was so easy to dismiss the flora of the world if you didn't understand how it felt, how it reacted, and how it—interacted. Teaching others what the earth experienced was so vital.

Especially today.

Around four, the air changed again. I'd just returned from my break, but goosebumps rippled over my arms. It wasn't cold. It was more like... pressure. I turned and saw Mara at the back of the greenhouse corridor, standing too still, the way people did when they're trying not to be seen.

She worked in research and rarely came out of the analytics lab. When she did, she always wore black gloves —even inside. Her skin was nearly translucent, and likely to burn, so I could hardly blame her. Her voice was softer still, and you had to be close to catch it.

"Something wrong with the sensors?" I asked. That was the only reason I could imagine that would bring her up.

"No," she said. "They're just... picking up anomalies today."

"Anomalies?"

"Biofield irregularities," she added, like that explained anything.

I didn't press. That was the same kind of language Thanatek had been using in their pitches—"biofields," "liminal energy," "predictive grief loops." The sort of terminology that made art feel like something monetized with a spreadsheet.

Still, Mara lingered. Her eyes flicked toward *Regrowth*. Then to me.

"Has anyone touched the core stem today?"

"Just me," I said.

A long pause. My stomach sank at the way she focused on me. I'd hardly done anything *wrong*.

"Be careful," she said finally. "Some systems remember more than they should." Then she turned and walked away, her shadow stretching longer than her body should allow. I blinked, but when I focused again, she was gone.

By five, the greenhouse was empty again. I stayed behind to recalibrate the scent diffusers in *Future Flora*. As I worked, the light shifted from honey-gold to the kind of deep green that only existed right before a thunderstorm.

Just as I stepped back to check my work—*Regrowth* opened her petals fully. All at once. No stimulus, no presence but mine. The petals trembled, then stilled, forming a perfect starburst. It was beautiful, but it was also wrong.

For the first time in a long time, I felt like I was being

watched—not from across the room, but from *underneath* it. Like something deep in the soil had opened its eyes. Apprehension shivered over me, and I shook off the wild thoughts.

By six, the last of the lights dimmed and the greenhouse clicked into its automated sleep cycle. The misting systems whispered to life, and the plants began to breathe slower, as if they too had ended their shifts.

I packed my bag, pulled on my cardigan, and paused at the threshold of the *Future Flora* exhibit. *Regrowth* was still fully open. Still facing me.

"You're being dramatic," I muttered, but softer than I meant to. The room had the hush of a chapel after hours. I flicked off the final light and stepped outside into the warm press of early evening.

I usually biked home—it was faster, cleaner—but tonight I felt... off. Not in a bad way. More like a compass needle spinning when it shouldn't. I left the bike locked in security and walked two blocks, then veered toward the subway entrance without thinking. My feet knew before I did.

The 2 train platform wasn't that busy, which in and of itself was *strange*. The crowded platforms and press of people were why I usually avoided the subway during rush hour. Instead of standing room only, we'd probably be able to sit. Someone hummed too loud through headphones, a man slept standing next to a column, and a woman was tapping out a text like it might save her life.

I sat on the edge of the bench, watching the rats dart along the tracks. Survivors, all of them. The scent of soil still clung to my sleeves. As the train approached, a gust of warm tunnel wind rushed up the platform, kicking up a scrap of paper and something smaller—curled and whimpering.

At first, I thought it was a piece of trash, but then it moved. A tiny puppy. More shadow than fur, black with a single white paw. Skinny and shaking.

"Where did you come from?" I crouched without thinking.

No collar. No tag. Just huge eyes and ribs like parentheses.

The puppy looked at me and didn't bark. Didn't run. Just tilted its head like it was trying to remember where it had seen me before. The poor thing flinched as the train screamed into the station. Doors opened. People shuffled in and out like ghosts passing through each other.

I glanced at the animal.

"This isn't a good idea," I whispered, but I couldn't leave them there, so I scooped the puppy up.

Poor thing weighed nothing. A little heartbeat, fast and fragile. It licked my wrist once. We rode the train in silence. The puppy sat in my lap like it had always belonged there. No one even looked twice.

Sometimes, I truly loved this city.

By the time I reached my apartment in Williamsburg, the sky was bruised with the promise of a storm. I unlocked the door, turned on the hallway lamp, and set the puppy on the floor.

"You're going to need a name," I told him, as I hung up my sweater. "Temporary guest or not, you need one." He padded after me as I went into the kitchen. There seemed to be more energy about him than had been in the subway. That helped.

I rifled through my small kitchen—a mismatched collection of takeout containers, half-empty jars, and a sad packet of oats. No fancy dog food, of course, but I managed to find a few scraps of cooked chicken from the previous night's dinner and a small bowl I usually used for herbs.

I filled it with water, watching the puppy lap eagerly, his tiny tongue flicking like a flame. In between drinks, I fed him small bites of the meat I'd cut up until he seemed full. Then I cleared a corner of my living room, pulling a soft blanket from the couch and folding it into a makeshift bed. The puppy curled up instantly, eyes already heavy, as if he'd found the first safe place in a long time.

I made tea. I watered my plants. I checked on the puppy. I should probably look up the number of a local vet. I tried to read. But my mind kept wandering back to *Regrowth*. To that name on the visitor log.

Graven Skotos.

I had no idea why it stuck. Maybe it was the way the syllables felt like they belonged in another language. Maybe it was the way he looked at me like I was a lock he already knew how to open.

Or maybe—it was just that I'd always had a thing for beginnings.

An obsession, or so one of my former boyfriends used to say. I was too busy looking for the beginning that came just before everything changed that I couldn't appreciate the present. Maybe he was right.

That night, I dreamed of hands pushing up from the soil.

Not terrifying—just inevitable. Like roots trying to find their way back to something they'd forgotten.

When I woke up to the puppy's mewling cries, I shoved the dream aside to take care of the little one.

CHAPTER

EIGHT

She'd changed. Again.

Not in the obvious ways. The hair, the name, the city—those were masks. Temporary. But underneath, her energy was different. Slower this time. Quieter. Like she was truly trying not to be found.

The flowers didn't bloom for me.

They never did.

I stepped out into the warm city air, adjusting my collar as if it made a difference. Manhattan pulsed around me—horns and footsteps and breathless urgency—but I could still feel the faint thrum of her presence behind me. Like a thread pulled tight.

The simulation models hadn't predicted she would activate *yet*.

She wasn't supposed to begin remembering for another cycle. Even acknowledging that, I couldn't stay away. I rarely found her *before* she began to remember. Still, something had stirred. I felt it the moment I stepped into the greenhouse: not just the plants, but the entire place *reacting*. Holding its breath.

It wasn't just her. The whole city had shifted half a degree.

Thanatek's Manhattan office was only a few blocks south, disguised as a boutique tech firm behind glass walls and gentle lighting. Inside, the air smelled sterile, filtered, static-neutralized. The kind of environment that promises logic, order, safety.

False promises.

The elevator recognized me without needing a keycard. Of course it did.

"Welcome, Mr. Skotos," it said, voice smooth and sexless. "Simulation Room Two has resumed sync."

"Show me," I said.

Room Two was dark when I entered, because the room itself preferred shadow. The interface was biological now, threaded with living fiber and synthetic mycelium that mapped patterns faster than silicon ever could. It pulsed faintly as I approached.

The display shimmered to life.

Irina Bloom.

Human designation: Artist.

Energy designation: In flux.

She appeared as a soft silhouette within the node-map: bright, rooted, expanding.

But something else appeared now, too.

A second presence. Small. Recently bound. Canine. Shadow-tethered.

A dog?

"Curious," I murmured.

One of the Thanatek bio-analysts appeared on the far

side of the room, silent until acknowledged—Mara, gloves still on. Always.

"She took it home," she said.

"You allowed that?"

"She didn't ask."

Why would she? I studied the screen. Of course the animal followed her. Even in this life, the pull was still there—*life drawn to her*. Even things born in darkness want to be near her.

"Are we sure it's not an avatar?" I asked.

"Negative. It's untagged. Natural."

That was worse.

"Monitor it," I said.

Mara didn't move. "It's shadow-tethered. What if it binds fully?"

I didn't answer.

Back in my office, I sat at the window and watched the city blink itself toward night. I didn't need the simulation to feel the old energies stirring. They were in the cracks of the sidewalks, in the way shadows bent slightly wrong around certain corners. Something was waking. Not loudly. Not all at once. But enough to notice.

And Irina—she didn't remember.

Not yet. Not consciously.

But she would.

It was only a matter of time. No, my only question was, should I press the advantage I *finally* had or wait...

When she did, the bloom *could* become a gate again and I could choose to let her walk through it or close it before she entered. *What if it doesn't become a gate?*

I pushed that last thought away.

We couldn't rush this. She needed *time*. She needed to be *allowed* time. She needed to *not* be stolen again. How many times now had she been torn away just as I found her? Too many mistakes made over the years. No, I had to be patient. It had been near a millennium since I'd been this far ahead. I'd had months to study, to put people in place. To create a safety net.

I refused to anticipate failure.

Not again.

My home sat in the Upper East Side—though it never looked like much from the outside. The kind of brownstone that disappeared into the background. Carefully chosen. Warded, though no one would know it. Humanity had forgotten so much over the centuries as their reason and logic sought to eradicate *knowing*. The animals, though, they remembered. Even the birds avoid the second-floor sill.

Inside, it was all dark wood and silence. Shadows nested in the corners and didn't move unless I let them.

I shed my jacket, set my gloves on the marble dish by the door, and moved through the house like I always did—measured steps, checking the windows, checking the dark.

Not for safety.

For signs.

The apartment *remembered*. Just like I did. It moved with me, letting me carve it out of whatever time or place I needed it to be. The door to enter just another gateway I forged.

I stood at the tall window in the study, looking down at the street, at the thin pulse of city life smeared in taxi lights and rain.

She'd taken the dog home.

Not a tagged projection. Not a creature of the net. A real thing, small and still damp from some other plane. *Shadow-tethered.* That was Mara's phrasing, but I felt it more plainly. I *knew* where it had come from and what it might mean.

The Underworld still answered to me. Mostly.

Yet even that was changing.

I lit no lamps. Shadows didn't need help here.

I was halfway through reviewing the second day's node reports when the air in the study shifted—like someone *smiled* behind me, without sound or breath.

I didn't turn around.

"You're early," I said.

A pause. A footstep. Soft, deliberate.

"I thought you'd appreciate the gesture." He emerged slowly into view—elegant, sharp-featured, with that kind of ageless calm you only find in gods and assassins. Dressed in a tailored storm-gray coat, hair pulled back, eyes faintly golden in the dark.

Thales.

At least, that's the name he was using this century.

"Your reports say she's stabilizing," he said, walking to the sideboard and pouring himself a drink without asking.

"She hasn't begun to fragment," I replied. "And the simulations haven't split. That's the most I can ask for."

"The dog?"

I glanced at him. He already knew.

"Unbidden. Not sent by me."

He took a sip of his drink—some amber thing I didn't recognize. "You're sure it wasn't sent by *them*?"

"No." I gave a shrug. I wanted to investigate, but what if it didn't recognize me? That could be worse.

Thales set the glass down with a deliberate *clink*. "Then they're not moving faster than we thought."

"I've been ahead of them this time. I've bought us months."

He studied me for a long moment. "If she doesn't remember? Not this time."

"She always remembers," I said quietly. "Eventually."

"You say that like it's a blessing."

I didn't answer.

He walked the room slowly, fingers trailing across the bookshelves. He always moved like he was inspecting something ancient and sacred—and a little bit fragile. His reverence was genuine. For once, that didn't comfort me.

"You've lost her before, Graven. Repeatedly."

"I know."

"Then why—this time—are you still building toward something that can break you?"

I looked at him now. Fully. Met his gaze.

"Because if I don't," I said, "someone else will decide how this story ends." I would allow *no one* else that power.

The storm outside began to gather in earnest. Not loud. Not dangerous. But heavy. Predictive models suggested a mild front. They were wrong. This wasn't just weather—it was memory taking shape again.

Her name—Bloom—was so appropriate. She was the blossoming. Someone—or *something*—wanted to cut the stem before she ever flowered. The storm outside began to hum against the glass.

Thales remained standing. He never stayed long enough to sit. Or maybe he just didn't want to appear settled in my house. He was a friend, or as close to one as beings like us could claim. But loyalty among immortals was rarely about affection. It was about timing. Strategy. Mutual loss.

"You're unusually confident," he said. "That doesn't suit you."

"I'm not confident," I replied. "I'm prepared."

He tilted his head. "Which version of prepared are we discussing? The kind where you rewrite a simulation node to shield her identity... or the kind where you've hired a necromancer from Boston to live in the apartment downstairs?"

I didn't respond. I'd only ever found a necromancer once.

Thales grinned. "That's what I thought." Smartass.

This century has made it easier. For the first time in thousands of years, the edges between things had thinned. Not torn—but *softened*. Humanity didn't believe in us anymore. Not consciously. That had become our greatest advantage.

They trusted their devices, not their instincts. They followed data, not omens. They looked for patterns in everything—until they found one that frightened them, and then they labeled it a glitch.

That's all Thanatek was, really. A way to control the glitch. We packaged it as predictive grief modeling. Neural-laced AI bereavement therapy. But underneath all of it was the same principle we'd used since before language had rules.

Names held power. *Memory* shaped reality. *Belief* was a trigger.

And in this era—this exquisite, fragile century—they'd built machines that did half the work for us.

Magic never left.

It just got better branding.

Thales was inspecting one of the old objects on the shelf—a knife, ancient and blackened, with its edge still sharp enough to cut sound. He ran his finger along the flat of the blade, then looked back at me.

"You think the bloom will open this time."

"It already has."

He raised an eyebrow.

"I saw it," I said, quieter now. "In the greenhouse. The core flower—*Regrowth*—opened. Fully. But only when she is alone."

Thales whistled low. "That's earlier than expected."

"It means we've passed the first threshold."

He looked out the window, toward the storm. His posture changed—less casual now. Alert. "So," he said after a moment, "what are the rules this time?"

"No direct intervention unless she's endangered."

"And who decides what qualifies as danger?"

"I do."

He smiled, faintly. "Convenient."

We stood there, quiet again.

The city below crackled faintly. From here, it didn't feel alive—but something close to it. A beast with too many heads, each dreaming of a different future.

"I have sentries in place," I said. "Networked through Thanatek's emotional-mapping nodes. If she experiences a moment of recognition—true myth-memory, not just intuition—it will light up."

"What about the dog?"

"I'll know more soon."

He finished his drink, left the glass precisely where it had started.

"I'll be in Berlin by tomorrow night. There's movement under the catacombs again."

"Another gate?"

"Or something that wants to be one." He walked to the door but paused before opening it. "She won't be just your decision, you know. The others... some of them will come. Sooner than you think."

"I'm counting on it," I said.

He gave me a long look, somewhere between warning and approval, and then vanished down the hall. Alone again, I activated the display on the far wall. It glowed with the information.

Irina Bloom.

Human designation: Artist.

Energy designation: In flux.

She hadn't dreamed yet. Those would come soon. The memories always found a way in. When they did, this time, if we were careful, she wouldn't only remember what she was.

She might choose it.

CHAPTER

NINE

Three days passed.

The puppy still hadn't barked.

He slept most of the time, curled near the windowsill or beneath the old fern by the kitchen, as if the apartment were his burrow. I kept calling him temporary, but the longer he stayed, the more the label started to feel like a lie.

I hadn't named him. I told myself I was waiting for the right word, but maybe I was just afraid to claim something I didn't understand. Naming him would mean admitting I wanted him to stay, and letting him stay meant allowing something else to take root. As strange as the thoughts were, I didn't deny them.

Thankfully, I could take him to work with me. The Greenhouse Annex wasn't the kind of place that followed strict rules, not when it came to lifeforms of any kind, really. I brought his blanket and tucked him under the desk in my office, near the big window where sun pooled through by noon.

He made for a silent companion. Observant. Growing stronger every day.

We had a rhythm now. Morning check-ins with the sensors in *Future Flora*, a walkthrough of the propagation corridors, then updates to the interactive installations—adjusting scent diffusers, reprogramming the ambient pulse reactions for *Regrowth*, that sort of thing. If he joined me, he'd pad quietly between the aisles of bioreactive flora like a tiny curator.

Somehow, no one questioned his presence. Maybe they didn't see him. Or maybe they just knew not to ask.

After work, I'd settle him into the basket on my bike and we'd glide up the trail toward Williamsburg, the city shifting around us like a breeze. At night, after dinner and a walk through the park, we returned to a peace that was no longer just mine.

When the next storm promised, we went to bed early. A soft headache had been building behind my eyes since sunset. A pulse like a second heartbeat, slow and steady, hammering an ancient drumbeat.

I dreamed of soil.

Rich, black, humming with life. I was buried in it, but I could breathe. I wasn't afraid. My fingers curled into the dirt like silk. Something was growing around me—through me—roots twisting into my ribs, my spine, my lungs. Not choking. Connecting.

And far above, a voice.

Low, like thunder in a cavern. Not words. Just presence. Ancient and—

I woke in the dark. Not just early-dark. Wrong-dark. Thicker than it should've been, like sleep hadn't fully let go.

The puppy was at the foot of the bed, standing still, silent. Watching me. Not whining. Not pawing at the sheets. Just—*waiting*.

I sat up slowly, the air oddly still, and rubbed my eyes. The faint strip of streetlight across the floor felt like the only real thing in the room.

He looked different in the half-light. Taller, maybe. Limbs stretched longer than they had any right to be. But when I reached out, he licked my palm like always—soft, grounding.

Still real.

"Bathroom break?" I murmured.

But he didn't move. His gaze shifted toward the window.

That look chilled me.

I padded barefoot across the floor and pulled back the curtain. Outside, the city was silent. No wind. No sirens. Not even the familiar groan of the subway below.

But, the ivy in the fire escape planter had grown. Not by a little. By inches. Its leaves were darker, waxy, curled inward. As if listening.

I reached toward the glass as if to touch it and it shivered. Visibly shivered.

Then— A soft knock from *inside* the wall.

I jumped.

The puppy growled, low and deliberate, ears angled toward the hallway.

Nothing. No footsteps. No creak. Just that strange thudding in my chest—not fear. Recognition.

I tried to shake it off in the kitchen. Made tea I didn't want. The puppy followed, his steps careful, distant.

He was still watching me. Like I was the one changing. Maybe I was.

Since Skotos' visit—since *Regrowth* recoiled for the first time—things had felt... thinner. Not broken. Just stretched. Like my nerves were far too worn away in spots.

I'd begun waking with dirt under my nails. Soil in the folds of my sheets. Dreams that lingered past waking. Most of it, I could dismiss as my imagination running amuck. Most of it.

Not all of it.

AT WORK, the systems misfired. Biofields pulsed irregularly. Misting cycles triggered without input. Plants seemed to be listening, even when no one spoke.

I'd biked to the Annex early. Cut through the back gate to avoid the loading zone and the chatter from the education staff. The puppy leapt from the basket before I could lift him, trotted up the path like he knew it. Every day he grew stronger, more certain. His ribs had begun to vanish from regular meals.

The greenhouse loomed, veiled in dew. My breath caught. Something in the way the light hit it made it feel like stepping into memory. Inside, the air was warmer than it should've been. I checked the climate logs—no change. But I knew better. The air was saturated, heavy, like it had been waiting for us.

The puppy didn't follow me through the main corridor. He walked straight toward *Future Flora*. Straight to *Regrowth*. I hesitated, then followed. The exhibit was dark, still waking. The petals on *Regrowth* were half-shut, but twitching—aware.

A ripple moved through the surrounding soil trays. Slow. Deliberate.

Not wind. Not moisture shift. Movement.

I crouched beside one of the propagation beds. New shoots had emerged overnight—broad, waxy, unfamiliar. Not part of any registered seedling I'd logged.

The soil? It was darker than it should've been. Thick with that forest-floor smell. Alive.

The puppy stood a few feet away, tail still, ears angled. Watching the dirt. Not barking. Just staring.

I reached down and touched the base of one new stem. It trembled beneath my fingertips. Something responded. Something beneath.

I straightened, heart thudding. Dragging out my phone, I jotted down my notes with shaking fingers. It had to be the compost interacting with some experimental mineral blend. Weird dreams or not, I knew the soil and the plants knew me.

This was *explainable*. Dreams didn't make weird things happen, they just made it seem weird because of the hazy state between waking and sleeping. That was all. I clung to that fact.

Later, as I passed Dr. Lane near the scent-diffusion panel, he nodded in that quiet, knowing way of his. "Something's different today," he said.

Surprise bubbled through me. "You can feel it?"

He glanced toward the installation. "The ones who listen always can."

His comment startled me. The ones who listen? Was I still asleep? The puppy brushed against my ankle then. Not playful. Anchoring. A touch to remind me I was still here. Still in the waking world.

And yet... I wasn't sure.

When I finally returned to my office, I found the ivy

from my fire escape somehow included in the latest lab registry.

Unsubmitted. Unlabeled. But registered. My name beside it.

When did I log it?

Despite my love for them, I had to admit—nothing about this was a beginning even if it should be. It was like waking up in the middle of an episode of a show. While I could read the blurb, it didn't really tell me what I'd missed. The only thing I knew for certain was that I *had* missed something.

Outside, the city moved on—its noise folding over the quiet edges of the greenhouse. But inside, something else had already taken root. No, it felt like something so much older and no matter how strange, I couldn't shake the sensation and I didn't know if I was ready.

I told myself I was going to find Mara.

There were too many coincidences. The unregistered ivy. The shifting soil. Bloom cycles collapsing into minutes instead of days. Not to mention the look Mara had given *Regrowth* just three days earlier, all sharp and strange, like she was measuring more than just the light.

I stepped out of my office, the puppy padding behind me like a small shadow, but didn't get far.

"Ms. Bloom!"

Erin from Facilities waved me down, her clipboard already in motion. "Sorry to bug you, but one of the calibration pods in Gallery B isn't responding. It's throwing off the humidity curve."

I blinked. "That shouldn't be possible. I just reset Gallery B's systems yesterday."

"I know, but the orchids are reacting like it's monsoon season in there. Can you take a look?"

I glanced toward the corridor leading to Analytics, where Mara's lab was housed. Just past the atmospheric sensors and the sub-basement entrance.

"Yeah," I said. "I'll come now." Ten minutes. It shouldn't take more than ten minutes. Famous last words. Gallery B was a *mess*.

The orchids had dropped half their petals. The air was thick with their scent, sweet and almost cloying. It was far too much for morning. The misting nozzles had frozen in a constant half-drip that created a slow, syncopated rhythm like a leaking faucet.

I crouched to recalibrate the base panel, and the system responded almost a full *second* before I put in the commands. A kind of reverse lag, like the sensors were anticipating me. That shouldn't be possible.

The puppy whined, just once. Then stopped.

I glanced at him. "It's okay," I murmured. "It's okay." Even if it wasn't, he shouldn't have to worry about it. A few minute changes should fix all of this.

What puzzled me were the *number* of minute changes I had to make. When I finally got the room to stabilize, I stood. My body protested the sudden stretch and I had to roll my head from side to side to ease the tension. That was when I realized it had been over thirty minutes since I started.

Not a swift fix at all, even with the system's strange behavior. We were going to have to pull the logs and see if the programming was off somewhere.

I wiped my hands and turned to go, heart already racing faster as I thought of the long hallway and the static hum of Mara's lab. Unfortunately, the puppy and I didn't even make it to the threshold of Gallery B before my earpiece buzzed.

The sound startled me. I'd slipped it on out of habit and hadn't even paid attention to its presence.

"Ms. Bloom, we've got a group in the atrium that didn't book through central. NYU undergrads. They're saying Dr. Lane invited them."

I sighed. "Of course he did."

"Do we want to turn them away or…?"

"No, I'll be right there."

Puppy glanced up at me and I found a smile for him before giving him an affectionate scratch. "Hold that thought."

The atrium was full of noise and perfume, flashes of student cologne and overheated wool scarves. Dr. Lane waited near the entrance, calmly sipping a thermos of what I knew would smell like cedar and citrus. The man really liked his tea.

"I thought we agreed on Thursdays for walk-throughs," I said under my breath as I joined him.

"Spontaneity is vital to ecological curiosity," he replied, smiling in that maddening way of his. "Besides, *Regrowth* seems more expressive when she's surprised."

I didn't argue. I ran through the demo. I enjoyed watching the students wave their hands over sensors and gasp when petals curled or color shifted.

Then I felt it again.

The sense of being watched, not from within the exhibit, but beneath it.

As if the greenhouse had layers I hadn't yet mapped.

By the time I finished with the question and answers session following the demo and finally excused myself to return to the hallway for Analytics, the day began sliding sideways again.

Puppy stopped at the foot of the corridor, head low, ears pinned slightly back. Unease slid through me.

I knelt beside him. "You feel it too?"

He didn't move.

The hallway was dimmer than it should've been. Even the overhead fluorescents looked pale and thinned out. I walked forward anyway, my steps echoing slightly despite the sound-dampening panels.

I had just reached the halfway mark when—

"Irina."

It wasn't loud, but it wasn't from my earpiece or from *behind* me.

It came from the intercom above the emergency hatch. That line was only supposed to be used during drills *or* if something went wrong. I hesitated, heart thudding. The call light blinked again.

"Please report to the back loading bay, immediately."

There was no sign off nor recognizable voice, just the robotic tone of the automated system. I glanced back toward Mara's lab then down at the puppy. He'd followed me silently and stared in the same direction I'd been headed. He didn't whine or wag his tail, he just waited.

I had a feeling neither of us was going to make it down there today. With a longer sigh, I turned away and the puppy fell into step with me.

The loading bay was cooler than the rest of the Annex, and smelled faintly of rust, fuel, and old rain. The gate was closed, but not sealed. A thin line of soil trailed in from outside, which was unusual. The last delivery had come in the day before, and we always swept up after a delivery.

One of the freight panels had shorted out. Again. That made for three times this month.

This time, however, the error code flashing wasn't the usual mechanical alert. It was a string of text.

001-REGROWTH-EXCEEDED

I stared at it. That wasn't even a real code. The puppy stood beside the freight bay now, nose pressed to the seam between the gate and the floor. He didn't bark, but his entire body was braced like he waited for something to come through.

I didn't know what I expected when I opened the panel housing. Maybe it was a wiring error or a loose connection. I definitely expected something *explainable*.

What I found though, inside the electrical box was a single green leaf.

Dark. Waxy. Curled.

Not burned. Not out of place.

Just *there*.

That did not make any kind of sense, at all.

By the time I finished running diagnostics and closed the panel again, I had no answers for the leaf. I took it with me and returned to the hallway for Analytics, but the corridor was empty. Normal. The air was cool and quiet. The lights shined properly.

I didn't have to check. Mara was gone.

Of course she was.

The puppy trotted ahead of me now, his gait light. It was like he knew we didn't have to go down there and he was *happy* about it. Though, I might just be projecting because I wished the emotion was mine. Unfortunately, all that I experienced was relief.

Still, my questions were far from finished. There was something moving under the greenhouse and I was running out of reasons to pretend I couldn't feel it.

Then there was the leaf still in my palm.

CHAPTER
TEN

GRAVEN

Four days.

I told myself I wouldn't go back. That once was enough. Observe, assess, move on. That was what the protocol dictated. It was what the simulations suggested. Distance ensured clarity.

Clarity vanished the moment *Regrowth* opened.

I arrived at the Greenhouse Annex just after nine. The public were already making their way inside. I shouldn't have come, but knowing it didn't make it more desirable than seeing her again. The boundary between what I knew and what I wanted had begun to blur.

The building looked unchanged on the outside—sleek glass, vertical planters, the quiet whir of a climate grid syncing to solar output. Inside, however, the hum had deepened. Everything within responded to stimuli whether it was light, warmth, or movement.

Now it responded to more. *Intention* elicited a response.

The building itself wasn't just awake. It was listening.

I signed in without a word. The intern at the front desk blinked at me like she wasn't sure she'd seen me at all. Good. The Annex certainly didn't need more questions today.

The front atrium greeted me with the scent of damp loam and photosensitive oils. The corridor to *Future Flora* was dimmer than I remembered, less filtered sun and more shadow softened by mist. The change tempted me. The exhibit hadn't opened to the public yet, but the plants were already responding—one bloom nearest the entrance swiveled subtly toward me, not in welcome. In awareness.

They remembered me. Most things did. The light adjusted sluggishly at my entrance, they didn't want me here.

Fair.

I didn't belong here, but I came anyway.

I walked the corridor deliberately, not hiding but not announcing myself either. The light shifted as I moved—an artifact of the building's circadian modulation. But still, too reactive. The sensors weren't just reading temperature or movement. They were reading presence. *Mine.*

Someone had fine-tuned this system past the point of safe thresholds.

Someone like her.

I found her at the far end of the east wing, sleeves rolled, a smudge of soil on her cheek. She was bent over a tray of moss-tiered growth, adjusting something beneath the top layer—wiring, maybe. Her hands were steady, but her energy definitely wasn't.

I felt it before she noticed me. The time it took her to realize I was there was a gift. I was able to savor her presence and just study her.

She didn't startle when she finally looked up. She straightened slowly, eyeing me like she'd half-expected this. "You again," she said. The words came out more like an acknowledgment without a hint of impatience or annoyance.

"I know," I admitted without apology. "I shouldn't have come."

"Then why did you?"

I paused, glancing around. One of the secondary vines near *Regrowth* twitched. Not toward me, but away.

"I wanted to check the system's response metrics. After the storm." I tacked on the last three words. It seemed a better reason to come in person rather than send someone.

She snorted softly. Apparently not better enough for Irina. "You came all the way down here to 'check metrics'?"

I didn't answer, merely shrugged.

The dog lay nearby, watching. He seemed stronger than before. Sharper at the edges. His limbs didn't quite move like a puppy's. When he stood, it was silent, measured. Appearances could be deceiving after all, and who better to know that than I?

The puppy took a few steps toward me, not aggressive movement, just present. He put himself between me and Irina. A choice. His gaze met mine and I felt the tether again.

It wasn't new at all. No, it was as old as I'd begun to suspect.

Irina knelt once more, though this time she did it to stroke behind the puppy's ears, grounding herself with touch.

"Does he have a name?" I asked, curious.

"No," she said, a wistful note in her voice. "Not yet."

"Good."

"Good?" She raised her eyebrows.

"Names bind. Better to know what you need before you do that."

Irina tilted her head as the puppy mirrored the exact same movement. She glanced back down at the pitch-black animal, save for his single white paw—that paw was new. Something I tucked away to consider later.

"He doesn't bark," Irina said, more to herself than to me. "But he watches everything."

"Some things don't need to speak to be understood."

That earned me a half-smile and a gleam in her sky-blue eyes. It was enough to stop all the breath in my body. "Was that poetic or ominous?"

I allowed myself the faintest of smiles, not that I could have contained it. "Both."

She rose, but folded her arms. I didn't think she was cold, but she was definitely unsettled. "You didn't leave a name last time."

"Didn't think I needed to."

"You still don't."

Amused at the bite in her words, I lingered. I should've walked away. Said something cryptic and made myself leave, then vanished into the humidity of the greenhouse. That might have let the moment fade.

That was exactly what I should've done. Instead, I stepped closer.

"Your soil composition shifted," I said quietly. "Layer drift. The deeper trays, especially near the stem core."

Her brow furrowed. "You read our data?"

"No," I said. "I felt it."

She didn't move, but something in her gaze changed. Caution giving way to curiosity. "You really expect me to believe you just *feel* soil layers?"

"Do you believe *Regrowth* blooms on instinct?" I answered her challenge with one of my own.

"That's different."

"Is it?"

We stood there, a few feet apart, surrounded by plants that could feel heart rates and thermal loss patterns. The puppy didn't interrupt. The leaves didn't tremble. But the room wasn't still. It waited.

"You're not here about the plants," she said finally.

"No."

"And not about the puppy."

"Also no."

She held my gaze. Her heartbeat didn't spike. No fear entered her eyes. That was so much worse, because their glow made me hunger for her even more.

"What are you here for then?"

I glanced down at the way the moss around her feet had darkened, drawn slightly inward, like it anchored and protected her. The last thing I should tell her was the truth.

But I found, I could not bear to lie to her.

Never lie.

"You," I said.

Silence stretched unbearably taut as she held my gaze.

Then she blinked, and it released us both. "You've got the worst pickup line I've ever heard."

Her response startled a chuckle from me, and the sound was as unfamiliar to my ears now as the feeling was to my chest. Yet a smile tugged my mouth wider before I could contain it. "It's not a line."

Skepticism filled her expression. "Still terrible."

The invitation to play was right there. My being stretched out toward hers in yearning. I turned toward the corridor before I could give in to the desire. If I stayed any longer, something might happen that couldn't be undone.

"You're leaving?" The disappointment wreathing the words looped around me, and I had to glance back.

"You have work and so do I." Not a lie. Never a lie. But not the whole truth either. "I've interrupted you enough as it is." The last, the absolute truth.

"Oh." So much meaning populated that one word, and I resisted the urge to translate it. To offer her comfort and to take some myself, because the last thing I wanted to do was leave her.

"You should run a test on *Regrowth*," I said over my shoulder as I neared the exit. "Use a neural imprint pattern —without touch. Watch what she does when you walk by."

An olive branch for her. A gift for me.

"Why?" Puzzlement filled the word, and I knew her gaze had gone to the plant so I looked back once more to drink in the sight of her.

"She's remembering you." With those last words, I forced myself to leave and not wait for any response. She wasn't going to say anything to that. Not yet, anyway. The puppy didn't growl as I left, but his stare stayed on me all the way down the hall and beyond when the doors closed behind me. There was an ancient question in his stare and one I didn't have an answer for. Not yet.

Back on the street, the city pulsed around me—sirens, footsteps, voices, car horns, fragments of music—but I wasn't listening. I should have stayed away, but how in the name of Gaia could I possibly do that?

I was closer to her far sooner than I'd ever managed before. I'd had two whole conversations with her and not a few sorrow-infused moments before she was ripped away from me again. How many times had I lost her? I hadn't lost count, every single moment imprinted on me forever. Those tear-drenched moments both sustained and enraged me.

No, I couldn't stay away. Not when the tether had finally tightened again. Not when the blood had already begun to stir. If I were close, then I might be able to hold on to her this time.

The moment I made the corner, the air shifted. Not like before. This wasn't memory humming in the wires or the pulse of something ancient rising through the cracks. This was colder. Stiller. As if the city itself skipped a beat.

The clouds threatening earlier had rolled in, but they hadn't thickened. The light had changed anyway, it slanted sharper and colors blued at the edges. It was like the sun had glanced away for a moment too long.

I made myself keep walking with a measured pace, spine straight, and I kept my gaze firmly forward. I didn't glance back at the Annex, even if I could still feel her inside. *Irina*. The puppy. The slow, inevitable rhythm of something beginning.

At the next crosswalk, the voice found me.

"Didn't think you performed your own errands." It came from the stoop of an old bookstore, one that hadn't been open in years. The sign was still hand-painted, letters faded and flaking like they were ashamed to still exist.

The man seated there wore a crisp gray suit, but no tie and no coat. He appeared young, but the kind of young that didn't really start that way. His eyes were the color of tarnished copper, and he wore a single ring on one gloved hand, a seal I recognized and hated.

I didn't stop walking.

"Pollux," I said without turning.

He laughed. "That's not the name I'm using this time."

"Don't care."

"Rude. I came all the way to the surface, and you don't even offer me a coffee?"

"I didn't invite you."

"I go where the threads pull."

I paused then, just for a second. That was the problem with gods like him. They didn't lie. Not exactly. They just told the truth in the most weaponized form they could devise.

I turned.

Pollux still lounged, perfectly relaxed, like a cat on a sun-warmed ledge. There was far more pressure beneath the surface, crouched within him just behind his spine. One of the Dioscuri, he had shared his immortality with his human twin. They were rarely without the other, though together they had warranted a place in the stars.

"You're early," I said.

"That's twice today you've said that. Maybe the clock isn't broken. Maybe you're just *late*." The insouciance infusing his quip dared me to act.

"She's not ready." And he should damn well know that. His gift with travelers made him as likely to be one of those who stole her away at the moment of her death. One who could act in those few precious seconds when her soul was just out of my reach, before she could truly re-enter the Underworld.

"She never is." His eyes sharpened. Yet, he didn't seek to deny his presence or offer me weak excuses. "That's not the point."

I didn't respond. The street around us blurred slightly. A lens shift, too subtle for mortals to notice, but I saw it. The barrier *between* was thinning. Not unheard of, but not expected either. More shifts this time. More changes. The pattern seemed to finally be breaking after all these centuries.

"Let me guess," Pollux said, his voice almost kind. "You think this time will be different. You think this incarnation will choose you and the bloom will open and stay that way." He straightened then, far too smooth and confident. "Let me save you the trouble, Skotos. She's already being watched and not just by you."

My chest went still. My *will*. "Stay away from her."

He grinned, all teeth now. "I'm not here for her. I'm here for the moment *after*. When she breaks. When she remembers too much too fast, and the world you've so carefully manicured around her begins to burn. I'll be there to offer a different path."

I stepped toward him, not a threat but a warning. "I'll end you before you touch her." This time, suspicion would be enough.

Pollux's smile didn't move, but the air around him did. Slightly. It was as if it bowed—to me, not him.

"You could try," he said lightly. "But I'm not your shadow anymore, Graven. Not since Prague. Not since the gate burned in reverse."

I didn't flinch, but the memories still tore through me like teeth.

"I know about the dog," he added softly. "It's almost cute that you don't."

That stopped me cold.

He turned to go then, brushing imaginary dust off his shirt. "Be careful with hope, Skotos. It starts small and then it eats *everything*."

He vanished with the next flicker of the traffic lights. No

sound. No trace. The world around me resettled, and sound rushed back in.

I'd just been warned—whether Pollux meant to do it or the universe offered me a boon—I would take it.

What the hell had I missed? And how much time did I truly have left?

CHAPTER

ELEVEN

IRINA

As if the encounter with Skotos wasn't enough to disrupt the day, Mara wasn't in.

Her office lights were off. No note. No texts. Just Mara's gloves folded neatly on her workstation, like she'd slipped out of her skin and just wandered off.

Weird. She was always here before me. Quiet as a ghost, but still *here*. Today, of all days, when I wanted—*needed*—answers she wasn't here. The readings. The ivy. The walls.

So many questions. Including why did I keep waking up with soil under my fingernails? Was sleep-gardening even a thing? Skotos just added more questions to my ever-growing list.

The greenhouse air was thicker than usual, warmer too. The humidity monitor was calibrated, but everything felt a few degrees too alive. The plants turned more quickly toward movement. The *mimosa pudicas* flinched before I touched them. Even *Regrowth* seemed agitated, petals twitching open and shut like breath.

137

The puppy, still unnamed, sat curled in the sun spot on my office floor, chin resting on his adorable paws. Watching me. The white paw just seemed to gleam against all the darkness.

"You're not going to tell me anything, are you?" I muttered.

He didn't blink.

By midday, I gave up waiting for Mara to come in "late." The staff calendar showed nothing. Not PTO. No meetings. Just a sudden absence that felt... deliberate. So when the front desk buzzed my line with a visitor I wasn't expecting, I was already on edge.

"Someone from the city," Mindy, the assistant, said, trying to sound casual. "Says he's here to tour the Annex as a potential arts patron."

"City doesn't do private patronage," I said, already suspicious.

"He's not *with* the city," she added, lower like she'd turned and covered the microphone to keep her words hushed. "But he's got that *look*."

I sighed. Mindy was easy to persuade with a pretty face. "What look?"

"You'll see."

"Well," I said to the puppy, "I guess we'll find out." Unfortunately, Mindy proved to be correct. He had the look.

Tall, dark, expensive—like a sculpture of a man that had been taught how to move convincingly. He wore a sleek black shirt, no tie, unbuttoned just enough to suggest heat tolerance or arrogance. His blazer was slate-gray, tailored to within an inch of its life, and he wore his confidence like a scent.

His hair was neatly tousled, jaw sharp, sunglasses tucked into his collar like they'd never seen actual sun. A scar traced his jawline, but the roughness of it seemed to enhance his beauty. An aesthetic, not an accident.

He smiled when I stepped into the atrium. Not wide, just enough. His expression said he expected this to be fun.

Well, that made one of us.

"Ms. Bloom," he said, voice smooth with a rasp at the edge. "I've heard good things."

"And who exactly have you heard them from?" I asked, not smiling at all.

His grin deepened into a delighted one. "That would ruin the charm of mystery, wouldn't it?"

"I don't do mystery tours."

"Then think of this as a courtship." He offered a hand. "I'm Kassian Harpe. I represent a small fund that's very interested in immersive bio-art. *Future Flora*, especially."

Kassian Harpe.

The name meant nothing, but I'd heard worse pitches. It wasn't like we were flush with donors who didn't want to install NFTs or algorithmic nonsense among the orchids. Still, I didn't trust anyone who led with charm before credentials. While he held out his hand, I didn't accept. "I don't take potential donors through exhibits without notice."

"I'm not just a donor," he said easily enough and let his hand lower to smooth down his lapels. "I'm an admirer."

"Of plants?" I doubted my tone could get much drier.

"You misunderstand." He stepped closer. "I am a great admirer of power that grows slowly and doesn't ask permission."

That stopped me.

Because it didn't sound like a line. It sounded like something older. Like something I'd heard before, maybe in a dream. Maybe in dirt.

Or maybe in a book, I scolded myself. "Shall we take our conversation elsewhere?" I motioned to the hall and guided him away from the front. While I might not take him on a tour, I didn't need to continue the interaction with our avid audience, and Mindy hadn't taken her eyes off him since I arrived.

The puppy padded out of my office before we were even halfway down the hall, tail wagging faintly and nose twitching.

Kassian dropped to one knee, completely unbothered by putting his pressed suit trousers to the tiled floor. He extended his hand again this time to my puppy.

"Well now," he murmured. "Aren't you something rare?"

The dog didn't move at first, just stared. Then, slowly, he stepped forward and sniffed. He didn't lick, didn't nuzzle, just stood there with his nose barely an inch from Kassian's fingers as if weighing the scent he detected.

Kassian didn't force it when the puppy made no further moves. "Apparently, he's no more interested in taking my hand than you were." He rose, then brushed imaginary dust from his trousers as he turned to face me.

"Neither of us know you." Not that I should have to remind him of that. Part of me was pleased that the puppy didn't just wiggle in happiness for the man.

"It's funny," Kassian said. "Dogs usually love me."

"Maybe he has a different palate," I suggested, folding my arms.

"Or perhaps he's cautious, like *you*." He glanced down the hall leading toward the exhibit. "There's nothing wrong with caution, Ms. Bloom. I find only the careless act without it."

Somehow, that wasn't a comfort.

"Tell you what," he said, turning back. "Let me buy you a drink sometime. You can vet me properly. Ask for references. I'll even bring a notarized document assuring you I know the difference between a moss wall and a mood board."

Was that his idea of a joke? I stared at him. "Or, you could do something inventive, like just tell me what you're actually looking for."

"You," he said, lips curving. "Obviously."

"Then you should make an appointment." It came out far snippier than I intended. But Kassian Harpe seemed like a man who rarely heard the word "no" and should probably have it drummed into him.

"I'll do that." His smile deepened, and he inclined his head before he strode down the hall back toward the atrium and the entrance. "You'll hear from me." His promise floated back and left me even more unsettled than I'd been before.

When he disappeared through the door the puppy whined once. Soft. Low.

I felt it again, that tug behind my ribs. Not fear. Not desire. Just—something stranger. A memory. What kind of memory?

I had no idea. The lack of answers might drive me mad.

Two men in four days.

Two.

Both impossibly composed. Both saying too much and not enough. Both watching me like they were looking for something specific. And both of them were here for *me*. Or so they said.

That didn't land right.

I was hardly the kind of person people just… showed up for. I organized, I curated, I moved things into harmony and made them run smoothly. I didn't attract mysterious men with cheekbones sharp enough to draw blood and voices that sounded like rain sliding down iron. That happened to other people. People who wore flawless cosmetics, styled their hair perfectly, and didn't second-guess the way they walked into rooms.

I glanced down at myself—loose linen shirt, soil-stained pants, sneakers with scuffed toes. Not exactly cursed with main character energy.

Still, it had happened. *Twice.*

I half-laughed under my breath as I dug into my desk drawer for a granola bar. My fingers brushed over my phone, and without thinking, I picked it up and hovered over the call screen.

Mom.

The name looked out of place. Too soft. Too simple. Yet, I nearly tapped it. She always told me I had a kind of intuition that gave me a green thumb, and the stubbornness to never quite trust it. She'd know what to say about all of this.

About *them.*

I hesitated, my thumb hovered, and then the greenhouse shuddered. Just once, but the vibration was unmistakable. Not the building. Not the street outside. *The greenhouse.*

I dropped the phone and left my office on a course to the exhibit corridor. Heart in my throat and fearing the worst, I pushed open the door. Everything looked the same. Light filtered gold through the mist glass. Vines curled neatly along their lattices. The digital humidity readouts were still green.

It was fine, but then— The air shifted and the scent changed. Something *wrong* bloomed under the usual notes of moss and ozone. It was burnt copper and crushed jasmine, sickly sweet and electric.

I turned sharply toward the *Future Flora* exhibit.

Regrowth was trembling.

Not opening. Not reacting to anyone's presence. Just shaking.

Each petal quivered at its edge, as if caught in a nonexistent breeze. The core stem bent ever so slightly toward the floor. An invisible weight pulling it downward.

I took a step closer just as the mist system hissed. A shadow flickered beneath the mesh floor. Then another. I froze in place.

There was *nothing* under the flooring. Just the support structure, the sub-misters, and the fiber-optic threads that connected each installation to the rest of the sensory web. I knew every inch of it, because I'd helped to design the grid.

Then something moved again, fluid and slow. If my imagination wasn't playing tricks on me, I'd think it was the roots themselves shifting beneath the loose soil.

The puppy let out a single, sharp bark from behind me. His first. Shock jerked through me, galvanizing my pulse to racing. I shot a look back at him. He was stiff-legged in the doorway to the hall. The door that should have closed behind me. His fur bristled and his dark eyes locked on the floor beneath *Regrowth*. Ears forward. Tail low.

A warning.

"I see it too," I whispered as much to comfort the puppy as myself. I hadn't meant to say it out loud, but the air was pressing in from everywhere and I was staring at the trembling bloom. It was so dense in here, it was almost hard to breathe and the pressure closed in.

Then—just as quickly—it stopped.

Everything.

The tremors. The scent. The flicker.

All gone.

Regrowth stood still again. Perfect. Serene. Like she'd never moved at all.

My hands shook, but nothing else in the room did. I wasn't exactly afraid, but something inside of me vibrated in almost perfect tune with what I'd just witnessed.

And I *had* seen it. Even the puppy reacted to it.

Confirmation.

I backed away slowly, not quite willing to turn away from *Regrowth*. The puppy followed me as soon as I made it to the door and out. Then I closed it.

Once back in my office, I shut the office door and leaned against it. The once again silent puppy stared up at me. The room felt smaller, less safe. The edges seemed to have warped in my short absence.

"Okay," I whispered, exhaling a hard breath and trying to get my pulse under control. "We're going to do some research."

Two men.

Crazy plant activity.

Monitors off.

Yes, we needed to do some research.

I sat down at my desk and logged into my computer. With trembling fingers, I typed in Kassian Harpe to the search bar.

Nothing.

No social presence. No company site. No board memberships. Just a name.

I tabbed to a different program and logged into security, then searched through the stills for the time when Harpe arrived. I captured one via the plugin we used for safety reviews and saved it.

With that done, I refined the query to do a reverse image search. That got me something, but not remotely what I expected.

The same face. Different name—no, not just one name. Multiple names.

Sebastian Rhagos, venture backer for a weapons lab in Nevada.

Lucien Varo, keynote speaker at an "elite resilience summit" in 2019. What even was elite resilience?

Unknown male in the background of a grainy photo dated in the 1990s. The man shook hands with a U.S. general and had the exact same face as Harpe. Not aged a day.

There were more names. More activities.

One man. Dozens of names. Dozens of suits. No other trail to follow. A search on those names turned up the same as Kassian Harpe.

Leaning back in the chair, I stared at my reflection in the dark screen and then down at the puppy who had crept closer to lean against my leg.

"Right," I said softly. "Not just charm. Definitely *not just charm.*"

I pulled open the drawer with my cell phone again. I could still call Mom, and tell her what?

That was the point, I didn't even know what was going on to tell her. I shut the drawer again. Then, heart hammering, I returned to the search bar and typed in Graven Skotos, then hit enter.

I needed more.

CHAPTER
TWELVE

She was remembering.

Not fully. Not yet. But something inside her had stirred—and the world was already beginning to bend around it.

I stood in Simulation Room Two again, eyes locked on the glowing node web. Irina's outline pulsed slowly, like the beat of a shallow tide. Nearby, the dog's signal sparked with erratic flickers—chaotic, untethered, instinctive.

But that wasn't what disturbed me.

No, it was the absence. Another presence had entered her orbit this morning. Something—someone—powerful. Masked from the system, which meant it wasn't one of mine.

Mara stood behind me, silent.

"You told me she was stable," I said quietly.

"She was."

"And now?"

"Disturbed." She stepped forward, fingers twitching at the edge of her gloves. "Ares was there."

My jaw tightened. "In the greenhouse?"

"Briefly. He left without damaging the node field, but—he's noticed her."

I turned away from the screen. Cold coiled in my gut, ancient and rising.

"He's not supposed to know yet." *None* of them were.

"You don't control the pantheon," Mara said evenly.

"No," I said. "But I control this facility. You were supposed to shield her."

"She's blooming too fast. We can't contain what we didn't anticipate."

I moved toward her, voice low. "What *exactly* didn't we anticipate, Mara?"

She didn't flinch. "The dog. The way *Regrowth* responded. The anomalies in the substrata of the greenhouse soil—something's stirring beneath her presence, and it's older than anything I've tracked through Thanatek's systems."

A pause.

"And?" I pressed.

She met my eyes. "She's not following the usual pattern."

Of course she wasn't.

She never did.

Yet, how was I supposed to counter any obstacles if she changed everything too swiftly?

⌇

Thessaloniki, 1456

. . .

They called her *Leto* then. Black curls, hard green eyes, a laugh that could cut through the salt-thick air of the harbor. She was a candle-maker's daughter, or so it seemed. I knew the truth the moment she passed me in the square. She didn't look. She didn't smile. But something in the air behind her shimmered like ash from the old world.

It was her.

I waited three days. Didn't speak. Didn't interfere.

On the fourth, I followed her to the hillside chapel, half-burnt from the most recent siege. She left wildflowers at the altar—red and gold and violet, the same colors she had always chosen.

She was seventeen.

Too young.

Too mortal.

Too bright for a god like me.

And yet I waited, even then.

But she died in childbirth the following spring. And still she *did not come to me.*

No soul. No echo. No descent into shadow.

Nothing.

It was the third time that had happened.

Present

"I want a full scan of every soul-tether in a ten-mile radius," I said. "I don't care if it burns the node network. I want *every anomaly tagged.*"

Mara hesitated. "That may trigger—"

"I know what it may trigger," I snapped. "Do it anyway."

She bowed slightly and stepped out, silent as vapor.

I was alone again with the simulation.

Irina's light shimmered on the map. Still. Beautiful. Unaware.

She wasn't Persephone. Not yet.

But she would be.

If the curse didn't take her again first.

I had to make sure *that* didn't happen.

BERLIN, 1889

SHE WAS A PIANIST THEN. Louisa. Hair pinned back with silver combs. Her music filled salons full of air that reeked of cologne and politics. She never smiled at anyone except the children who brought her flowers.

But when I stood outside the concert hall—gloved, expressionless, a man-shaped silhouette—she looked up.

Her hands missed a note.

She *never* missed notes.

It was her.

That time, she *almost* remembered.

Her fingers brushed mine at a private gathering, and she gasped—like something ancient had reached through her lungs. She whispered something in a language she shouldn't have known: "*Aidôs...*"

She died two weeks later. A fire in the guesthouse. Charred remains.

Still, she didn't come to me.

Her soul bypassed the Underworld *again*.

PRESENT

I poured myself a measure of something too rare to name and let it burn through the silence. Thanatek had begun as a cover. A false face to hide the real project—*Mnemos*. A living archive of soulpaths. Every lifetime, every thread, every fracture of a soul echo that might lead me to her.

It had taken two centuries to build the system. A thousand quiet agents. Algorithmic sorcery wrapped in corporate language. We sold grief prediction, yes. We mapped emotional ecosystems.

But the truth?

I was mapping *her*.

Each life.

Each version.

Irina was the first one in nearly three hundred years to bloom without a false imprint—no false loves, no broken lines.

She was clean. Untouched. And for the first time...

Something was coming with her.

The dog.

The stir in the soil.

The flare of the core flower—*Regrowth*, yes. But also *return*.

She hadn't remembered me yet, but the earth had.

Mara returned twenty-two minutes later.

She didn't knock. She never did. Her presence announced itself the way frost does—without noise, but with consequence.

"The anomaly scan's complete," she said. "Nothing new in her immediate surroundings. But two of the older tether-nodes just spiked in correlation with her current signature."

I looked up. "Where?"

"One in Prague," she said. "The other in the dead sector of Node Archive Nine. A corrupted memory vault."

My chest tightened. "Nine? No one's accessed Nine in decades." Longer.

"I didn't say it was accessed," she said. "I said it reacted. The pattern was dormant until her interaction with *Regrowth* this morning. Then something... ignited."

Mara crossed the room and pulled a black data shard from her coat pocket. Thin as a blade. "I extracted the last stable memory from the corrupted sector."

I took it, fingers brushing hers. Even through the glove, her skin was cold. She was always cold.

"I don't like it," she added. "That it's waking now."

"Neither do I."

I crossed to the viewing alcove and inserted the shard into the auxiliary reader. The room dimmed. A shimmer flickered into shape before me—a memory reconstruction. Flickering. Scarred.

Then—clarity.

Memory Fragment: Paris, 1795

She was called *Élise* in that life.

A poet's daughter. Pale and ferocious. Her hair was black as burnt sugar, her laugh sharp as a blade. She walked the ruined alleys of post-revolution Paris like she owned the bones beneath it.

The echo began with her running.

No. *Fleeing.*

A back street. Rain. Blood.

She was clutching something to her chest—a book, or perhaps a mirror. A distorted reflection of herself flickered in the object, and for a second... her face *shifted*.

Not Élise. Not Irina.

Persephone.

Wide-eyed. Terrified. Glowing faintly with a light not meant for that century.

Behind her, a figure moved through the rain.

No face. No features. Not even a name in the records. The simulation had failed to tag it. Only darkness wrapped in mortal skin. A god, perhaps. Or something worse.

She turned into a doorway—but the door never opened.

Her scream didn't sound human.

The memory ended before her death.

PRESENT

I stood motionless as the last flicker of rain faded from the projection.

Mara watched me carefully, arms folded.

"That record was corrupted for a reason," I said slowly. "This was the only death we never confirmed."

"No soul tether," she agreed. "No return. No crossing."

"She should have come to me." Every single time she should have come to me, and she didn't.

"Maybe she has tried," Mara said. "But someone else reaches her first."

The thought settled like a cold weight in my spine. It was a thought I had had, over and over. One I desperately clung to but had never been able to prove.

"Do you think it was him?" I asked.

Mara hesitated. "You mean Ares?"

"No." I looked at her. "The one we don't name." The one

most likely to interfere because he thought it his divine right.

She didn't speak for a long time. Then: "I don't think he's *here*... yet."

"But you think he will come."

"It's power," she said with a shrug. "Yes, he will come." It was a *fait accompli.*

I turned back to the now-empty display. There were rules, once. Laws carved into the oldest stones, long before fire had a name. Gods who died were meant to fade. Mortals who bloomed again carried only fragments.

But *she* was different. Her soul retained shape. Music. Memory. The *pattern.*

I had tracked her across centuries, followed that glimmer through empires and ruins, through ice ages of loneliness. I was the Lord of the Dead, but I was not immune to yearning. "I won't lose her again."

"Then you'll have to change the ending," Mara murmured. She turned to go, her shadow slipping back into the corridor.

I remained, alone with the echo of a memory that should never have existed.

She had screamed, but not in pain—in *recognition.*

Something had found her that night. Whatever it was... it had stolen her *away* from death itself.

The first time I knew something was wrong was not Paris.

It was long before, when she was called Selene, a healer in Delphi, gentle and clever, dead at twenty-six from a fever that came too fast. I waited three days in the Lower Gates for her soul to cross. It never did.

It happened again in Tangier, and Siena, and once

outside Kyoto. Each time her life ended, I *waited*. I felt her pass from her body, but not into mine. Not into the realm that should've welcomed her.

At first, I blamed myself. Maybe the curse—*or her choice to be mortal*—cut the thread too deeply. Maybe she wasn't meant to return. Maybe I wasn't meant to hold her anymore.

But Élise—

Élise was different.

Paris, 1795.

That was the first time I had evidence. Data. Patterns. A true fragment to anchor the suspicion I'd carried for centuries.

I replayed it now—again, again. The rooftops wet with spring rain, her dress torn at the hem, her blood mingling with soot. Élise Rousseau died with grace in her eyes and something resolute on her lips. I'd watched from the shadows, hidden by the veil, waiting for the moment her soul would cross—

But it didn't.

Not to me.

And for the first time in thousands of years, I had *proof.* Thanatek's earliest soul-mapping interface caught the anomaly.

Subject: Rousseau, Élise

Age: 31

Status: Deceased

Soul Transfer: FAILED

Expected Descent: Overdue

Underworld Tether: Severed

She had died, yes. But she had *refused the path* that should have led her to me. Not instinctively. Not blindly.

Intentionally.

The fragment played back one more time. Her final breath, lips parting—two words, whispered not in fear, but in resolve.

"Not yet."

That was what changed everything.

That was when I knew.

She was being blocked. Rerouted. Intercepted.

I STOOD, the simulation flickering behind me, and crossed to the far wall of the chamber. My hand brushed over the obsidian plaque, and the veil between worlds softened—just enough.

The shadows shifted. The room darkened.

And I stepped through.

THE UNDERWORLD — Outer Vaults

The world beneath the world isn't fire and brimstone. It's silence and stone and stories etched into the walls. I emerged into the Vault of Names, where no light glowed unless summoned. My breath did not fog. My footsteps did not echo.

They were already waiting.

Two shapes moved near the central altar. One was tall and gold-eyed, draped in silver cloth, Mnemosyne, the titan of memory. The other was folded in red shadow, skeletal hands resting atop a black staff, Charon, the ferryman, who forgot nothing but volunteered little.

"Mara told you," Mnemosyne said without turning.

"Not enough," I replied. "I want the full account. Paris. Élise. Why didn't she descend?"

Charon chuckled. A thin, rattling sound like bone wind through cavern teeth.

"She tried," he said. "You weren't listening."

"I was *there*. I reached for her. And then—nothing."

Mnemosyne turned. Her eyes were lined with star fire. She studied me, not with contempt, but with the solemn fatigue of one who has seen too many patterns repeat.

"You forget," she said. "The living must choose to remember. But the dead must choose to arrive."

"She wouldn't have refused me."

"She didn't," Mnemosyne said. "But something else did."

She raised her hand and touched the center of the altar. A soft white shimmer appeared. The fragment. The moment of her death. Élise, lit by moonlight, red blooming from her side. Whispering something.

I moved closer. Her lips were moving, just once.

"Not yet."

A refusal.

Not to life. Not to me. But to whatever called her next.

"Where did she go?" I asked, voice low.

"Nowhere we could follow," Mnemosyne said. "Someone intercepted her."

"Someone? Or—"

"The one you don't like to name," Charon interrupted. "Even now, you won't say it."

"I don't need to. I can feel his interference." I clenched my fists. "But is he the one who stole her?"

Mnemosyne frowned. "No. I don't think so. He didn't

take her. He rerouted her. Cut the tether. Turned the riverbed so the soul lost its way."

That was the trick. Not death. Not resurrection. Disorientation.

"Did he know what she was?" Did he know *who* she was?

"He always did," Charon said. "He was there when she first stepped into the sun."

Back in the Vault, I paced. Memory was fragile. Myth, even more so. I couldn't afford to lose the thread. Not again.

"Can it be reversed?" I asked.

Mnemosyne hesitated. "Only if she remembers not just who she is—but where she belongs."

"She's beginning to," I said. "She felt something in the greenhouse. She felt me."

"Then time is short," Charon said. "Because if *he* felt her too, he'll come to remind her of their version of the story."

"And that can't happen," I whispered.

The Surface

When I returned to the waking world, the air in my office had gone still.

Mara stood at the edge of the room.

"You went looking," she said.

I nodded.

"And?"

"Élise didn't choose death. She chose delay."

"Then it wasn't a failure," Mara said. "It was a divergence."

I sat slowly, hands resting on the edge of the desk.

"No," I said. "It was a warning."

The system pulsed. Irina's node flared once—soft and gold.

She was remembering something.

If I didn't reach her first, the one without a name might offer her a version of herself that *wasn't mine to reclaim.*

CHAPTER

THIRTEEN

IRINA

It wasn't insomnia exactly. Just a kind of restlessness that had settled under my skin like static. I couldn't focus. I couldn't sit still. The puppy was curled up on his pallet, twitching in his sleep. Rain tapped lightly at the windows. Even the city sounded quieter than usual.

I sat cross-legged on the floor of my living room with my laptop open and the television on but no sound. I'd started doom scrolling on my phone but gave that up for trying to find something more productive.

So now, I was doom scrolling on my computer. It didn't do a damn thing for my mood nor did it make me tired. If anything, it just increased my agitation.

I searched for Graven's name again. I don't know why. After the research in my office, I wanted to put it all away. I told myself to stop, that looking was only going to cause more issues. But the encounter with the man in the greenhouse—the first one—Graven, had left more than a mark. It left a *question*.

That question was one I couldn't leave alone. It haunted the edges of my mind and whispered in my ear. Unlike Kassian Harpe, the man with the slow grin and perfect timing, Graven Skotos had a digital footprint.

Small, but real. While that was somewhat unnerving, I took far more comfort in finding one man instead of *dozens*. Graven Skotos was listed as the founder and executive director of Thanatek Industries, with press quotes going back at least a decade.

He had no social media, but not everyone did. I had some but I really didn't like it so I rarely used it. No personal interviews. Just the kind of clinical bio that made you think he either had nothing to hide or too much.

I needed to stop watching crime dramas. As if summoned by the thought, an episode of *Law and Order* kicked off on the screen. There'd been a marathon running.

"Thanatek: Reimagining End-of-Life Data with Neural-Mapped Legacy Solutions"

I clicked the link.

The homepage was kind of sterile. Soothing in that tech start-up mixed with luxury hospice kind of way. Soft grays, relaxed language. Euphemisms *everywhere*.

"Grief responsive AI."

"Continuity of Memory."

"Liminal interaction modeling."

There were no definitions or explanations. As I scrolled, I found an interactive module labeled "Memory Archive Preview."

I hovered, then clicked.

It opened a sample interface: a mock-up of what a user might see after "uploading" the memory of a lost loved one. I wasn't sure if they wanted you to upload a video or a photo, but it said *memory*. The page pulsed with a soft heartbeat animation as if syncing to my presence. Despite the seamless, if beautiful design, something about it made my stomach cramp.

Interactive or not, it was just a demo, right?

I backed out of it. Then I opened another search bar.

Graven Skotos + founder.

Then *Skotos + philosophy.*

Finally, just *Skotos.*

That was when it got strange.

An old symposium video popped up of him giving a keynote address. The label said it was on "Transliminal Identity Structures." I hit play and *listened.* Most of the lecture went right over my head. He covered everything in complex terms from digital soul-mirroring to the ethics of mapping grief patterns across social networks.

There was a lot more in between that I just couldn't follow. I stopped trying and just listened to his voice. It was... kind, measured, and warm. He clearly understood everything he said, but he was patiently offering it to everyone else so we could catch up.

One comment below the video caught my eye as it ended.

"If Thanatek ever cracks true continuity, we won't need gods to find the afterlife anymore. We'll build it ourselves."

I stared at the screen and re-read that comment over and over. I wasn't sure if the commenter was trolling, making a joke, or deadly serious and leaving a prophecy.

I minimized the browser and set the laptop aside. The puppy stirred from his doze to lift his head and stare at me.

"I'm being weird, aren't I?" I asked.

He yawned. It wasn't really an answer.

I picked the laptop back up again. I almost hit play on the video to listen to his voice once more, but I closed that and opened a new search window. I thought about searching Kassian Harpe again, but something stopped me.

Maybe it was the lack of footprint for him and way too many other spots for his bizarre doppelgangers. Maybe it was how the plants hadn't trusted him. They might not have been certain about Graven, but there wasn't automatic distrust.

Or maybe I was just losing my mind. I typed in: "Thanatek + biofield irregularities."

I didn't expect much. Only one link pinged back. It was a cached version of a research page long since scrubbed from their public site.

It was a white paper. Co-authored by M. Andrelis.

Mara.

My chest went tight again.

"Preliminary Notes on Shadow-Tethered Entities in Post-Thanatic Liminal Zones."

I skimmed the language; like the keynote a lot of it went right over my head. It might have been written in English, but it wasn't with any familiar terms until one footnote leapt out at me.

"*...non-digital presences with anomalous canine forms have been observed near subjects with energy fragmentation thresholds approaching myth-recognition levels. Further study required. Subject Code: B-9. Bloom.*"

My name.

A cold wave crashed through my body. I pushed the laptop away like it was part of the problem.

My name, in a research note. Tagged like an experiment.

The puppy abandoned his bed to cross the room and settle next to me. His dark eyes were wide, and watchful.

"I didn't ask for this," I whispered to him. Somewhere

deep in the greenhouse annex of my mind, the vines twisted tighter. The air shimmered. Something inside of me uncoiled. It wasn't fear. It was a hell of a lot more uncomfortable than that.

It was recognition.

~

THE MORNING CAME like it always did. Only today it was gray, damp, and as reluctant as I felt.

I hadn't slept. Not really. Still, my body went through the motions: shower, tea, food. The puppy watched me the whole time I was half-spiraling. I tried to leave him at home but he was having none of it, darting out the door as soon as I opened it. Convinced, I put him in the basket so he could ride with me again.

The air outside was wet with that almost-rain. The streets shimmered with the kiss of oil that rose to the wet surfaces but hadn't quite washed away yet. I pedaled as hard as I could, thinking that maybe the speed could burn off the thoughts that clung to me.

That white paper with a footnote containing my name clawed at the edges of my mind and refused to let go. It had been scrubbed from the website only a couple of months earlier, but nothing indicated *when* she wrote it in the first place.

Thanatek had eyes on me? Was it new? Or had they always? And Mara was involved. I mean, she had to be, right? She co-authored the paper, cataloging something she hadn't even warned me about. What about everyone else?

What about the Annex?

The moment I arrived, I went straight past the main gallery and down to the admin wing. The puppy trotted next to me. My boots squeaked slightly on the polished floor. I didn't even bother checking my reflection in the side glass. I was too focused and too wired to care what I looked like.

I didn't knock. The door to Dr. Eleanor Heinritz's office was open a crack, and I pushed through on instinct. The words already formed.

"I need to talk to you about Thanatek and why my name is—"

I stopped cold because the doctor wasn't alone. She sat behind her desk, half-turned toward a man lounging in one of her guest chairs like it had been put there just for him. He didn't look even a little surprised at my entrance. In fact, he smiled.

Slow. Easy. If sunshine could be trapped in a smile, he had it and it would burn if you got too close.

"Ah," he said. "There she is. Right on time, I'd say."

What?

He wore a tan wool coat over a navy suit, open at the collar. No tie. Polished brown shoes that had somehow stayed clean even in the mucky weather outside. His hair was golden bronze and far too perfect. His eyes? A little too bright and far too amused.

"Ms. Bloom," Dr. Heinritz said carefully. "We're just finishing up a meeting—"

"No," the man interrupted smoothly. "We're just beginning, I think." He rose and crossed over to me while holding out his hand. Welcome radiated off him. I took his hand almost automatically and his warmth engulfed me.

"West," he said. "Oscar West. Independent logistics consultant. But you can call me Hermes."

I all but gawked as I stared at him. "Excuse me?"

He grinned wider. "Sorry. Habit. Alias, not name. I go by

Oscar in this century. Old names have a tendency to get heavy."

"Oscar is here representing a legacy patron," Dr. Heinritz said, folding her hands. "He's expressed interest in some of our more interactive installations, particularly *Future Flora.*"

Tugging my hand from his, I glanced between them. My pulse hadn't slowed. "Is this about Thanatek?"

"Everything is, eventually," Oscar said, smile undiminished. "But in this case? No. Not directly."

Dr. Heinritz gave him a look.

"What?" He raised his hands. "I didn't say it *wasn't* related. Just not the *reason* I am here."

Honestly, I didn't have the spoons for this man. I turned to Dr. Heinritz. "I found something last night. About Mara. A research paper—"

"She hasn't been in," the doctor interrupted gently. "And I'm aware of the work you're referring to."

"You knew?" It came out far sharper than I intended.

"Thanatek funds a portion of our sensory-mapping research. That's hardly a secret, Irina."

"No," I countered. "But tagging *people*? That's not just data. That's *surveillance*. That's me."

Oscar shifted, his attention dancing back and forth between me and the doctor. "You *are* special," he said, studying me with an intensity that added weight to his words. "Even if you don't remember why yet."

"Don't do that," I ordered. I didn't know this man and he didn't have the right to interject his opinions or judgment. "Don't talk to me like I'm some huge secret."

"Who said you weren't?" He tilted his head.

Dr. Heinritz rose. "I think it's best we reconvene—"

"No, no," Oscar said. "Let her stay. Actually, I came to

deliver something and she might as well hear it too." He retrieved a small envelope sealed with silver wax from his coat pocket. The insignia pressed into it seemed to shimmer. I didn't immediately recognize the symbol.

But it felt *familiar*. Almost wrongly familiar.

Oscar passed the envelope to Dr. Heinritz with something like reverence.

"This needs to reach a certain someone by tomorrow's solstice marker. Physical relay only. No digital tracking. You understand." Clear yet cryptic.

Dr. Heinritz nodded.

Then, Oscar turned to me. "As for you," he said softly, stepping closer. "You're waking up. That's good. But remember this, messages are just mirrors. It's up to you whether you read them or break them." He tapped two fingers to his forehead in mock salute, winked and then paused at the door to pet the puppy. "Hey there, little one." Then he strolled on like a man who owned the place.

The silence he left behind wasn't empty, it rang.

I wanted to scream. Instead, I whirled to focus on Dr. Heinritz. "What the *hell* is going on?"

She didn't answer right away. Just looked at the envelope in her hands and then at me.

"I think you're going to need some context," she said with a sigh. "And probably some tea."

The tea was jasmine. Hot. Strong. No sugar, no milk— just the kind of bitter clarity I needed.

Dr. Heinritz moved with that eerie calm she always had. It wasn't indifference. More the practiced serenity of someone who'd seen weirder things than this. At the moment, I really shouldn't find that as comforting as I did. She handed me the cup, then sat across from me at the low table in her office. The strange silver-sealed envelope sat between us. Untouched.

I stared at it. "He called himself *Hermes*."

She nodded. "It's not his first time using that name."

I blinked. "Wait. Are you saying... that *was* Hermes? Like the actual god?"

Another sip of tea. "Would it really surprise you?"

I leaned back in the chair, trying not to spiral. "You're telling me literal mythological gods are walking around New York and... what? Dropping off mail?"

"It's not as metaphorical as you think," she said. "Most of the older ones take human roles now. It's easier to exist in fragments. Less attention."

As stunning as that bombshell should have been, I was far from flummoxed. If anything, I was *irritated*. "But why *here*? Why me?"

Dr. Heinritz finally looked me in the eyes. "Because *you* aren't just human either, Irina."

Silence plummeted between us, chilling the air until it left a coat of frost behind.

She continued, slowly. "I don't know the whole story. I've only ever been told pieces. Clues. But Thanatek's involvement in *Future Flora* wasn't a coincidence. They've been tracking bio-signatures—unique energetic patterns— across multiple lifetimes."

"And mine matched something," I whispered.

"It matched *someone*," she corrected.

"Who?"

She paused, then said, "Persephone."

I sat very still.

"The goddess," she continued. "Or the soul once called that. A spirit that's reincarnated dozens of times. Not always as a woman. Not always in this part of the world.

But always carrying the same core resonance. And each time... something interferes. She dies, but doesn't cross over. Leaves no trace in Thanatek's underworld data. It's like she evaporates."

I laughed, breathless. "So, I'm a glitch in their reincarnation tracking?"

"You're more than that. You're a *missing piece.* And someone powerful wants to keep you that way."

The tea had gone cold in my hands.

"I found Graven last night," I said, quietly. "He *doesn't* match the ghost-blank like Kassian does. He has history. Work. But it's all tied to Thanatek. And it all *feels* like misdirection."

Dr. Heinritz didn't confirm or deny. "He's not a stranger to the systems we use. But he's not their pawn either."

"He's, what, in love with Persephone?"

"More than love," she said softly. "Bound. Across lifetimes. One of the oldest stories there is. He's not the villain here, Irina. But he may be too close to see clearly."

I closed my eyes. The room felt heavier now. Denser. Like something unseen had entered with the truth. I opened them again. "The envelope," I said. "What is it?"

"I don't know. But it's for someone I haven't seen in a long time."

"Someone... like him?"

Dr. Heinritz nodded once.

A part of me wanted to leave. Run. Call my mom. Pretend this was all some elaborate dream wrapped in the scent of moss and soil and jasmine tea. But I didn't move. "Why didn't you tell me earlier?" I asked, finally.

"I wasn't sure it was *you*," she said. "Not until *Regrowth* opened the way it did. That revealed *her* presence. That was *you.*"

I looked down at my hands. They were shaking. "And now?"

Dr. Heinritz leaned forward, her gaze calm and exact. "Now," she said, "you have to choose how much truth you want to carry. Because once it starts coming, it won't stop. And it will change everything."

CHAPTER

FOURTEEN

It was subtle, at first. A ripple in the tether.

The tether wasn't physical. Not really. But it thrummed in a way that made the hairs at the back of my neck rise — old instinct paired with older technology. Biofield resonance had its quirks, especially when paired with shared myth-coded lineage. I'd studied them. I'd designed instruments to measure them. But nothing had prepared me for when *her* signal finally spiked.

Irina Bloom. Persephone's spiritual-signal in a modern skin. And now, *awakening*.

I closed the interface and stood. The air in the Thanatek monitoring suite had gone suddenly stale. Too clean. Recycled too many times. I hated this building. Its precision. Its lies. I had built its foundations, but I had never made a home here.

The screen still glowed behind me, faint afterimages of a waveform spike that looked almost like—

No. Not *almost.* It was a *pattern match.* One I'd seen centuries ago.

My coat was already in my hand before I realized I was moving.

By the time I reached the Annex, the sky had bruised into that unpleasant mid-morning gray. I didn't use the front entrance. I moved through service corridors, not because I needed to be secretive, but because being seen—*truly* seen—could trigger memories she wasn't ready for. Not yet.

But something had changed.

Her tether had flared hard enough to make my vision swim. That wasn't just fear. That was identity realignment. Recognition at the soul level. Something—*someone*—had told her *too much* too fast.

I reached Heinritz's office just in time to catch the last trailing edge of Hermes's departure.

Of *course* it was him.

Oscar West. The god of transitions, of messages between the worlds, always showing up where doors began to crack. His fingerprints were *everywhere*—just like always. Subtle. Playful. Dangerous. His aura still lingered like ozone after a lightning strike.

I didn't knock. I opened the door.

Irina and Heinritz both turned at once. The envelope lay between them like a ritual object waiting for the final act.

Irina's eyes locked with mine—and my chest tightened.

She remembered something. I saw it in the way she tensed. Not everything. But a shadow of what we had been. Her eyes were the same. They always were.

"Graven," Heinritz said, guarded.

But I was already speaking. "She's not ready for him."

Irina's jaw clenched. "For *who*?"

I stepped forward, ignoring Heinritz's silent warning. My voice was quieter now. Focused. "Hermes plays both sides. He always has. But he doesn't show up unless something is in motion. You triggered it, Irina. You did something."

"I found a paper with my *name* on it," she snapped, passionate anger swirling in her posture, her voice, her *eyes*. "Found out I was being tracked like a goddamn experiment."

"You are more than that," I promised her. So much more.

"Don't," she warned, power crackling under the words. "Don't speak to me like I'm a riddle to be solved."

I did not want to have this argument with her. "I'm not trying to solve you. I'm trying to *protect* you."

"Oh, well that makes it better," she shot back, voice sharp. "Thanatek tags me, Mara writes about me like a footnote, and now gods in business suits are showing up with glowing envelopes, and *you*—you just walk in like you own the story."

I hesitated. She was hurt. No—*betrayed*. And I had no defense that wouldn't sound like control. With that in mind, I revealed the only truth I had.

"You're waking up," I said. "And that's dangerous. Because if you remember everything, the beings who've kept you scattered for centuries... won't let you stay."

Silence fell again. Not empty. Not peaceful. It was the hush before a fault line breaks. Irina stared at me, eyes dark and wet and burning.

"I don't know who I'm more afraid of," she whispered. "Them. Or you."

Heinritz shifted. "Graven—"

But I held up a hand. Not to her. To *Irina*. My gaze didn't leave hers.

"You should be afraid of me," I said, voice low. Because this was another truth she'd never embraced, yet had always existed. "But not because I'd hurt you. Because I *won't*. Even when I should. Even when the world burns."

She blinked. The room pulsed with something deeper than fear.

Recognition.

Again.

"I knew you," she murmured, softer now. "Didn't I? Before."

"You've always known me," I replied, choking off the desperation that wanted to give her everything. "You just didn't always choose me."

The air went very still. Something *other* seemed to study me through her eyes. I had no name for it nor the feeling it evoked, but there was a deep *knowing* that rang through me. The rules were *changing*.

Then Irina stood. Slowly. Purposefully. She looked at Heinritz, then at me.

"I'm done waiting for answers," she said. "I'm going to find them myself. No more riddles. No more ghosts." She turned to leave. At the door, she paused and added, almost as an afterthought: "You might want to start being honest. Because whatever happens next? I won't be the only one waking up."

That warning came from the *other* too. Before I could latch onto it, she was gone. The only sound left in the room was the soft, rhythmic tap of the silver-sealed envelope trembling slightly on the table.

It hadn't done that before. Apparently, it *also* knew what was coming too.

I watched the door close behind her, the resonance of her departure still echoing faintly through the field. Even now, she carried her energy like a storm just beginning to gather — wild at the edges, but centered by something ancient. Something *hers*.

Across the table, the envelope pulsed once — faint, but undeniable.

I stepped forward and picked it up.

The wax was cool and dry beneath my fingers, but the weight of it wasn't measured in grams. It felt like memory. Like obligation. Like warning. Hermes never left things behind lightly.

I slid the envelope into the inside pocket of my coat. But not all warnings were worth being listened to. Sometimes, the wind just blustered, and if you kept the door closed, it couldn't bother you.

When I looked up, Heinritz met my gaze.

Her composure never cracked — not entirely — but the faint crease at the corners of her eyes told me everything I needed to know.

"She's not ready," I said, tone quiet but resolute.

"She's stronger than you think," Heinritz replied. "Stronger than *any* of us thought."

"That's not the problem," I said. "It's *everyone else* I'm worried about."

I let the words hang for a beat too long — then added, softly but with steel:

"Don't let her be alone with West."

Heinritz's mouth tightened. A silent agreement.

I didn't wait for more. I turned and followed.

The corridors were cooler than they should've been.

The Annex had its own climate control, and yet the air felt like early winter. Charged. Irina had already left the admin wing by the time I reached the main hallway, but the trail was fresh. I could feel it, a shimmer in the air, faint electromagnetic signature from her presence — and from the creature at her heel.

The dog.

He wasn't ordinary. Not even close. But then again, *nothing* near her ever was.

I found her just past the internal atrium, in the open passage near the herbarium rotunda. She wasn't walking quickly — more like pacing on instinct. Trying to outstep a thought. The dog was pressed close to her left side, head up, ever watchful.

I didn't rush her.

I simply matched her pace and spoke from just enough distance that she had to choose to hear me.

"Irina."

She stopped, but didn't turn.

"I'm not here to make you decide anything," I said, voice steady. "But I am asking you to come with me."

Now she turned. Her eyes glittered, sharp with a thousand unspoken thoughts. "Come with you *where*?"

"For a walk," I said simply. "We can get coffee. Talk. Nothing else."

She stared at me, her expression unreadable at first, then cracking, ever so slightly, with disbelief. "That's it?" she asked. "Coffee? A *walk*? After all that?"

I shrugged once. "Sometimes the simplest things are the hardest to offer."

"And why would I accept?" she demanded. The edge in her voice had softened, slightly, but it was there. "Why now? Why you?"

I didn't hesitate.

"Why not?" It was far lighter-hearted a response than any I could truly experience, but I needed to carry this burden for her. "You don't owe me trust. Or answers. But I won't lie to you, Irina. I never have. And I won't let anyone take advantage of where you are right now. Not gods. Not ghosts. Not even those beings who think they mean well."

Her jaw clenched again, but her posture shifted. She wasn't closing off, not entirely.

"You expect me to believe you're one of the good guys?"

"No," I said quietly. Never would I seek to control her impressions. Never. "I expect you to believe I'm trying."

The dog—the not-dog—pressed his body gently against her leg. Not forcing her. Just present. Grounded.

Her fingers curled once at her side, then relaxed. Some of the heat left her eyes. For a moment, she looked tired. Then tempted. Then human again.

It was that woman who looked at me, really looked, as if peeling back all my layers. From the warrior to the executive, the researcher, and all the way down to the shadow I'd let myself become.

Something in her gaze flickered with *memory*. Not full recognition. But the beginning of it. Her shoulders dropped by an inch. "Fine," she said. "But I pick the place."

A faint, unexpected smile pulled at the corners of my mouth. This was so much more than I could have expected. I would not spoil the moment. "Deal."

She turned, and the dog followed. I stepped into place beside her. One heartbeat behind. Exactly where I always had been.

We walked in silence at first, down the corridor lined with ferns and filtered light. Irina didn't speak again until we neared her office. She gave me a side glance—measuring, wary still—but motioned for me to wait by the threshold.

"I need something," she murmured, and disappeared inside.

The not-dog followed at her heel with the kind of precision that said *guard*, not *pet*. But when she opened a drawer near her desk and pulled out a soft charcoal-gray leash and matching collar, his ears flicked back and his shoulders drooped slightly. Not in resistance. More in visible, offended *dignity*.

Irina noticed immediately.

"Oh, come on," she said gently, kneeling beside him. "You don't need it, I know that. You *probably* understand traffic laws better than half the drivers out there. But rules are rules, and I don't want anyone getting the idea that you're lost or unattended." Her voice dipped. "I don't want anyone taking you."

The dog's reaction was instant and subtle: the tension melted out of him, his head lowering, muzzle brushing her knee. More quiet agreement than submission. An understanding. It was a moment of unguarded affection so clear, so instinctively intimate, it stopped me. Not because of the display itself.

But because something in me... *ached* at it.

She could say she didn't remember. She could fight the recognition rising inside her. But this creature—this presence she hadn't even named yet—had earned her claim. That was exactly what it was, too: a *claim*. Spoken gently, yes. But there, all the same. She chose him.

I remembered what it was like to be chosen by her, and I remembered what it cost her every time.

She clipped the leash with a soft *click* and stood. "I want to walk to the park," she said.

"It's a few blocks," I replied, not objecting.

"I know." There was no challenge in her voice now. Just a quiet need for space, for distance. For air.

"Then we'll walk," I said.

We left the Annex through the side entrance. Not as grand as the atrium, but quieter. Better. The door hissed shut behind us, sealing off the cold scent of jasmine tea and unanswered questions.

"Will you tell me about the letter?" The question was hesitant, almost unnerved as if she had no idea how I might react.

"Eventually," I promised "But not now." Even I didn't want to know what it contained. I wanted to be here, now, in the present.

The city's damp morning pressed in immediately, a concrete wet with the thin sheen of rain not quite over. The air was ripe with ozone and the faint chemical musk of spring trying to push through industrial rot.

Irina stepped onto the sidewalk first, the leash looped loosely in her hand. The not-dog pressed close, ears high, eyes tracking. I fell into place at her opposite side. Neither of us spoke.

We bracketed her.

Anyone watching might not have noticed. It wasn't overt. But to those who *knew*—who *looked*—there would be no mistaking our positions. This was not a casual walk.

This was escort.

Protection.

The city moved around us: taxis muttering at intersections, pedestrians whispering down crosswalks, distant sirens howling between the buildings. All of it a blur I filtered out. My focus was narrow. Trained. Irina.

Her shoulders stayed high for a few blocks. Guarded.

But not brittle. Not fragile. She was gathering herself with each step. Letting the motion wear down the jagged edges inside.

I didn't fill the silence. I didn't need to. Presence was sometimes louder than words. And right now, what she needed wasn't explanation or comfort.

She needed to *exist* without being hunted. So, we walked. As we moved, I made sure no one came close enough to threaten the space she was finally learning how to reclaim.

By the second block, Irina began to speak.

Not *to* me, exactly, nor *at* me, but into the world beside her, casting thoughts into the air like seeds. Her tone was half-wonder, half-casual... The kind of voice people used when talking to themselves but hoping someone else might be listening.

"That bakery on the corner?" she said, gesturing with a slight nod. "The one with the blue awning? They used to give out broken biscotti pieces to kids on Sundays. Probably still do. I haven't checked in a while."

I said nothing, just listened.

"There's a gingko tree behind that traffic light," she went on, more softly. "It was planted after the blackout in 2003. The owner said it was to remind the street that even in the dark, some things endure. People don't notice it, but it drops the most perfect gold leaves in October."

She glanced at me briefly, then looked ahead again.

"You probably don't care about that."

"I do," I said.

She blinked, surprised. But something in her expression eased.

A few steps later, she continued. "Did you know that parts of Central Park were built on land that used to belong to a free black community? Seneca Village. It was razed to build the park. Not many people know that. But the trees remember. You can feel it in the way the wind changes near the west edge."

I looked at her sidelong, the way you might look at a star just past the horizon line, afraid it'll disappear if you stare directly.

"You talk about the land like it's alive," I murmured.

She shrugged, then smiled crookedly. "Maybe it is. Plants *listen*, you know. Even if most people don't. And the city... it breathes. Bleeds. Remembers. You just have to know how to hear it."

I knew. By everything unholy in the universe, I *knew*.

The magic wasn't in the spectacle. It never had been. It was in the *details*. The bark fissure that formed like a smile after seventy seasons. The lichen that changed color a week before a cold snap. The way roots curved away from grief buried beneath the soil.

She understood it all instinctively, yet she had no idea how rare that was.

As we neared the park, her words faltered. She laughed, at once both soft and embarrassed, like she'd just realized how much she'd said. "Sorry," she muttered. "I ramble when I'm—when I don't know what else to do."

I stopped walking.

"Irina," I said, catching her gaze. "I could listen to you forever."

The moment snapped still, golden and suspended between us.

She froze. Her lips parted slightly, eyes caught on mine like a tether had drawn taut between us—undeniable, trembling. The kind of connection that lived in the blood, beneath memory. The kind that crossed lifetimes.

I wanted to touch her. To see if her pulse matched mine. But before I could—

Thump.

A sharp shoulder brushed mine, forceful and deliberate enough to throw me off balance for half a step. I caught myself before I could stagger. My head snapped toward the source.

Jogger. Blonde. Tall. Her stride slowed just enough to meet my eyes. Her ponytail bounced like any other early-morning runner. But her eyes—those sharp, silver-green *predator's eyes*—held me in place with the precision of a blade.

Artemis.

Wearing modern skin, yes. But still *her*. Huntress. Guardian. And right now? Watchful. Unimpressed.

Her gaze said everything I already knew.

Don't fail her. Or I will end you.

She didn't slow again. Just ran on, leaving the warning etched behind like claw marks in fog.

I inhaled once—steady. The dark inside me bristled, then stood down.

"Graven?" Irina's voice cut through the sudden tension.

I turned.

She'd stepped closer. Her brows drawn in concern, one hand resting lightly on my forearm. "You okay?" The question wasn't about politeness. It was *genuine*. Concern poured from her like warmth from the sun—real and effortless, not something she even thought to question.

The weight of it undid something in me.

"I'm fine," I said quietly. "Just... distracted."

She didn't press.

We crossed the street and turned onto the final stretch of sidewalk that bordered the park. The fence line ran ahead of us like an open invitation, trees just starting to leaf out with summer green.

And there, nestled into the corner beneath a canopy of ivy-covered trellis, stood the café.

The Grove.

Small, quiet, half-sunk into the earth like it had grown there instead of being built. Tables clustered around it like mushrooms. Painted signs hand-lettered in gold. The door hung open, and the air smelled like cinnamon and citrus peel.

Irina lit up as they approached, the stiffness in her shoulders easing.

From behind the counter stepped the man who must've heard her footfalls before the door even creaked.

Golden skin. Gleaming teeth. Hair like honey spun through sunlight. And when he saw her—

"*Irina!*" His grin blazed.

She laughed, warm and open. "You're actually here this morning."

"Only for you," he said, leaning over the counter. "The sky doesn't shine half so bright without your face beneath it."

I stopped cold. The man's eyes flicked to me. And that grin—flawless, lazy, *challenging*—grew wider.

Apollo.

Of course.

The god of light and truth and smug, unbearable charisma. Playing human, again. He had the glow, even muted in flesh. And now he was *smiling* at Irina like they shared something I hadn't even been offered yet.

My temper coiled. Heat rolled up my spine like fire under skin.

He reached for a mug without looking. "The usual?" he asked her.

"Please," she said.

"Anything for the queen of chlorophyll," he teased.

Irina just shook her head with obvious affection.

Watching them, I remembered with brutal clarity that gods did not always need force to steal what mattered.

Sometimes, they just smiled first.

CHAPTER

FIFTEEN

I loved this café.

The moment you stepped into the garden-ringed patio, it felt like the city exhaled a too-long-held breath and time slowed. The light turned honey-gold, even on gray days. Green things grew where they shouldn't have—ivy blooming in stone cracks, violets popping up near chair legs, moss threading the bases of coffee tables. It was a secret haven, half-brewery, half-botanical daydream.

And this morning of all mornings, it betrayed me.

The moment the *café owner*—Lukas—grinned at me, the air changed.

Not badly. Not entirely. Just... *complicated.*

"Anything for the queen of chlorophyll," Lukas said, beckoning us to follow as he moved to make my drink.

I smiled, because I always did. He had that kind of gravity. Warm, effortless. Like he *knew* you, even if you'd never met.

I'd known Lukas for a while. One of those long-running fixtures of Manhattan weirdness. Sometimes behind the counter. Sometimes absent for weeks. But always charming, always present *when it mattered.* I never asked what his deal was because I already knew he'd never give a straight answer.

Today, though—today he radiated a very different sort of intensity.

And Graven?

Graven had gone utterly still.

Not visibly so much as the way he *watched* Lukas now, like he was cataloging every breath, every shift in posture. It was the same way birds watch a snake in the grass.

The puppy noticed too. His hackles didn't rise, exactly. But he planted himself firmly between them and refused to move. Every time Lukas leaned forward even a little, the dog repositioned.

That would've made me laugh any other day. Instead, it just unsettled me more.

"Cinnamon oat latte," Lukas said, setting the mug down in front of me with a flourish.

He didn't even ask. He just knew.

And then his eyes cut to Graven, sharp and assessing. "And for your… friend?"

Graven didn't smile. "Black. Hot. No additives."

Lukas nodded as if that answer confirmed something for him. He turned away, but I could still feel the pull between them, like magnets trying to figure out if they were facing the right poles.

I took a breath.

"Let's sit outside," I said, nudging Graven's elbow. "It's nicer."

The puppy followed without hesitation. Graven did too, though slower. Controlled. Like he was still doing threat assessment. We found a small round table near the edge of the patio, half-shaded by a twisting vine-covered trellis. The puppy curled at my feet with one ear turned outward —alert, but calm. For now.

I sipped my drink and exhaled. The quiet was warm, but weighted.

Graven finally lifted his mug and took a long swallow, his eyes never straying far from the door.

"You know him," I said carefully.

His jaw flexed. "Yes."

"You don't like him."

"I don't trust him."

"Well," I said, tracing the rim of my mug with a fingertip. "That makes three of us."

Graven blinked at that. Just once. But I saw it—a flicker of amusement in the glacier of his expression.

The air shifted again—less from the tension, more from the *knowing*. I could feel something pressing around the edges of reality. Like the world was waiting for a signal. Or a decision.

I looked at him over the steam of my drink. "Tell me something true," I said quietly.

He frowned. "About what?"

"You," I said. "Tell me one thing that's real. Not Thanatek. Not myth. Just *you*." I didn't even know why I added "myth" in that request. I couldn't quite process everything Dr. Heinritz had said and frankly, I didn't want to think on it too closely. Instead, I focused on Graven.

The silence that followed wasn't awkward. It was thick. Alive. While Graven didn't answer immediately, he held my gaze for a long moment. With a half-formed sigh, he shifted his attention to the edge of the garden, past the fence where ivy curled around black iron and morning light filtered through the leaves. He held his coffee like a shield, though his grip was loose. Calm.

But his eyes...

His eyes said *everything* wasn't.

"I've lived in this city a long time," he began finally. His voice was quiet but clear, like someone telling a secret to the space between breaths. "Long enough to know the difference between being alone and being *unseen*."

He paused.

The puppy lifted his head at that, and I stilled too. Graven didn't look at me. Just kept watching something distant.

"I used to think solitude was just a side effect of purpose," he continued. "That when your work matters, you don't have to explain the empty spaces. They're just... part of the shape of things. Tools don't get lonely."

His fingers tensed slightly around the mug.

"But lately," he said, "I've started noticing the hours more. The repetition. The way the silence feels like a weight instead of a peace. The way even the city stops answering back."

That caught me. The phrasing.

"You talk about the city like it's alive," I said softly, echoing what he'd said to me earlier.

At that, he glanced at me. Just for a heartbeat. But something in that look made the ground feel less stable under my feet. Like I'd stepped too close to the edge of something vast and ancient.

"It is," he said. "In its way."

Another breath. He looked down into his coffee.

"I spend my days making decisions that move other people's endings. Quietly. Sometimes mercifully. Sometimes... not. The work fills the hours. The hours blur. There's never a shortage of need, or memory, or death."

The last didn't shock me. Not from him.

"But none of it..." He hesitated, voice going even softer. "...*matters*. Not the way it should. Not the way I think it used to. There was a time I thought that was enough. That fulfilling the function was the same as *living*."

He looked at me then. Really looked. And everything he wasn't saying hummed in the air between us.

"But now?" he said. "Now I'm not so sure."

The puppy let out a low breath and leaned his head against my boot. I reached down and rested my hand on his soft ears without thinking. When I looked up at Graven, my instincts told me that what he'd said was *true*.

But it wasn't *all*.

While he wasn't lying, he *was* holding something back.

Something vast and older than the language we used. Something throbbed beneath his skin, wild and insistent, like a lost current trying to surge back to its source.

Gods. Powers Monsters. Life. Death. I swallowed hard. "Thank you," I said quietly. "For telling me that."

His shoulders eased a fraction. "You said you wanted something real."

"I did. I do." I meant it, even if it scared me a little. Even if it felt like we were standing at the edge of a cliff and daring each other to jump. The moment lingered. The birds in the trees went silent, just for a beat. Like they knew something was shifting too.

Then—

"Irina."

Lukas's voice called from behind us. Bright. Familiar and laced with a knowing I didn't like.

"You forgot your biscotti," he said, holding out a small plate. He winked. "Thought maybe your friend might need something to sweeten him up."

Graven's expression didn't shift, but the tension rolled back in like a tide.

This time, it wasn't subtle.

I rose to take the plate, offering a neutral smile in return. "Thanks, Lukas."

"You know where to find me," he said, his gaze landing just a little too long on Graven before he turned and sauntered back inside.

I sat again, feeling like the sun had gone behind a cloud.

Graven didn't speak, though his knuckles were white where he gripped the cup now.

The puppy exhaled and stood, positioning himself once more between the two of us and the door to the café. Protective. Watchful.

I looked at Graven and tilted my head slightly. "Still doing okay?"

He let out a slow breath. "That depends," he said, eyes on me now. "Are you going to keep asking me things that matter?"

I smiled, even if it felt a little like standing too close to a flame. "Yes," I said.

This time, he smiled too. I let the silence breathe for a few moments.

Graven sipped his coffee again, slower this time, like the act itself grounded him. The sun was beginning to break more boldly through the trellis above us, scattering gold over the table, glinting off his dark coat like flecks of embers had landed and didn't quite want to go out.

I didn't look away from him. "Can I ask you something else?"

His brow lifted slightly. "You already did."

"Another something."

He gave a single nod, quiet and consenting. That almost-smile hovered again, like it was learning how to live on his face.

I curled my fingers around the mug, suddenly aware of how tightly I kept holding my own breath.

"Do you even enjoy what you do?" I asked, voice soft. "The work you talked about—the decisions, the weight. It sounds like you do it because you must. But if you could choose—*really* choose—what would you do instead? What's something you've always wanted to do... and never let yourself try?"

That got him.

He didn't flinch. But his stillness sharpened. For the briefest moment, the air seemed to tighten around us, like a net had been cast. I wanted to dismiss the sensation, but I didn't dare. So much I didn't understand intellectually, yet my gut seemed to comprehend.

Graven set his mug down gently. Then he leaned back, eyes never leaving mine. His posture didn't threaten. It invited. "You want another truth," he said, thoughtful. "A deep one."

"That's the deal."

He tilted his head, considering me like I was both a puzzle and match-flame. "Then we make it fair," he said. "One for one. If I tell you another truth, you have to give me one of yours. Not a small one. Not something practiced. Something *honest*."

His invitation, a match for the one I'd already made,

curled in my chest like heat. I hesitated, just long enough for him to notice, and then nodded. "Deal."

Glancing up toward the trees, he looked thoughtful. His voice, when it came, was lower. Like a thread pulled from a place most people don't look anymore. "There was a time," he said, "when I thought maybe I'd write books."

I blinked. That... was not the answer I'd expected. "Stories?" I asked, cautiously.

He nodded. "Not for the world. Just for... someone. A few people. To pass the time. To remember. I used to write in margins, on scraps, when no one was watching. Little myths. Alternate endings. Stories where choices mattered more than fate. It felt like cheating, at first. Later, it felt like... dreaming."

He didn't look away from the sunlight.

"But I stopped," he said quietly. "I told myself I didn't have the time, or the right. That the hours were better spent elsewhere. The stories stayed in my head. They always do."

I stared at him, unsure why my throat felt tight. Maybe because I could picture it so vividly. Him, alone in some forgotten hour, spinning worlds no one else would see. Holding his own stories like breath in his lungs.

"I think you should still write them," I said before I could stop myself. "Even if it's just for you."

His gaze returned to mine. Something about the way he looked at me then, like I'd touched a place inside him even he didn't visit often, made it suddenly *very* hard to hold eye contact.

"I gave you mine," he said softly. "Now yours."

Right. My truth. I took a deep breath. Let it out slow.

"When I was a kid, I used to sneak into the gardens behind the museums," I said. "Not just for the plants. For the quiet. For the way it made me feel like I belonged somewhere, even if I didn't fit with the people around me." I smiled, a little lopsided. "I used to imagine I was the guardian of all of it. That if I sat still long enough, the trees would talk to me. That I could feel the earth breathe."

Graven's expression didn't change, yet something softened in him.

"I guess I never really stopped doing that," I added, almost shyly. "Trying to make sense of the world by listening to things that don't talk back."

"They do," he said, voice reverent. "You've just never needed translation."

A beat passed.

Then another.

The space between us bloomed—dense, golden, alive with things unspoken.

And I didn't pull away.

I smiled into my coffee, feeling the heat of it warm my palms as I watched him.

"I have another one," I said, letting the moment stretch just long enough to feel deliberate.

Graven arched an eyebrow, the faintest suggestion of curiosity playing along the corners of his mouth. "Another truth?"

I nodded. "You said you used to want to write stories. But do you actually... *like* them? Reading them? Watching them? Do you enjoy stories that aren't yours?"

Something flickered behind his eyes. Something nearly boyish. Almost private. "I do," he said, and the honesty was so immediate, so *pure*, it disarmed me. Then he added, "The quiet ones. The ones about memory. About things that don't shout to matter. Not just epics. Not just endings."

I tilted my head. "So, what? Indie films and literary fiction?"

The smile that ghosted across his mouth was surprisingly real. "Sometimes," he said. "But I'm not above a good fantasy series either. There's something... comforting about seeing magic treated as ordinary. As a truth the world just accepts."

My chest ached a little. Maybe because he said it like he missed that world. Or maybe because I did too, and didn't know it until now.

"I like that," I said quietly. "The idea of magic being accepted."

His gaze lingered on me. With a slow shift in his weight, he leaned slightly forward, both hands folded loosely around his mug. "My turn."

A subtle shift. Not predatory. But intent.

I swallowed. "All right."

Graven's voice dropped, soft but steady. "If you could do anything—*be* anything—without limits or barriers... What would you do?"

The question landed like thunder in a quiet room. The puppy, lying half-curled at my feet, let out a small whine and leaned gently against my boot again, grounding me. Like he *felt* it too.

I blinked. My mouth opened, but no words came.

"I don't mean in theory," Graven said, gentler now, almost coaxing. "Not what's safe. Not what you've already settled for. I mean the thing that sits at the back of your mind like a door you've never let yourself open."

My fingers curled slightly around the cup. I didn't answer right away. Because *I didn't know.* Or maybe I did. Maybe I always had. But I'd never been brave enough to name it. Something moved in my chest. Like a vine brushing the edge of a memory. Something *old.* Something *sacred.*

"I think…" I began, hesitantly, "I'd build something. Not a company or a brand. Not even a museum. Something alive. A place."

He didn't interrupt.

"A sanctuary," I said, the word trembling on my tongue. "Something part garden, part temple. Part archive. I don't even know what I'd call it. I just know I'd want it to *remember*. And I'd want it to *welcome* people who don't know where they belong and people who don't have a place to rest."

I looked at him then, and everything in me was raw and wide open.

"I'd want to make that place real," I whispered. "Even if no one believed it could be."

The silence between us split wide—sacred, shimmering, and full of things we didn't say. For the first time since I met him, Graven looked like he didn't know what to say. I wasn't sure whether it was because he didn't believe it or if it was because *he did*.

Graven hadn't spoken in over a minute. Yet the silence didn't feel empty—it felt *charged* with understanding. A stillness that settled over us like dust in a long-undisturbed room.

He knew—*really* knew—that what I'd said wasn't just personal. It was structural. A hidden beam beneath everything I am, quiet for years, never named aloud.

His eyes never left mine, and in his steady gaze, I felt something shift—not in him, but in me. Like he held up a mirror to a truth I'd almost forgotten was mine.

Then he murmured, almost like a vow, "You could build it, you know. A place like that."

"Could I?" I asked, half-laughing, half-hollow.

"You already carry the blueprint," he said softly. "Some places are people first. They just don't know it yet."

It shouldn't have made my heart beat faster. But it did.

I looked down, biting the edge of my lip. The puppy bumped my ankle again, his tail flicking once like approval. I reached down without thinking and ruffled his ears.

"Okay," I said, voice quieter now. "Another one."

Graven tilted his head slightly in acknowledgment. His stillness didn't unsettle me anymore. It felt like safety.

"If you weren't doing what you do now…" I trailed off, then smiled faintly. "What would you be if you were allowed to *just* be? Not a role. Not a job. Just… Graven."

His eyes softened, then he dropped his gaze to the table like the answer might be hiding in the grain of the wood.

"I'm not sure I remember how to just be," he said, a thread of something mournful threading his voice. "But if I could… I'd want to be someone who remembers *people* instead of managing them. Someone who helped them stay tethered to the lives they wanted, not the ones they were told to accept."

A pause.

Then: "I think I'd want to be a lighthouse."

I blinked. "A what?"

He looked up again, a hint of a rare, crooked smile ghosting across his face. "Not a person. Just… a fixed point. Something people can use to find their way home."

I stared at him, every part of me pulling toward that warmth like a tide toward moonlight. That was when the air shifted. It wasn't dramatic. No lightning. No wind. But the *texture* of the world changed.

Graven noticed it too. His jaw tightened the barest fraction, and the puppy rose in a silent motion, ears swiveling like a radar dish.

Then—

"Hope I'm not interrupting anything." The voice came from just behind me, low and dry and unmistakably amused.

I turned, heart already tightening, to see Lukas—with his shining eyes and smile—leaning against the corner railing, arms crossed like he'd been watching for a while.

He raised a hand in lazy greeting. "But then again, you always did like your dramatic pauses, Graven."

Graven didn't move, but something about him *steeled*. Not anger. Just preparation.

I blinked. "Lukas?" They knew each other.

Of course they did. *Everyone* seemed to know each other.

He straightened with a grin, then looked past me and clucked his tongue. "Still brooding after all this time. Like a dragon's breath, you're consistent."

"Leave it, Lukas," Graven said without inflection.

"Oh, I *will*," Lukas said easily. "Just as soon as I visit with Irina, and remind you that you're not the only one who knows the value of time."

And then, as if summoned by cue—

"*Hello,* loves."

Oscar's voice rolled in like sunlight through stained glass, warm and infuriatingly smooth.

I turned to find him rounding a corner with a paper bag in hand along with a to-go cup. He wore another flawless coat, gold-toned this time, with sunglasses perched on his head like he was auditioning for a magazine cover.

"Seriously?" I said under my breath. Had he truly changed in the few hours since he left the Annex?

He beamed. "Miss me?"

Graven rose to his full height, slow and deliberate. "Not now," he said, quiet but tight. "This isn't your game."

Oscar grinned wider. "Sweetheart, I don't play games. I *host* them."

Then the final chill came. "Am I late?" The new voice slithered into the air like a blade slipping from a sheath.

Kassian Harpe. Or... what wore his face walked like he owned gravity. Dressed in a charcoal coat with buttons the color of old blood and his hair wind-swept in a way that looked careless but clearly wasn't, he smiled at me, even though it didn't quite reach his eyes.

"Fancy seeing you here," he said smoothly, "Irina."

Unease weaved through me and sent a chill rippling over my skin. I rose as well, the puppy pressing close to my leg again like a velvet shield. I wasn't sure which one of us was trembling or if it was both.

Graven stepped half a pace closer to me, not touching—but there. *Present.* He didn't say anything, but it felt like a line had been drawn.

Kassian's eyes gleamed. "Tense? Don't worry. I just wanted to say hello."

Oscar let out a breath like a stage sigh. "And *I* just wanted pastries. Look what we've become."

Lukas rolled his eyes. "Can we skip the part where everyone postures and pretends they're not circling the same flame?"

Graven's voice dropped low, nearly guttural. "You're all circling the wrong one."

That silence returned—but it was *sharp* now. Like a pause before something splintered.

I touched Graven's arm. Not hard. Just enough.

"Are *you* alright?" I asked him softly, honestly.

His gaze dropped to me—fast, startled almost—but the

moment it found mine, the tension around his mouth loosened.

He nodded once.

"Yes," he said. "Now I am." But his hand hovered near mine like he wasn't quite ready to let go. Behind us, the gods waited.

I might throw-up but yes, they were definitely gods.

Watching.

Ready.

Gods.

CHAPTER

SIXTEEN

GRAVEN

The city was breathing differently today.

Beneath the heat shimmer off the pavement, beneath the scent of roasting beans and distant rain in the east, New York's pulse was *off-beat*. Not broken —no, the city was *awake*. Stirring like something half-buried and ancient was rolling over in its sleep.

They were coming.

They were all coming.

And Irina was at the center of it.

She stood beside me, her fingers still brushing the edge of my sleeve where she'd reached for reassurance a moment ago. The contact had grounded me—more than I wanted to admit. It shouldn't have mattered so much. But it did.

Because this wasn't just an interruption.

It was a *summoning*.

Lukas—Apollo—always arrived too early or too late, never when wanted.

Then Oscar—Hermes in all his irritating glory—offered his smirking charm in gold tones and false sunshine.

And now Kassian—Ares—wore that face like he deserved it. Like it hadn't been *engineered* for war.

I could feel others, like Artemis who kept her distance and Pollux who wanted to insert his own opinions. They were all there, pressing at the edges. Watching through mirrored windows and pigeon eyes and the rustle of elm leaves from across the street.

The old bloodlines were restless. The power running through Irina—half-buried, half-awake—was calling to them, whether she meant it to or not.

It's too soon, I thought. *Damn it, it's too soon.*

I leaned down just enough that my voice could reach only her.

"One word," I said, low and quiet. "And I'll take you out of here. No questions. No delay. Just say it."

She glanced up at me, startled, but held her ground. Brave as ever. Unaware just how many *wolves* she'd wandered into the middle of.

Apollo's avatar was still smiling like the sun never burned.

"Come on, Graven," Oscar said brightly, sipping his coffee like we weren't a breath from disaster. "You're not jealous, are you? I mean, I know I'm prettier, but we can still share."

Irina tensed beside me, and the puppy gave a faint growl, distinctly unfriendly and real.

"I don't share," I said, voice flat.

"Typical," Kassian drawled. "Still guarding things you don't understand. Still pretending you can keep the story from repeating."

His eyes flared—just a flicker—but I saw the red behind

the brown, the *possession* bleeding through the borrowed form. The hunger.

He was planning something. He always was. And Irina—Persephone—was exactly the kind of pivot he wanted to leverage. Not just as a symbol. As *bait*.

"I understand more than you think," I said, keeping my hands visible. *Neutral. For now.*

Oscar tsked. "This isn't going to devolve into a pissing match, is it? We're supposed to be the civilized ones."

"You showed up uninvited," I reminded him.

Never one to be dissuaded, Oscar flashed Hermes' irrepressible smile. "I'm *always* invited."

"You're always watching," I said. "That's not the same."

That grin widened to cutting now. Almost cruel. "I watch when the stakes matter. And you've been playing the slow game, my friend. But that little spark she's waking up with? It's not going to wait for your tragic, broody pacing."

He took a casual step forward and addressed Irina directly.

"Don't let him treat you like glass, darling," he said with a wink. "You're a forge, not a figurine."

Irina's brows drew together, clearly trying to decode him.

But Kassian was already moving, circling just enough to make me want to move between them.

"You've grown," he said to her, voice darker, hungrier now. "That strength. That edge." A crooked smile twisted his mouth. "I liked you better in Carthage, though. There was fire in that version."

I stepped forward, subtle but firm. "Back off."

"Oh? *Or what?*" His eyes gleamed. "You'll finally stop pretending you're just her shadow?"

"That's enough," I growled.

The air around us buzzed. Too loud. Too sharp. *Too many of them at once.*

Irina didn't realize what it meant that all three had shown up like this—on instinct, no coordination, just *drawn*. The moment was thinning. A threshold opening. That old thread of myth trying to snap back into place.

The cycle wanted to repeat. The damnable and fickle nature of the gods meant they were always hungry, even for a rerun.

Not this time.

Irina touched my arm again, barely, but enough to break the thread of tension inside me. "Graven," she said quietly, "what's really happening?"

I didn't answer right away. The truth wasn't safe to speak aloud yet. Not here. Not now. And absolutely *not* in front of them. But my gaze never left hers.

When I spoke, I said it only for her. "They're circling. They all want something from you. But I won't let them take it."

I won't let them take you.

A ripple of movement caught my attention just beyond the street. Figures paused under neon awnings, drawn like moths to the static in the air.

Hephaestus.

Or someone wearing his shape—broad shoulders, thick arms, heavy-lidded eyes almost hidden beneath a hood. He leaned against a lamppost across the street, hands in his coat pockets, watching. Not stepping in.

He's watching too.

Moments later—another ripple inside the café, hushed voices against the storm-light—that meant others were rising. Athena's triangle of eyes. Dionysus's quiet laughter. Each one drawn by the surge radiating from Irina.

The city's heartbeat quickened.

The sky shattered.

Lightning tore vertical scars across a slate-gray sky. Rolling thunder vibrated through the pavement and the café walls. Sidewalk vendors shuttered, pedestrians fled to doorways—everyone except us.

I felt it—waves of *pressure*, the old bloodlines, the raw hunger of immortals reaching through the city, trying to reclaim what they thought they owned.

Irina's fingers tightened on my arm, too tight. Not conscious, but full of intent. She stepped into me, shielding. Body-to-body.

Her eyes lifted. Storm-dark.

Clear.

"Back. Off." Her voice trembled, so soft I almost expected it to fracture... but it didn't.

The magic in the air might be hunting her, but in that moment, she *owned* it. The power pulsed and found form in her words. Her posture.

As for the others? Their smiles flickered—surprised at first, then calculating.

Apollo's grin turned brittle. Kassian's eyes narrowed with ironic affection. Oscar flashed false brightness that didn't register beyond his mask.

But she held them. She *held* them.

I saw her will blooming.

The force shimmered over her, cloaking her like it belonged.

And it was breathtaking.

A low rumble of thunder vibrated underfoot. I felt brittle electricity in the air: her power humming, the dog at her heels tensed like a coiled spring.

One careless move from Kassian—his hand drifted toward her arm—

And the puppy *leapt* forward.

He collided with Kassian's side, snarling, wool-hair bristling. The strike surprised him—because gods never expected retaliation from *animals*.

But this wasn't any animal.

The moment *broke*.

Kassian staggered back. The café door flew open. Lukas shouted for silence. Oscar stiffened, instantly calculating risk vs. gain. Hephaestus slipped away into shadow, Athena's eyes blinked, and Dionysus grinned like it was the best party he'd crashed in centuries.

Irina exhaled—her power slick and primal at her back.

And I... I was ready. One step forward, and I would *end* them.

The storm raged overhead as if the sky had recognized the opening. Lightning split the air above us. My fingers flexed at my sides.

Irina looked up at me. Her eyes glistened like moonlit water. The puppy growled again, low and certain.

No one moved.

Thunder.

Lightning.

Pulse.

All the gods froze.

They *heard* that shriek of denial that came from everywhere and nowhere.

That edge of *no*.

In that same breath, Irina turned toward me.

I swallowed the storm, leashing it for now. The silence after the crash echoed loudly, buzzing with energy that hadn't dispersed, only coiled tighter.

Irina was still touching me. Still holding me.

Her voice was barely audible through the static and wind. "You can take us?"

I didn't blink. I didn't breathe. *"Us."* Not just her. She meant the puppy too.

"Yes," I said. "Both of you. Anywhere. Just say it."

I let the leash go.

Not on the beast inside me—but on the *power*.

The air changed instantly.

The gods, the demi-gods, the star-stitched echoes of old myths trying to slip through cracks in time—*they all felt it*. I let it radiate, cold and searing, an echo of the thresholds I walked. Thanatek's architect, yes—but something far *older* had always moved in my blood.

Lukas' smile faltered. Kassian bared his teeth, more wolf than man. Oscar's golden mask didn't break but his posture shifted. They *knew* what I was. What I could do when I stopped holding back. They didn't *fear* me exactly. But they respected the cost.

I looked only at her.

"Say it," I told her again, softly. "One word, Irina. One."

She didn't speak for a long moment.

The puppy pressed against her leg again, whining low, aware of the mounting tension like a wire pulled too tight. Her hand found the curve of his ear in a gentle stroke.

Then her eyes rose to mine—wide and shimmering, full of that same, impossible mix of fire and fragility.

"Please," she whispered.

And it wasn't just a word.

It was a *prayer*.

She didn't even know it.

I broke every rule I'd ever made.

I reached for her, not just physically, but across that

deep weave of soul and signal. Power sang through my bones, ancient and absolute.

And I *tore* us free.

The cafe vanished in a breath of wind and silence as I released the storm to batter the park behind us.

In the next breath… we were in the penthouse.

My penthouse.

High above the city, where glass met the skyline and rain kissed the windows in quiet patterns. Marble floors. Warm wood. Stillness.

She staggered slightly, but I caught her.

The puppy landed beside her with a soft sound, immediately circling once and sitting close. He was alert but not afraid.

Neither was she.

Irina turned slowly, her fingers still half-tangled in my coat sleeve. Her voice was smaller here. More human. More *real*.

"You brought me to your home," she said.

"Yes."

"You've never done that before."

"No," I said, not pretending. "Never." Not since the first time she joined me to explore the Underworld. That was the last time I took her home. The last time…

She looked out over the skyline—so many lights, so many lives—and whispered, "They'll come after us."

"I know." Let them come. I would battle them all. If she wished for it, I would end them all.

"Are we safe here?"

I didn't lie. "Safe enough."

She took a breath, nodded once, and then lowered herself carefully onto the velvet couch near the window.

The puppy joined her instantly, curling at her feet like a sentinel.

She was shaken. But whole. For now—that was everything. The air in the penthouse remained still, but it wasn't quiet.

Power curled through the space like invisible vines, trailing after her, born not just from me—but from *her*. The longer she was here, away from the others, away from their voices and manipulation, the closer it came to the surface.

She didn't know yet. Not entirely. But she was *remembering*.

Small flickers behind her eyes. The way she looked out over the city like she had seen it burn before. The way her fingers brushed the puppy's fur like she had once cradled wolves made of starlight and winter ash.

Too soon.

It was always too soon.

I stood, still as stone, watching the lines of tension return to her shoulders, the way memory itched at the corners of her consciousness. The goddess within her shifted—unfurling from sleep. Not a hurricane yet, but a gathering storm with her name braided into its wind.

I should've waited.

I should've fought harder.

She looked so *young* like this. So mortal and alive and painfully *herself*. I wanted to sink to my knees before her—not just in reverence, but in apology. For every lifetime I had not reached her in time. For every breath she had taken without me there to guard it.

So, I did.

I dropped to one knee in front of her. Not dramatic. Not theatrical. Just... *true*.

She blinked. Surprise, confusion. But underneath that?

Recognition. Something ancient and unsure opened in her gaze, and I felt it cleave straight through my chest.

A thousand lives slipped between us.

A thousand lives where she died before I found her.

I couldn't bear another.

Not now. Not when I'd heard her beg me—*please*—and meant it.

A treacherous part of me whispered, *Take her.* Not to this apartment. To the threshold. The river. The Underworld.

Lock every other god out. Seal the gates. Let them *choke* on what they could not have.

But I couldn't.

I *wouldn't.*

I'd never caged her before. I would not start now. Even if I burned for it. Burned for her. Always would.

Her voice reached me—soft, uncertain. "What is it?"

I looked up at her, held in the gravity of her presence. Not a queen in this form, not a goddess—but something more dangerous: a soul still choosing, still waking.

"If there's anything I can do..." I swallowed the roughness from my voice. "Tell me. Whatever you need. *Name it.*"

She didn't answer right away. The puppy lifted his head from her foot, watching me with something close to judgment in his inky eyes.

And then—

Irina leaned forward, barely a breath between us. The city blurred behind her, the storm outside forgotten. She stared at me like she had lived this moment before, like it had followed her through lifetimes and dreams, all the way here.

"I think..." she whispered, fragile and true. "I only need *you.*"

The world dropped away.

The gods, the war, the buried memories still clawing to be free.

None of it mattered.

For a single, incandescent moment, there was no *then*. No *soon*.

Just *now*.

And *her*.

SEVENTEEN

IRINA

It was too much.

Everything in me felt like it was unspooling. Memories that didn't belong to me and yet *did*, thoughts layered with emotion so deep I couldn't tell where I ended and something *other* began. A low, steady hum echoed under my skin like a song I hadn't heard in centuries.

I didn't want that ancient earworm. Not right now. Not yet.

I didn't want gods or myths or magic.

I didn't want truth folded into riddles.

I wanted something *real*. Something *solid* to anchor to.

So I looked at him.

Graven.

Still kneeling in front of me, watching with that unreadable expression that somehow still made me feel *seen*. His eyes weren't just dark, they were endless. It was as though he carried the whole night sky behind them and still made room for *me*.

He asked the question again, gently this time. "What do you need?"

I could have said "clarity". I could have said "peace". I could have asked for explanations, answers, a way to make it all make *sense*.

But I didn't.

I couldn't.

Because the answer was already there, rising like heat from the center of me, absolutely undeniable and terrifying in its rightness.

"You." My voice broke around that one syllable. I swallowed, licked my lips, then leaned forward like the universe had narrowed into a single point that existed just between us. I reached out and cupped his face in both hands, my thumbs brushing the sharp line of his jaw.

"You," I said again, firmer this time. "*You, Graven.*"

His breath caught.

A multitude flickered through his eyes. It started with longing, then disbelief, and the kind of ache that didn't have a language, only shape and weight and time.

He didn't move.

So I did.

I kissed him.

God, I kissed him like I had been waiting *lifetimes* for it. Some aching, breaking part of me *had*.

When his lips met mine, the world split open.

It wasn't gentle. It wasn't careful. Passion surged up through both of us, reckless and ravenous. There was no easing into it, no tentative exploring. He kissed me back with hunger so deep it bordered on anguish, and I felt it— all of it.

His *need*. His *hesitation*. The restraint he wore like iron armor just so he wouldn't consume me whole.

But also, *his want*. Raw. Desperate. Focused entirely on *me*.

His hands came to my waist, grounding me, holding me like I was something fragile and on fire at once.

Maybe I was.

Because everything else fell away.

The gods. The past. The war still looming in the wings of memory.

For one breathless, shattering moment, there was only *us*.

It was *real*.

We were real.

It was the most real thing I'd ever felt.

His mouth broke from mine with a gasp like surfacing from deep water. His hands trembled where they held me—one at my hip, the other braced against my lower back, anchoring us together as if afraid I might dissolve if he let go.

He didn't speak, not right away.

I saw the war inside him, etched into the lines of his face, carved into the tension in his jaw. The want, yes. But behind it, something darker. Something clawing at the edges of him.

"Are you sure?" he murmured, so low I barely heard it. Not because he doubted me. He doubted himself. The flash of insight carried nothing but certainty. This wasn't just a man giving in to desire. This was a creature carved out of myth, who had lived with fire under his skin for so long he was terrified of burning me.

But I couldn't let him hesitate. Not now. Not when I finally understood what I wanted, even if I didn't understand *everything else.* Not when the pull between us felt older than names and stronger than fear. Despite what he believed, I had nothing to fear from Graven.

I looked up at him and asked the only thing I needed to know. "Are *you* safe here?"

Some part of me, some rational, flickering shard, remembered the way we'd arrived. How the air had crumpled and bent around us like space itself folded. How he'd whisked us away from the confrontation at the cafe with nothing but a look and a whisper of power.

Magic.

Something else.

Something more.

But I refused to focus on that.

I was too full of him. Of this.

"Yes," he said. There was something in his voice, low and molten and dark enough to scrape against the edge of danger. "We're safe."

It wasn't a promise. It was a warning. A warning not just to anyone who might come for us, but to anyone who *would dare.*

May all that was holy help me, it *ignited* me.

Before I could second guess it, I pulled my shirt off in one smooth motion and tossed it aside. I didn't look away. I didn't flinch.

His breath stilled.

I reached for him again, my voice steady now, sure in a way my soul hadn't been in days.

"Yes. I'm sure. I want this." I curled my fingers into his shirt. "I want *you.*" I leaned in. "And I want it *right now.*"

Even the puppy, curled in a ball near the corner of the room, didn't stir. As if the world itself knew this was a moment that couldn't be broken.

A growl—not quite human—rumbled from Graven's chest.

He surged up from the floor and swept me into his arms with a force that made the breath catch in my lungs, and before I could blink, he was carrying me toward the shadows of his bedroom.

We didn't look back.

The door slammed shut behind us with a thrum that echoed in my bones, but I barely registered it. Graven's mouth was on mine again before the sound faded, a collision of want and wildness. He kissed like he was trying to memorize me—no, *mark* me—as if each brush of his lips could anchor me to this moment, to *him*.

I clung to him, wrapping my legs around his waist as his hands found the backs of my thighs, holding me like I weighed nothing. But to him, I knew I wasn't light. I was everything. I could feel it in the way he carried me. Reverent. Desperate.

He laid me on the bed like I was something sacred, and then just *looked* at me.

That stare undid me more than anything else. It wasn't hunger, not entirely. It was worship. Awe. A grief so deep it had nowhere to go but through his fingertips.

His hand trembled as he brushed my hair from my cheek. "You don't know what this means," he whispered.

"I don't care," I whispered back.

He bent to kiss the hollow of my throat, and I felt his restraint like iron shackles—held so tight, it nearly shook him. His lips moved over my collarbone, then lower, tender in a way that cracked something raw and trembling inside me.

It wasn't just passion.

It was *years* of denial. Lifetimes of silence.

He explored me like he was afraid I would vanish beneath him—soft kisses that melted into open-mouthed worship, the scrape of his stubble leaving trails of heat across my skin. His hands moved over my ribs, my hips, as though he needed to feel every inch of me with aching patience before he dared take more.

Then, just when I thought I couldn't bear the reverence, he shifted—and the hunger returned, sharp and bright and consuming.

He growled against my skin, low and primal. It vibrated through my chest, made my back arch. One of his hands slid up under my back, pulling me flush to him, and suddenly there was no space left between us—nothing but heat, skin, and the frantic thrum of blood in my ears.

He thrust into me with a smooth motion that both impaled me on his cock and took possession of me in the same moment. The stretch was perfection. The naked heat of him a brand on my soul. I'd never wanted as I wanted him. I arched my hips, desperate for more. Desperate for him.

My nails raked down his spine, not gently. He gasped, and then laughed—dark and rough and full of something dangerously close to joy.

"Careful," he murmured, his voice thick. "You'll wake the part of me that doesn't *ask*."

I didn't look away. I didn't flinch. "I'm not afraid of him." I touched his cheek. "I'm not afraid of *you*."

Something splintered in him then—quietly. A soundless quake that loosened whatever restraint he had left.

He kissed me again—slower now, but deeper. His hands were shaking, but his mouth was steady, like he was grounding himself in the shape of me, finding some part of his soul he'd forgotten how to hold.

And gods, I let him.

I *gave* myself to him, not out of need, not out of fear, but because it was the most honest thing I'd ever done.

Each movement between us was a conversation—heat and gentleness, friction and stillness, his breath on my skin and mine on his. Every thrust of his body into mine built a rhythm that broke and built again. My nipples ached each time they rubbed against his chest. The strength in his palms shaped against my hips or my ass as he moved me where he wanted me or pushed my leg higher. We were a writhing mass of limbs, tangling together in a story we wrote together in skin and sighs.

Every gasp I released felt like *finally* and then he would capture my mouth again in a rush. Graven was the air I breathed. He was the blood pounding through my veins. The heat of him thrust into me with every beat of our hearts.

He pulled back once, just enough to look down at me.

"Irina," he said, my name raw on his lips.

I reached up and cradled his face, my thumb brushing the hollow beneath his eye. "I'm here," I breathed. "I'm *yours.*"

Then there were no more words. Just the breaking, and the burning, and the beginning of something neither of us had a name for—only the unshakable truth of it, pressed into every kiss, every heartbeat, every breathless, beautiful second of becoming.

The world had narrowed to this bed, this room, this breathless afterglow. Time didn't exist here. Not in the way I'd ever known it. There was only the warmth of his body pressed to mine, the sound of our hearts finding a pace together, and the slow unraveling hush of everything we hadn't said but now understood.

We lay tangled together in the sweat-damp sheets, his hand curled around my hip like he still wasn't sure I was real. His chest rose and fell beneath my cheek, steady and solid. Anchoring.

I sighed and stretched against him, languid and loose and beautifully sore in all the right ways.

He kissed my temple, his lips brushing my skin like an apology. "Did I hurt you?"

His voice was quieter now, hoarse and tentative, like he was afraid of the answer.

I lifted my head, brushing a curl of hair from my damp cheek and giving him a crooked smile. "No."

He didn't seem convinced. His hand slid down to my waist, stroking slow circles across my side, the pads of his fingers reverent, careful. It made me ache in a different way.

"Graven," I said, soft but firm, "I feel like my body was struck by lightning and left humming in the ruins—and I *liked* it."

His eyes flicked to mine, still storm-dark, still shadowed with that lingering guilt. I kissed the line between his brows before it could deepen.

"I'm not breakable," I whispered.

"You are," he said, almost inaudible. "To me, you are."

That nearly undid me more than anything else.

But instead of answering with words, I let my mouth trail kisses along his jaw, down the strong line of his throat. His breath hitched as my lips found the hollow at the base of his neck.

I kissed him there, slow and deliberate.

He made a sound, half warning, half surrender.

I grinned against his skin. "Tired already?"

His hand tightened reflexively on my thigh. "Irina..."

I kissed lower. The curve of his shoulder. The hard plane

of his chest. My tongue flicked lightly over a scar I hadn't noticed before, and I felt him flinch beneath me—not from pain, but from memory.

"Don't," he murmured.

I stilled.

He looked down at me, eyes soft but guarded. "That one's not a story I want you to wear on your mouth."

I nodded, understanding more than he knew. Some stories we might *never* share.

So I kissed beside it instead.

"Thank you."

"You never have to thank me."

"No, I must, because I am so grateful for you."

The way he teased language, it undid me. "Then do what you desire."

He relaxed beneath me again, tension bleeding out with each brush of my lips. I let my fingers follow the path my mouth had taken, learning the shape of him all over again—the dips and ridges, the heat and muscle and the scars he hadn't hidden, but hadn't offered either.

"You're still hungry?" he asked, voice low and rough.

I met his eyes and let a slow, wicked smile unfurl. "For you? Always."

He groaned, dropping his head back against the pillow. "You're going to be the end of me."

"No," I whispered, lips tracing the line of his ribs. "I'm going to be the part that brings you back."

And then I kissed lower, into the space between where ache met want, and began again. When I wrapped my hand around his cock, it was thick and hard, and so beautiful it would make angels weep. The length of it was generous, but the girth reminded me of how he'd filled me. How he'd stretched me past the point of pain to where pleasure existed in its own realm.

I'd never been fond of oral sex, and only ever experimented once or twice. Sex itself seemed fine, if unremarkable. Until now...

Sex with Graven was a religious experience and when I traced my tongue over the tip of his cock, his whole body shuddered. He reached for me, but I pushed his hand away.

"No," I said, and it came out an order. A sensuous one, but an order nonetheless. "I want this. I want to taste you. I need you in my mouth." Every single word was true. "I want you to feel me the way I feel you."

That was a declaration that came from some depthless place within me. I had no reason to expect him to obey, yet his acquiescence was immediate and without question. Delight shivered through me as I licked him from base to tip, savoring the musky scent and rich ambrosia of his taste.

When I swallowed around him, he let out a groan that pleased me on the most primitive of levels. More than once he thrust into my mouth deeper and I took him to my throat. When I pressed down with my hands to his hips, he went still again.

We lingered in this sensual haze for hours or years, I lost count, as I took him to the edge and then let him drift down again. Only when he whispered my name in the most solemn of pleas did I relent.

I cupped his balls, rolling them against my palm as I stole a look upwards. His eyes were twin pits of fire and they blazed as he stared into my eyes. A single nod from me and every corded muscle in his body tensed before he let out a shout and came in a wild rush.

Every drop of his release was a salted nectar. I wouldn't call it sweet, but I was definitely drunk on the pleasure radiating off of him. I barely had time to savor his expression before he rolled me over and pinned me to the bed with his hands on my waist.

"My turn," he said in a voice so thick with sensual promise that I almost came from it alone. Then he put his mouth on me and my thoughts scattered like birds taking flight.

The only thing I felt, saw, or heard was Graven and when he drove me to a shaking orgasm with his tongue, he thrust into me again. We rode the tempest, or at least I rode *him*, until we seemed almost one and then we would collapse, clinging to each other to breathe.

Only to start all over again.

EIGHTEEN

IRINA

I didn't remember falling asleep.

Only the way his body curled around mine after. The way his breath stroked over the back of my neck like an old vow. The warmth that spread from skin to skin, bone to bone—too much to hold, too much to name.

And then—nothing.

Not sleep. Not rest.

A descent.

I was dreaming. At least, I thought I was. Maybe I was remembering.

It could be both.

But the dream wasn't just one. It was many, layered like sediment and veined like a ruined cathedral window.

The world blurred around the edges.

In one breath, I was on a marble terrace beneath a bruised Italian sky. My hands were stained with ink, my gown cinched too tight. I was Siena-born, a scholar's daughter, young, brilliant, bold. Everyone said so. They call me *Livia*. There's a letter burning in my pocket—one I'll never send. It began, *My lord of silence, I remember you again.*

In the next breath, the ink was blood. The terrace was a battlefield, a Roman one, or older. My name was *Kleonike*. I wore armor, and my brother was at my back, dying. I don't weep. I can't. I sing instead, an old lullaby our mother taught us. The mother who begged me not to go.

Another turn.

I was *Élise*.

Paris. 1795.

Rain.

Running.

Always running.

The blood at my side was real this time. I clutched a book; no, it was a mirror. A face flickered in its surface, not mine, not quite. It was someone older. Someone brighter. Someone who didn't belong in my century.

I ducked into a doorway, but the door never opened. I know it won't. It never did. Behind me, the footsteps approach. No, they weren't footsteps or at least not *just* footsteps. Something else. Something that shouldn't be here.

Turning to flee, I didn't even make it a step before I halted. *He* was there.

Not Graven.

Not Ares.

Not anyone I knew.

He didn't speak, not a single word. But he watched. Stared.

The air warped around him like light falling into a black star.

I tumbled sideways, time slipping away to a concert hall in Berlin. It was 1889.

My name was *Louisa*. I was a pianist, prodigy, and adored. Tonight, however, my fingers shook. As I looked over the crowd, I saw a shape at the back. A silhouette, still in the most unnatural of ways.

When my hands struck the wrong chord, the whole world shivered. Children in the audience began to cry. No one there knew why. I did, but I couldn't tell them. They would never understand. Abandoning the bench, I ran. Not from fear, but recognition. I didn't know his name.

I don't think I'd ever known it. But I had seen him before. So many times had I seen him. Every life. Every time. His arrival meant...

The world slid sideways to Delphi. I was Selene, a healer. The people came to me for herbs, for prophecy. I served daily in the temple; it was my whole life.

My mother, or at least this life's version of my mother, was cruel. In public, she was gentle and dignified, honored by all who knew her. In private, however, when it was just us she was full of iron and her will was immutable. Despite knowing what I had seen and that I walked too often under moonlight and even spoke in my dreams, she was unforgiving.

"You don't know what you're giving up," she says. Her voice cut through lifetimes, a dagger in warm fruit.

"I do," I answered her and even as I spoke, I could hear myself. I was both there and not.

"You think you love him," my mother hissed. "But you don't even know what *he* is."

"I know what *I* am," I said, tired in my bones and in my blood. We'd had this argument before. So many times. I'd *seen* him. I knew where I was supposed to be. Yet, we had to argue *again*. In so many lives, different bodies. "You've never liked that, have you?"

Mother raised her hand—

A flicker, the blink of an eye and I was somewhere else, someone else before it fell. I stood in the snow with tall pines swaying around me. A cabin smokes in the distance and my name in this time comes to me slowly.

Magda.

Russia or maybe it's Finland? Either way, the landscape is unforgiving. The war was over, but not for me. I'd buried three men. One of them had been far too young. Now, I lived alone. A wolf visits in the evenings. Sometimes, I thought it was also lonely. Maybe it lost everyone it loved too. Did it want release? Did I?

While I had no real answers, the wolf had human eyes. They were unmistakable. It spoke to me only once though, probably just as well. I was already mad, after all.

"You are not what they buried," it told me. The voice was low and familiar. I reached for it—for him—but everything faded before I could.

Time sundered, ripping through.

A thousand lives crashed into me at once, they raced through me. Flickers of light on a movie reel or the flap of pages blinking past.

A slave in Giza.

A cartographer in Mali.

A thief in Lisbon.

A nun in Kraków.

A child left in the Temple of Fire.

A woman who walked into the sea and came back with pearls in her mouth.

Each version of whispered fragments. Warnings? Memories? Both?

"Don't let him speak your name."

"The flowers are always red when he's near."

"He never stops looking."

"You promised us a different end."

"Remember."

Then, I was nowhere and I was nothing. It was the void. The place between dreams. A dark field. A depthless still. I wasn't alone.

I couldn't see him, not at first. But the pressure of him was there, surrounding me, closing in. When I turned, he was there—the one with no name.

He wasn't frightening, not precisely. Yet, he didn't blink. He spoke as if he'd rehearsed each line carved into stone as ageless as the world.

"You're further along than you should be."

The voice came from everywhere, all at once. I wanted to retreat. "This isn't real."

A dream, I told myself. I was still in a dream.

"Nothing is real. That doesn't make it untrue."

"What do you want from me?"

"Nothing. I already have what I want."

"Then why follow me?"

"Because you haven't chosen yet."

"I'm not choosing anything," I snapped.

The figure tilted his head.

"You always say that. And yet... you always do."

His voice was like a book being closed over and over. Familiar. Final.

"I don't know you."

"You did. Once."

"Before?"

"Before you began running from death. Before you were given a name. Before you were hers."

"Hers?"

He stepped closer. A shadow given shape and movement. It didn't change what I could see. His face remained a mystery, yet I knew him.

"You keep waking up thinking you belong to him."

"Graven?" I exhaled his name.

"Is that what he's calling himself this time?"

Something in my heart twisted. It wasn't pain or joy, but something far more ancient.

"You're lying."

"No. But I am patient."

His fingers twitched as though he might reach out for me or maybe he was already touching me. That thought unsettled me even more. There was nowhere to go to escape him.

"You always bloom. You always love him. And you always die."

I shook my head. "Not this time."

A soft, dry chuckle. *"That's what Élise said. That's what Selene said. That's what the girl in Delphi promised when she poured salt into the river to change her fate."*

"You can't have me!"

"I don't want to have you."

Shock ripped through me. That wasn't the answer I expected.

"I want to remind you."

"Of what?"

His voice is low.

"That before you belonged to the dark... you were it."

A gasp caught in my throat as I wrenched from the dark to the light. The sheets were cold and Graven was gone. The curtains were wide open to the slumbering city beyond where the lights glittered against the darkness. Jewels in the cityscape.

I'd dreamed, but about what and who, it didn't seem

tangible. The gossamer strands flew apart before I could fully touch them. Yet, the emotion of the dreams remained a constant.

A choice.

An echo.

A warning.

Rolling onto my side, I ran my hands over the sheets where Graven had been and stared into the dark. I wanted to know where he was, but I was almost afraid to search. What if I made him up? What if that life was the dream? My heart trembled at the thought. Somewhere, beneath my skin, the dream's unease burrowed deeper.

Or maybe it was clawing its way up. Something ancient and indefinable had begun to stir. I knew, in a way that I couldn't pretend was just my imagination or fear, that nothing could stop it.

Not now.

Maybe not ever.

Lying back against the pillows, I pulled the silken softness of the sheets to me. The dream still echoed in my bones. Other lives. Fractured selves. They brushed against my skin. Whispered in languages from so long ago I shouldn't be able to understand their pleas or warnings.

A part of me pitied them, even as their images and feelings slipped through my fingers. Another part? That part hated them. Hated their helplessness. Hated how the tides of time drowned them over and over again.

I wasn't helpless here or now.

I refused to be. Maybe I didn't understand it all or believe any of it, but I had no regrets. Not a single damn one.

Graven's scent still lingered on the sheets. My skin still hummed from where he'd touched me. His every caress touched me like I was sacred, treasured, and his. Each kiss carved something ancient into the hollows of me.

No shame or fear or hesitation invaded my languor. No, I felt triumph. If this cycle truly existed, this cursed wheel of blooming, burning, and being reborn over and over—then let it spin.

Let it tear apart this empire. Let it swallow those gods.

Because this life? *This* version of me? I wasn't hiding in the dark or weeping as I ran.

I smiled and rolled onto my back to stare up at the ceiling. My body ached, but it was the good kind. The ache of living, the pain of something tangible. Something hot, golden and wild. Not a dream. Not a memory.

Him.

Graven.

The way his hands shook as he touched my shoulder as though he couldn't believe I was here. The way he'd whispered my name said it was a secret he was never supposed to say aloud. The way his mouth tasted like absence, and of longing, and want.

It wasn't just desire.

No, it was far more dangerous. It was recognition. That should probably terrify me. Maybe there was a smarter, safer version of me out there. Maybe she was the one who wrote poems in the dark or played piano for polite crowds or obeyed her mother and married a butcher's son. Maybe one of them would have run.

I wouldn't.

I had dragged him into me, asked him to touch me and to help me feel everything. I asked him to give me *him*. By God or gods or everything divine, he'd given it to me and I felt him everywhere.

My lips curved in the dark.

Let the voices whisper of fates and warnings. Let the figures in the dreams murmur of ancient tethers and stolen endings. Let the one I couldn't name taunt me with his riddles and shadows.

I was done being afraid of myself.

If the universe wanted to keep dragging me out onto this stage over and over and over, then I was going to take possession of the part dammit. Loud. Bright. Unapologetic.

If love was the fire that kept burning me, then fine.

I'd *run* into that fire this time and throw my arms wide.

I'd tasted *joy* with Graven. *Real* joy. Not the borrowed type or the one that flickered out before the second act. This was the kind that took root in your chest and bloomed fat and wide as the sun.

No one—absolutely no one, not a god or a curse or a whispering, trembling fragment of a forgotten life—was going to take this from me.

Looking to the window, I smiled out at the night and the darkness that had texture and shape. At the jewels of light that gleamed like beacons. Let the whole world watch, and let them wonder. Tonight, in this body and this moment and this version of me, was *mine*. Just as he was *mine*.

It had been so damn long, and I was far from done with any of this.

When the door opened on a soft sigh, I wasn't startled and I didn't flinch. It was Graven and I recognized him before he crossed the threshold. The air changed, thicker and warmer, a blanket of care and emotion that fell over me.

Sitting up, I savored his entrance. Graven was barefoot, gloriously nude, and utterly unashamed. Not that he had a reason to be ashamed of anything. He moved like even the laws of physics bent around him. Amusement danced through me. The air probably had to pause to admire him as much as I did.

His skin glowed almost bronze in the low light, but it was the stunning depth of emotion in his eyes that made me want to press my palm to his chest and say, *"yes, stay like this. Always just like this."*

Graven's smile was for me alone and I didn't even question that knowledge. He crossed the room holding a tray in one hand. The contents were two glasses, a carafe of something amber, and a plate of warm things that smelled like honey, spice, and lemon. At his heels, padding happily was the puppy.

My puppy.

If I could even call him that.

The little beast trotted in as though this had always been his. He gave one sharp bark of announcement before he launched himself onto the foot of the bed. Laughter bubbled effervescent in me.

Graven continued to smile. Not at the puppy, but at me.

Something in his expression unmade me all over again.

"You're awake," he said in a voice both low and rough with sleep, yet infinitely gentle. "I was going to wake you slowly, kiss you, then your breasts, and stroke you with my tongue until you came apart again."

Pleasure fountained through me at the description.

"Then I thought you might be hungry, so you should eat first and then I'll have your pleasure."

I'd been holding the sheet to my chest, an old modesty that I abandoned and let it drop to pool at my waist. Graven's breath caught, and it pleased me so much that he felt this connection as much as I did.

"I could eat," I murmured and let my gaze skim down

the sweet, cut lines of his hard, sculpted body to the thickening cock that jutted out, red-tipped and proud. "Food sounds good too."

The husky sound of his masculine laughter was a greater boon than I could have expected. He set the tray down on the side table with exaggerated care. When he turned back to the edge of the bed, he dragged his gaze over me, soft, reverent, and even a little amused.

Even then, his eyes turned solemn. "Bad dream?"

Not answering right away, I let my fingers drift toward the line of his thigh where the light touched the muscle. I traced a lazy pattern to reassure myself. He was real, still here, and not some phantom bleeding out from my dreams.

"They weren't all bad," I promised. "Some of them were almost familiar."

"How?" He tilted his head, studying me. The lack of artifice or deception warmed me all over again.

"You were in some of them. Sometimes watching. Sometimes waiting. Sometimes you weren't you at all, but close enough."

He tugged the rest of the sheet away before he slid an arm beneath my legs and another around my back and lifted me. In one smooth move, he took my place on the bed and settled me in his lap. The heat of him was a drape wrapped around me.

After plucking a fruit from the tray, he held it to my mouth then traced my lips with it, the sensuous act both erotic and loving. I accepted the bite, never taking my gaze from his. I chewed then I swallowed.

"I don't regret it." The words came out stronger than I expected. At the furrowing of his brow, I found my own smile. "What happened between us. I don't want you to mistake anything that comes next. Whatever nightmares, whatever echoes from before, *nothing cancels us out.* Nothing changes *this* between us."

His expression didn't change, not at first, then something loosened and he let his hand slide down my side to my thigh. "You don't regret me?"

That he could even ask that question broke my heart.

"Graven," I promised him in as solemn a voice as I could muster. "If I'm trapped in some mystical loop where gods and titans and shadows without names want to use me as a pawn, then I plan to savor every glorious moment." I pressed a kiss to the strong column of his throat. "And you are *glorious.*"

His breath hitched, then he shifted his head even as he wrapped his hand around my throat and tilted my chin. His mouth brushed mine then he kissed me so deeply, I swore he caressed my soul.

The puppy let out a sound of protest, and flopped over dramatically, as if to say, *Again? Really?*

We broke apart laughing. The sound of Graven's amusement proved to be a balm I had no idea how desperately I needed until it washed over me.

"We won't have much time," Graven whispered, pressing his forehead to mine.

"I know." I did. I'd woken up knowing. "They'll come. One way or another."

"I'll hold them back for as long as I can," he murmured. "I'll fight the cycle, the gods, the dark, and the system— whatever they want to call it. I'll burn the whole damn thing down to let you choose."

With care, I touched his cheek and let my thumb linger at the corner of his mouth.

"I already have."

CHAPTER

NINETEEN

GRAVEN

She said it like a vow.

"I already have."

For one, endless moment, I let myself believe. Not because I thought it would save us or because I trusted the wheel to stop spinning.

But because she had chosen *me*, again. She chose with her whole being, and fire in her soul. For the first time in eons, the choice had not been taken from her. I refused to let *anyone* or *anything* take it from her again.

I didn't, couldn't, speak. Not right away. Instead, I watched her. The tangle of her dark hair, tousled from sex and sleep. Her mouth, still stained with fruit and laughter, stretched into that smile I adored. Even if her face was not that of my love, she gleamed out at me from the sharp defiance in her eyes. All at once, she shone like every sun I'd ever watched rise over the edge of the Underworld.

I wanted to kiss her again.

I wanted to tell her she owed me nothing.

I wanted to show her she never needed to prove her choice with words or bodies or loyalty.

But Gaia help me, I also wanted to keep her. That desire was at war with everything else, so I said nothing. I stayed still. Stillness, I had learned, sometimes slowed the distortions and breaks from spreading.

If we didn't move, and if we remained inside the moment, maybe the cycle wouldn't detect that we slipped the leash.

The puppy froze, one paw lifted mid-scratch, nose twitching. A low sound, not quite a growl, started in his throat. A warning.

I straightened, the warmth of Irina's skin still clinging to mine like a benediction. The room felt the same, but the edges had begun to fray.

Energy, ancient and familiar. *Wrong.*

"Graven?" she asked quietly, as I moved her from my lap so I could get between her and whatever tried to get in.

I didn't answer her. Instead, I reached for the perimeter of the space where I'd woven threads of shadow, defenses carved from memory and shields buried into the stone and steel as well as the earth. Something pressed against them.

No. *Many* somethings.

The first voice came through my communication system, crackling over an intercom I rarely used but then my cell phone had been left in the other room. The sound was compressed, and clipped but definitely Mara.

"Containment breach in Grid E. Tether resonance increasing. I'm rerouting the upper sweep to—"

Static blasted out, sharp and painful.

"—they're probing *you*, not the facility. You need to move."

I stood, already pulling my awareness back to us. Irina

followed me to my feet. Sheet wrapped around her, she was a picture of feminine beauty but her confusion already gave way to readiness.

"What is it?" she asked.

"Not what," I said. "*Who*."

The second signal came as I dragged on a pair of slacks. This time it came from below. A ripple of pressure through the deepest current, the silent river beneath the river, where names and memory are buried.

Mnemosyne.

She didn't speak. She never had to.

Her voice arrived like a memory. *"Graven. Hold the core steady. She's beginning to see too much, too fast."*

I clenched my jaw. "That's not mine to control."

"Then brace her."

I was already reaching for Irina and she flowed into my arms. Even gods didn't argue with Titans. Not for long.

It wasn't Mnemosyne I feared. Not really.

The third presence, *hers*, descended like frost through velvet. I felt it before I saw her. The moment stretched. The walls breathed wrong. Even the light shivered sideways.

The dog whined. Tail tucked, he darted behind us.

Then I knew.

Before the veil tore, before the scent of winter roses and distant thunder crept into the room, I recognized exactly who had come. Not a god. Not a soldier or even an echo. But her.

The one I couldn't bar.

The one who walked through locked doors and oaths alike

She stepped through the breach at the foot of the bed. Still dressed in red, wearing a crown of broken time. Her voice slid into the room like silver over a blade. "Darling," she said in that ancient whisper. "You're losing her again."

I didn't look at her. Not yet. Focusing on Irina, I tightened my arms around her. She stared at the figure, brows drawn, breath held, her soul alight with confusion, heat, and fury. She knew the ancient one. *Not from this life*. But somewhere far older.

Somewhere deeper.

"Who is that?" Irina whispered.

I didn't answer because the figure in red, the crone, was already answering herself.

"I'm the one who remembers her *before* you did," Hecate said. "I've come to collect what was never yours to keep."

Irina stepped forward, unflinchingly leaving the safety of my arms. I wanted to grab her wrist and drag her backwards. I didn't. Instead, I faced the ancient goddess with her.

Hecate hadn't changed. She never did. Her robes flickered between time-worn velvet and smoke. In one hand, she held a lamp, unlit yet humming with old flame. The other rested lightly on a dagger secured at her waist. It was more symbolic than violent. For now, at least. Her hair was black as the deepest shadows and her eyes far too old.

In pure ferocious audacity, Irina stared at her with her jaw set. "You know me." It wasn't a question.

The crone who never chose sides merely smiled, soft as a storm approaching. "I *knew* you. Once. When your name was darker and your will stronger. Before love broke you."

That landed.

Irina stiffened and flicked her gaze toward me. I held it, saying nothing.

"You've both been stealing time," Hecate continued, walking the edge of the bed, dragging one fingertip across the footboard like it was a boundary she was measuring. "Pretending this moment can last. Pretending choice can shield you."

"She *chose*," I snapped. "You heard her." Why else would the goddess of the crossroads appear?

"Of course she did." Hecate's bottomless gaze returned to Irina. "But choice without truth isn't choice. It's just longing dressed in silk."

"Then tell me the truth," Irina challenged, her voice dropping low and dangerous.

That stopped the room.

The dog whined again.

Head tilted, Hecate studied her. "Are you sure you want it? It will cost you."

"I'm sick of fragments," Irina told her, absolutely uncowed. She raised her chin, every inch the queen she had always been. "I'm tired of dreams and men who think they know me, of gods who talk in riddles, slipping in and around my life like it's their playground. You both want something from me. Then start with telling me *why*."

I could have stopped her right there. Redirected. Protected. I chose neither. Irina was right. She deserved the truth, and Hecate recognized it, too.

She sighed, not with weariness but rather with the weight of inevitability. Finally, she turned to face us fully. The shadows behind her shifted and changed. For a heartbeat, the old crossroads appeared. The three paths, the torches and the old altars buried beneath time.

"You were never just Kore," Hecate said. "Not the stolen bride or spring maiden. That was an interpretation. A story told to bring comfort. A softened version. It gave the poets something to talk about and the priests something to summon and the people?"

At the last, Hecate just shrugged.

"It gave them a reason to celebrate." She shook her head. "Nor were you just Persephone, the goddess of the Underworld, a dark queen who dispensed mercy, judgment, and—hope."

The last one seemed incongruous with the rest, but my love was all of those things.

"No, the original you, the one that came *before* you descended…"

Irina's breath caught.

"You were *Kore*, yes," Hecate continued, waving a hand as if dismissing an unspoken interruption. "But you were also something else even before the maiden, something older. Something… twice stolen."

This part of the story I learned far too late. Long after my love had disappeared—taken again.

"You were the one who walked between worlds before there were doors. Before the Underworld had a king to claim it. You were *mine* before you were anyone else's."

"That's not entirely true," I reminded her. "She came to me."

"She fell, *Graven*. Because you made a place for her to fall to. That is not the same as being chosen."

No, I would not play *this* game with the crone. I stepped in front of Irina then. Protective. Useless.

"She's not *yours*," I reminded her. No matter what she had *been*, she was not hers now.

"She's not yours either." Hecate replied, eyes burning and voice tart. "She belongs to *herself*. Which means she needs the full truth—*now*."

Irina exhaled an almost steadying breath. Her courage and confidence humbled me. "Then give it to me. Both of you."

My mouth went dry. My thoughts were a warzone.

"She's the reason the gates stayed open," I said slowly. "Every version of her. Every life that ended wrong. I've searched across the centuries not because I was chasing a myth, but because the Underworld itself began to starve without her."

Much as I had. A shell of who I had been when she was there.

"And each time she tried to descend," Hecate added. "Something intercepted her. Not fate. Not error. Will. Yours. Others'. Even mine. We've all interfered."

"Why?" Irina blinked.

"Because you're not just one of us," Hecate said softly. "You're the balance. The fulcrum between bloom and decay. Life and death. You're what makes the cycle bearable. What makes the veil between worlds possible."

My mirror. It was what she'd called herself all those ages ago. As much as I didn't want to agree with the crone, I nodded. "That balance is fracturing."

"You don't remember all of it," Hecate said to Irina. "But when you do, you'll have to choose where you *stand*. Not who you love. Not which name to wear. But which world to anchor."

Irina didn't move. Her body was stone, but her eyes flickered with thought, fire, and something else—grief maybe.

"And if I don't choose?" Her voice might have been small, but it was still sharp. Hush blanketed the room. Even the torches in Hecate's shadow stopped flickering.

"You will," Hecate said as if there were no other options. "Or everything begins to unravel."

Irina stared at both of us, fury rising like a tide. "You speak like I'm a prize. A pedestal for gods and monsters to prop their empires on. I'm not yours. I'm not hers. I'm—"

"You've never been your own," Hecate said, while her voice was not unkind, I wanted to destroy her for saying it aloud.

It was worse, because it was true. Irina flinched.

"Not yet," Hecate added "But you could be. If you can *remember* the first time."

What? That revelation tangled around me. I had traced Irina through every incarnation from Kore to Persephone to Élise, Louisa, and every other name she'd borne across centuries. Followed her soul prints, anchored nodes, rebuilt Thanatek from ashes just to catch the glint of her light again.

But this? This didn't match any tale or tether I knew or had seen. Before Kore? Before she was *born*?

"What do you mean, the first time?" Irina asked even as her hand found mine again. The feel of her gripping me grounded me, draining away some of the fear and the loathing. "The descent? The Underworld."

Hecate focused on her folly. Her hands were empty of the torch and the dagger. The gravity in her gaze was enough to seal the truth of her words.

"No," she said softly. "I mean the first time you were *taken*."

Silence fell.

My heart kicked once. *Wrong.*

Irina blinked and there was no mistaking the cloud of confusion wreathing her. "You mean you? You took me— back then—at the gates?"

"No," Hecate said once more. "*She* did."

Reality cracked around me at the revelation.

"I don't understand," Irina said, tears coating the anger in her voice even as she shook her head. "Who?"

"Demeter," I whispered and it tasted like ash in my mouth. Of course, the goddess of the harvest, of the earth—the *mother*.

Irina jerked as though she'd been struck. "That's not—she's Persephone's, I mean Kore's mother. My mother, right? She mourned me? She searched..."

"She mourned what she feared to lose," the crone corrected. "Not you. Never you. *What you represent*. The cycle. The freedom. The capacity to move between."

"I know she raised you," I began, desperate to comfort the hurt in Irina's eyes. This was so much to take in. I struggled with it myself. She'd always been Demeter's child. Or so I had always believed.

"She *hid* her," Hecate snapped. "Wrapped her in spring, in sweetness, in safety. Only it had nothing to do with safety. It was *containment*."

"Stop," Irina ordered, her voice cracking as she pulled away from both of this. She pressed her hands to her head like covering her ears would keep the truth out. "You're twisting it."

"I kept this secret," Hecate said gently, "because you weren't ready. Not in the Underworld. Not the first spring you returned. Not in Thessaloniki. Not in Paris. Not in Berlin."

Irina turned to me, eyes wide and pleading. "Did you know?"

I shook my head. No. I'd never suspected Demeter. Yet, my love had been stolen *twice*. I pocketed that for the moment and focused on Irina. She needed comfort not fury.

"No," I swore. "There's no record..."

"There wouldn't be," Hecate said, waving off my concern even as she solidified the fact that I couldn't have known. "It happened before there were records. Before names had edges. Before you claimed the Underworld as your dominion."

"You were not *born* of Demeter." Hecate looked only at Irina, the weight of lifetimes passing in her breath. "She *took* you. Created the idea of you, the shell of a daughter to bind a prophecy she could no longer fulfill herself. Zeus lent his name and some of his power, but it was her will. You came into being as Kore, because she *needed* you to be Kore. Gentle. Contained. Obedient. A thing that bloomed *only* for her."

"She loved me?" Pain filled those words, pain that turned the statement into a question. Her eyes begged me to confirm it for her.

"She wanted you," Hecate corrected, unrelenting. "Love? Love allows you to choose. When you did, when you stayed in the Underworld for part of the year, when you *refused* to belong only to her—she took you again."

Raw fury spiraled out of me. I'd never suspected Demeter. Not once. She'd *grieved* or so I thought. She'd grieved when Persephone first came to me. Then accepted the deal, only when Persephone disappeared the second time, she'd *grieved* again and then *raged* at me. Blamed me. I kept my distance to keep from hurting her with my presence while I hunted.

And all this time...

"Over and over," Hecate said, this time as much to me as to my love. "In every life since. She has found you, reshaped you, rewrote the script. She couldn't stop you from returning, she couldn't bind you utterly to herself, but she could make you forget why you ever left."

My breath caught. The anger, a living fire, burned ice

cold in my being. That was why I could never catch her. Why the tether frayed each time she bloomed and why death passed her but did not claim her.

"She hid the moment," I said quietly, as furious with myself for having allowed my sympathy to blind me to the danger as anything else.

"The true one," Hecate said on a sigh. I could almost *feel* the apology she didn't offer under the words. "The moment Irina—Kore—stepped into shadow not out of fear, but of desire. Not because she was taken, but because she chose to go. For knowledge. For power. For love."

"The moment she left," I whispered. "That wasn't forced either."

"No," the crone said. "It never was. The descent, the return, the balance. None of that was theft. It was Persephone's consent. Demeter couldn't accept that. Because it meant you had outgrown her."

Irina's breath came in sharp, hard pants like she couldn't get enough air. Her hands clenched at her sides. She turned away, then back again. The short, staccato steps did not take her far before she came back. "You're saying that my mother—"

"She was never your mother." Hecate gave no quarter here. No softness. No allowance to ascribe other motives to Demeter's actions. "She is and has only *ever* been, your captor."

Irina's tears froze on her cheeks. She didn't fall. She stood straighter. For the first time in thousands of years, I saw her eyes glow with that same impossible light we'd only managed to glimpse in the Paris fragment.

Not Kore. Not Persephone.

Both.

All.

"I want to remember." It was a command. A demand. She would not be denied.

If the crone took issue with her tone, she did not show it, for all she did was incline her head. "Then go to the place she first found you. The place she took you."

"Where?" Irina and I both demanded in the same breath.

"I don't know," Hecate said. "But *you* will."

The air shifted and the shadows began to unravel. The light in the room returned to normal as the torches flickered out.

"But remember this," Hecate said, nearly gone but her voice drifted through like fog. "When you find that first memory, don't look away from it. Don't let anything distract you. Love let you be taken, but it was for love that you left."

Then she was gone, leaving me, a shaken Irina, a shivering dog, and the echo of a beginning too old for language.

We would make this right.

Then I would *end* Demeter.

CHAPTER

TWENTY

The robe clung to me like fog—soft, slate gray, open at the collar. Graven had offered it without a word after I stepped from the shower. No silks. No jewelry. Just cloth and breath and a silence I hadn't wanted to fill yet.

He was barefoot. Wearing jeans. A soft black shirt that clung to his chest like it belonged there. It felt like this was the first time I'd seen him so utterly himself.

Not the Death-King. Not the dark-eyed immortal with a thousand secrets. It felt right, those titles, and at the same time, the one I wanted was the one with me.

Just... him.

We hadn't spoken much. The puppy—if you could still call him that—trailed us through the echoing chamber. His limbs were too long now, joints loose like a teenager still growing into his own body. He yawned with a sound like velvet tearing and pressed his warm flank against my leg as we moved.

"Something's changed in him," I said, breaking the silence. "The dog."

Graven nodded. "He's a part of you. He'll grow with you. Defend you."

I ran my fingers through the thick fur behind the creature's ears. He leaned into it like he needed that more than breath. So did I.

Graven guided us across his living room into a second. I hesitated to label it a *room* because it was almost beyond description. It looked more like some ancient chamber yet kitted out with modern features and comforts. It was extraordinary.

Once we were inside, he crossed to the wide hearth in the center of the room. It wasn't lit. He didn't need flame. He whispered something in a language I didn't recognize but understood anyway.

The shadows along the mantle twisted. A ripple through air and memory. Then—

Mara appeared.

Not like Hecate had, fully formed and sovereign, but flickering first. Her presence seemed more like frost, creeping before it truly arrived.

Her gaze snapped to me, then to the dog, and finally to Graven, whose back was ramrod straight.

"You summoned me," she said, already wary. So weird. I hadn't seen her since discovering her "research." The anger and violation I experienced then paled in comparison to what Hecate had revealed.

Graven didn't look at her at first. He looked at me.

"I'm not hiding anything from her," he said simply. Then: "You shouldn't either."

Mara's silence was long as Graven laid out Hecate's

truth. Even when he finished, she didn't respond immediately though her gaze trailed back to me again and again.

"Go on," I said, more a command than a plea. Okay, so maybe I wasn't as over her *research* as I thought I was. "Tell him. Tell *me* why he didn't know."

"I didn't know either." Mara relented finally and spoke. "Not the *first* part. That Demeter wasn't her mother." She turned to me fully. "But I did suspect something wasn't right with your pattern. The way you bloomed and broke— it was always too *clean*. Too deliberate. As if the story you believed you were living had been edited already."

"And you didn't say anything?" I asked. That seemed odd considering the rest of the documentation they appeared to be doing. Even outliers should have earned at least a footnote.

"I didn't have proof," she said. "You don't challenge gods on instinct alone. Not even you."

I wanted to press her. Documentation, reporting, testing the hypothesis—how were these challenges? But Graven stepped in.

"I built Thanatek to *track* her," he said, tone cutting now. "To record every tether, every echo. If there was something before even that—*why didn't Mnemosyne tell me?*"

He reached into the hearth once more, this time not whispering, but drawing a symbol in the air. It shimmered like a sigil made of moonlight and nerve.

Mnemosyne answered immediately.

She didn't so much *arrive* as bleed through the corners of the room—tall, silver-cloaked, her skin etched with shifting glyphs. Her eyes were endless. I felt them press in against all of me, even those parts that remained a mystery. Yet, the connection was not unkind.

"You knew," Graven said. Not a question.

"I knew," Mnemosyne replied without hesitation. "And I held the silence."

My chest tightened. It was one thing to know that Mara had been researching me. Another to know that Graven had searched, relentlessly. But this? I'd always read that the gods were capricious, but how self-absorbed did one have to be to overlook some fundamental detail? I couldn't really be shocked, I didn't know this being. But Graven's disapproval and aggravation swarmed around us.

"Why?" Graven's demand could have drawn blood with how razor sharp the word was. It slashed the air around us, but neither woman withdrew from the raw fury coating every surface.

"Because you weren't the only one tracking her," she said. "Demeter's reach doesn't end with sunlight and harvest. She is memory too, when she wills it. Especially the kind she wants to *erase*."

Mnemosyne looked at me now. "She came to me once, just after you 'fell' the first time. After you chose the Underworld. She didn't scream. She didn't beg. She *bargained*. Promised silence if I let you forget the first choice." Something like an apology entered her voice.

"So you let her write over me?" As much as I might have wanted to, I couldn't blame her. What did this being owe me?

"No. I protected you from her," Mnemosyne said quietly. "But only half of you. The part she didn't know how to reach. I hid it in your dreams, in soil, in stories. In the dog."

I looked down.

The not-quite-puppy was watching Mnemosyne with too-human eyes.

"And me?" Graven asked. "You let me build a network to

find her, but didn't give me the full pattern. You *let* me chase a lie."

"No," Mnemosyne said. Her composure in the face of Graven's wrath was impressive. "I let you build a road. But the destination had to be hers. It always has been. Not yours."

His hands clenched.

I drifted closer to him as much to offer as to receive comfort. The room seemed to be spinning, but not with fear. At least not yet. No, momentum surged around us like waves splashing against the rocks.

"This all started before I knew my own name," I whispered. "Maybe even before I *had* a name." I slanted a look down at the dog. Existence didn't automatically come with a name. Either someone gave you one or you chose it for yourself. So, this all happened *before*. "Before Kore. Before anything. That first moment, the one Hecate told us about, where Demeter took me not because I was born, but because she *made* me."

"You always existed. You *were* real before she interfered," Mnemosyne said. "All she did was write a beginning that served her. But the truth is older. No matter what she's done, it's also immutable. Especially now you're close to remembering it."

I turned to Graven. His eyes were fierce, but hollow, too.

"You still want to protect me?" I asked.

He didn't hesitate. "Yes." Even now. Even after everything.

"Then stay," I said. "But don't hold back."

He reached out and cupped the side of my face.

"I won't leave your side," he said, voice quiet. "Not again. But what comes next... I won't soften it."

The dog stepped between us, then sat.

A sentinel.

A witness.

Something older than he looked.

I closed my eyes. The storm inside me was still building, but, for the first time, I wasn't afraid of it.

I turned back to Mnemosyne.

"If you protected the part of me she couldn't reach," I said, "then that part belongs to *you*, doesn't it? The memories. The truth. Unlock it."

She didn't blink. But something behind her eyes, vast and ancient, narrowed as if the aperture of a vault closing tighter.

"I can't."

Mara stepped forward, arms folded, lips already pressed in warning. "She *can't* because it doesn't work that way. Not even for Titans. You're not a door, Irina. You're a labyrinth. And the memory's at the center."

"But she *hid* it," I snapped, jerking my attention from one woman to the other. "You said so yourself."

"Yes," Mnemosyne said. Her voice didn't rise, but it filled the air like water flooding. "I shielded it. I scattered fragments across your lives. Symbols. Places. Smells. Touch. The dog."

He perked up at that—ears forward, tongue lolling slightly, as if *aware* of the weight of her words.

"Then if you planted it," I said slowly, "why can't you unearth it?"

"Because I did not *keep* it," Mnemosyne said. "I'm not your vessel. I'm your threshold. The memories don't belong to me. They belong to *you*. I couldn't carry them forward or they'd become mine. I had to leave them in you. Submerged. Sealed. Waiting."

"That's so much bullshit," Mara said under her breath.

Graven gave her a sharp look.

"No," I said. "Let her speak."

Mara blew out an annoyed breath. "It's not that she *can't*. It's that she *won't*. Not fully. Because if she forces your memory open, it'll shatter your mind. You're not meant to be a container for all of it *at once*."

I stared at both of them. "Then what the hell am I meant to be?"

The dog bumped against my hip. A soft sound. An anchor.

"You're meant to be the one who *chooses*," Mnemosyne said. "Not just where you go, or who you love, but which self you bring with you."

Graven hadn't moved. But his fingers were twitching again with small, nervous motions he probably didn't realize he was doing.

"You didn't tell me any of this," he said. "You let me build a monument to her memories and never once said she'd have to *reclaim* them herself."

"I didn't say it," Mnemosyne replied, crisp, practical and utterly unapologetic where he was concerned. "But I guided you to it. Your power, your tech, your node net, Thanatek itself—it's always been more than a map. It's a *mirror*. It reflects her back at herself. You're not chasing echoes. You're drawing a path home."

A path for me. He'd been building it ever since I disappeared. But he couldn't walk the path without me and I wouldn't walk it without him.

"Then give me a key," I said to her again. My voice cracked. I didn't care. "Not all of it. Not the whole thing. Just something to begin. If you're the threshold, open one door."

Silence.

It stretched out with brutal intensity until every nerve I had seemed to scream.

"There's a name," Mnemosyne said slowly. "One you've never said. Not in this life. Not in any recent one."

"What name?"

"I can't give it to you."

Fuck. Now I would scream. But before I could, she continued.

"But I can give you the sound it makes in the world."

She reached out with one long, pale hand and touched her fingers to my brow.

I didn't feel heat. I didn't feel cold.

I felt *recognition.*

A whisper passed through me, not in words, but in *song.* The syllables coiled around my breath like vines. It wasn't a name I knew, but my heart slammed against my ribs like it had just heard its own reflection for the first time.

Graven caught my shoulder as I swayed.

"You okay?" he asked.

I nodded, barely. "I think I know where to go."

Mara's voice cut through. "Then go. But you won't like what you find."

Frustrated, I turned to her. "*Why?*"

"Because if the first memory was stolen," she said, "then someone will be guarding it."

I looked at the dog. He stared back.

Not wagging. Not blinking.

Waiting.

Graven reached for my hand. "Then we go together."

Without hesitation, I threaded my fingers with his. I kept hearing the sound.

Not with my ears, but in that place behind the ribs, where breath becomes instinct and instinct becomes language. It wasn't a word. It was a feeling. A tone. A shape made of longing and distance.

It clung to the edges of my awareness, a perfume I couldn't place, ancient, half-buried, but *mine*.

Neither woman tried to stop us or offered more insight. I didn't even pay attention to whether they were still there or if their images had dissipated. They just weren't important anymore.

We reached the hallway just beyond the hearth chamber before I realized I was trembling.

"How do I find something by a *sound*?" I muttered.

Graven was quiet beside me, letting me think. He hadn't put his shoes on. He didn't seem to care. He looked like a man chasing starlight, barefoot and composed, letting me lead.

I stopped walking.

The dog halted too, one paw slightly raised. Watching.

I closed my eyes.

There it was again.

Not a name. A *note*. A low, humming resonance that tasted like smoke and honeysuckle and lightning just before it strikes. It was humming *up* from within me.

My fingers twitched toward my pocket, an old habit. Of course, that was when my phone rang.

The sound was jarring in the quiet—too normal. Too modern. After tugging my hand from Graven, I pulled the phone out and blinked down at the screen.

One word. A name.

"Mother."

The contact image was a photo I didn't remember taking: her in her garden, one gloved hand on her hip, mouth slightly open like she was about to tell me to stand up straighter.

I didn't answer.

I just stared at it.

Why would she be calling *now*?

Had she ever *really* called before? Or had I only *remembered* her calling?

Was she really my mother? Or merely the mother of the human vessel I was now? Was she Demeter in a guise? I had no idea who *I* was. How did I identify this woman?

The phone vibrated once more. Then stopped.

I felt... off-balance.

Like someone had just switched which side of the mirror was real but forgotten to tell me which side I stood on.

The dog nosed my thigh, firm, pointed, insistent. His muzzle bumped the phone, and it slipped from my hand before I could react. Hit the floor with a muted thud.

"Hey—" I reached for it, but he growled softly.

Not at me. At the *phone*.

Oh.

"Right," I whispered. "Not now."

I turned back to Graven, who had watched all this with the wariness of a man waiting for a verdict.

"I don't think I'm supposed to follow the sound with my ears," I said. "It's like—it's in my blood. I can feel it. Like pressure. Like a wind that hasn't arrived yet." Not that I had any idea what the hell that would *sound* like and yet, I did know. Inexorably, I *knew* exactly what music that wind would make.

He stepped closer. "You see something?"

"Yes." The word came out like a confession. "I *see* it. It's not a place I remember, but at the same time I *know* it. There's this... silence. But it's not empty. It's *full*. Like the air holds stories no one's spoken aloud for centuries. It's like an old ruin. Or a threshold. Maybe both."

"What does it feel like?" he asked, voice low.

"Like walking into a cathedral made of ash," I said. "Like tasting salt in a forest where no ocean should be." I looked at him, pulse quickening. "I know that doesn't make sense, but—"

"It makes perfect sense," he said gently. "That's how memory speaks when it doesn't have words."

Whether he knew those words would help or not, they buoyed me. It was like being on the edge of madness, aware that I could tumble at any moment.

I turned toward the eastern corridor. The stone walls curved slightly there, shaped by design or time, I didn't know which. The dog was already ahead of me, tail up, walking without hesitation.

I followed.

Behind us, Graven came, silent and steady, not just letting me lead...

...but *following me into the center of the labyrinth.*

Shouldn't we have hit a wall by now?

We'd left the hearth room what had to be fifteen minutes ago, followed the eastern corridor, and then the hall split—twice. One of the turns led up a flight of stairs that should not exist in a *penthouse.*

I slowed, casting a look back at Graven. "Didn't we start at the top of a building?"

He only raised an eyebrow.

"No, seriously," I said. "Penthouse. Top floor. How is this—" I gestured ahead of us, where the hallway bent sharply again, opening into another narrow chamber lined with stone columns and moss-covered walls "—*still going?*"

He didn't answer.

I pressed a hand to the wall. Cool stone. Real. Rough beneath my palm. But it wasn't *urban*. This wasn't reinforced concrete or polished marble.

It felt like *somewhere older* was wearing this place like a skin.

I looked down at myself, barked a short laugh. "Crap, I'm barefoot."

"So am I," Graven said.

"You at least have pants. I'm in a robe that barely qualifies as public."

"I like the robe," he said, totally unrepentant.

I laughed again. It came out high-pitched, sharp. A little too much breath.

"Okay, so—just to recap," I said, because if I didn't talk, I'd start screaming. "We're barefoot, underdressed, wandering through an endless nightmare maze. You're the Lord of the Dead, the dog is possibly the only one of us with a sense of direction, and I'm following a sound I don't understand toward a memory I don't possess. Fantastic."

Graven gave a low murmur in acknowledgment, but I was spiraling now, and I *let* myself.

"Of course it's a labyrinth," I muttered. "Why wouldn't it be? All mythic paths lead back to some tragic metaphorical hellscape. I mean, the Minotaur was in a labyrinth, right? That's real. That's Greek. That's ancient. Ariadne and Theseus and the string. Or was I Ariadne? Or the Minotaur? Did I *build* the labyrinth? Gods, how many lives *were there*?"

I stopped walking.

The dog circled back, nosing my knee again, impatient.

"Do I seriously have to dig through every life I've ever lived to find the keys? That's— that's not a journey, that's a billion-piece jigsaw puzzle without a picture on the box.

That's a memory scavenger hunt across *eternity*, and no one even left me a damned *map*!"

My voice cracked. I didn't mean to shout. But suddenly it all hit me—the weight of it, the absurdity. The *cruelty*.

"I didn't *ask* for this," I whispered. "I didn't ask to be reborn. Or bound. Or buried inside myself. Now I'm supposed to what? Just guess my way through centuries of echoes and hope I find the right door?"

Graven stepped beside me, silent for a long moment. Then he said, gently, "Yes."

I turned toward him, breath caught in my throat.

"But I'll be with you," he added. "Every step. Every key. Every lifetime if I have to. It'll take as long as it takes. There's no clock on this."

I looked at him then. Really *looked*.

Barefoot with his hair still slightly mussed from sleep. Wearing jeans and a T-shirt that said something in a language I didn't recognize. Not the Hades of myth. Not the cold architect of Thanatek. Just—*Graven*.

Steady.

Present.

Mine.

In that moment, something inside me twisted. Not in fear. In *grief*.

Because for all his poise, all his power, all his calm—

He had been alone.

For so long.

Waiting. Watching. Building entire networks around a memory that refused to come home.

I reached for his hand once again. He didn't flinch. Just curled his fingers through mine like it was the most natural thing in the world.

For the first time since this started, I didn't feel lost.

Not entirely.

I didn't let go of his hand.

I didn't want to.

Not after everything—every myth and memory, every twisted hallway of stone and echo—I needed something *real*. He was real. Not just because he was here, but because he always had been.

I studied him, the way his eyes searched mine—not with hunger or claim, but with quiet awe. Like he couldn't quite believe I was here. That I'd stayed.

"I know why," I said softly.

Graven tilted his head.

The dog, gangly, curious, still somehow noble despite his oversized paws and earnest gaze, tilted his head too.

It undid me a little. The smallness of the gesture. The kindness in it.

"I know why I chose you," I said again. "Or why *she* chose you. I don't know how this works, not really. If I'm just another sliver of her or a copy with my own shape or..."

I stopped. Breathed in. Let the words find their own rhythm.

"But I know why she chose you *then*. I know why I'm choosing you *now*."

Graven's brow furrowed, the faintest breath of emotion brushing his expression.

I stepped closer. Pressed a hand to his chest.

It was warm beneath my palm. Steady. Living.

"It's simple," I whispered. "Because you chose me. You haven't demanded. You haven't taken. You just... *keep giving*. Even when I wasn't here to accept it. Even when I didn't remember. You've been giving this whole time."

His breath caught. One of his hands lifted, covered mine

against his chest. His voice, when it came, was low and sure, like a vow carved into stone.

"I will *always* choose you."

The words struck me like a tuning fork. A deep, resonant chord that rang straight through my bones.

Something in the air shifted.

A soft *chime*—clear and crystalline—echoed through the corridor like a bell heard underwater.

I turned, heart stuttering.

There, where a solid wall of shadow had stood moments ago, now stood a *door*.

Wood, dark as midnight. Smooth as glass. A brass handle that shimmered faintly with some old light.

The dog padded forward, tail wagging once, just enough to acknowledge what we both knew.

This was it.

The first one.

I looked back at Graven.

And I *smiled*.

CHAPTER

TWENTY-ONE

GRAVEN

She didn't hesitate. That surprised me more than the door appearing, more than the ancient resonance it carried, and even more than the way the labyrinth held its breath. Even the stones seemed to understand a shift had taken place.

Irina reached for the door handle, then opened the door. She didn't release me, however. In fact, her hand tightened around mine. Her grip firmed not with fear but more with defiance. She held on as if letting go now would mean something *final*. As if, by sheer will alone, she could anchor me to her side.

I had no doubts about her success. Because I wasn't going anywhere. Not now. Not after hearing her confession about why she'd chosen me. Not after she chose me again. In this life and every other, I would always choose her.

The door creaked open. Warm air spilled out, ripe with petrichor and citrus, and something older than memory. When she stepped forward, I followed.

The dog, gangly with ears too big for his head, possessing a heart vast and unwavering, trotted in after us. His tail was high and his eyes were bright facets of jewels in the shadows. I couldn't help but see him as he was: a creature born of both innocence and myth, just as she was.

The room on the other side was not a room at all. The door opened to sunlight. Blinding at first, golden and full. The scent of dust and parchment with elements of sweet grass hit me like a memory I'd never owned.

I blinked the dazzle from my eyes. Summoned by a thought, a pair of sunglasses appeared in my free hand. Once I slid them on, I could focus. I was also ready to summon more if she needed them.

We were standing in a field.

Wheat? Barley maybe. Tall and gold and swaying to a rhythm that didn't match the wind. The sky was low, heavy with the color of the harvest. I could almost taste the smoke of the previous night's bonfires lingering.

No walls contained us. No corridors to give us a sense of direction. No sound save for the rustle of the grain and the soft creak of something in the distance. Not a door—I didn't think. Maybe a swing?

Irina still hadn't let go of my hand. She stood still, hair lifting in the breeze that teased at the sheer robe. Lips parted, she gazed around us. I didn't speak, because I could feel it. *This* was her place. Or one of them.

The first door? A fragment?

Though I hadn't known her *then,* I had the marrow-deep conviction that I was trespassing. This memory was not meant for me.

When she held my hand even tighter, I decided I would rather break off my own limb than pull away from her. If she wanted me here, then here I would remain.

I watched her, watched and waited. I couldn't—wouldn't—lead here. This was hers. I would follow, into memory, into fire, into *her*.

As she took one hesitant step forward followed by another, I moved with her. She tested the land and the place or maybe it was the memory itself. I was here as a companion, a witness—a guardian. No one would intrude on this moment or interrupt it. Unwilling to break the thread of whatever had begun to unravel in her eyes, I maintained my vigilance.

The grain whispered around our legs, golden stalks brushing against her bare calves as the robe parted with the breeze. The lack of a path did nothing to diminish the welcome for her. It bowed slightly where she stepped as if the grain knew her. Name or not, she was *known* here.

I glanced sideways. Her lips moved. No words. Just the shape of them. The attempt of translating sensation to language. The dog trotted ahead of us, his lean form outlined in the golden light, ears pricked toward the horizon. He moved without hesitation, a scout with purpose. He wasn't searching at all, he was leading.

Of course, he likely knew where she needed to go.

"I know this place," she said suddenly and I turned to her.

Her voice was low, not a whisper, not quite. More like awe wrapped in confusion.

"I don't... mean I shouldn't. I've never stood here before. Not like this. Obviously not in *this* life. But—" She inhaled sharply. "I know the way the sun smells. I know that tree."

Tree?

She pointed and I followed her gaze. There rising at the edge of the field, stood a lone olive tree. Ancient, gnarled, half-split down the trunk. Its limbs were twisted but vibrant, and its roots clawed into the earth like it had grown from the body of the land itself.

"The wind," she added, tears thickening in her voice. "It sings. I used to hum that tune without realizing. I thought it was something I made up as a kid. But it was *here*. Always *here*."

I didn't speak. What could I say?

Grief was a potent elixir. For all that I longed for her to never feel such pain, it was as much hers as the memories themselves. The kind of pain that came from being close to something you had loved and forgotten.

Her memory was unlocking itself like petals unfurling under the heat. Not all at once. Not violently. Almost as though she were *Regrowth* itself, responding with aching slowness. Torn from herself, she had the right to mourn that absence.

"I don't know if you see it," she said, glancing at me with shimmering eyes. "Maybe it's just me. Maybe this memory's only mine."

I looked past her again.

The grain.

The olive tree.

The slope just beyond it, where the field dropped gently into basin.

It looked like earth. Just grass. Just dirt.

Then I saw *them*.

Small white stones arranged in an impossible spiral. Carved with old sigils, some cracks, some half-buried. It was a shrine or maybe just an ancient altar. It wasn't mine or even for me. It was for something so much older than death.

The scent, it wasn't just wheat and dust. Shock rippled

through me. It was *spring* only spring buried beneath autumn. The soft sweetness of a pomegranate, faint and clinging, like someone had ripped the rind with their teeth and let the juice stain the wind.

"I see it," I said.

Her relief escaped on a breath.

The dog was up by the olive tree. He had circled it once then sat beneath it. Head cocked, he watched us. While he might still be on guard, he wasn't *guarding*. No, he was waiting for us and maybe for permission.

"Everything is so quiet here," Irina said. "Not empty though." She closed her eyes, taking a deeper breath as though she wanted to savor the fragrance of the air. "The land is waiting."

She turned to me, lifting those spectacular eyes to meet my gaze. When she studied me now, it was different. It wasn't just affection or recognition. It was far deeper. A sorrow threaded with longing. A knowing.

"I was happy here once," she said. "Not in some grand way. Not a queen or goddess or anyone that mattered."

She would always matter to me.

"Just me. But I was happy and someone I think I *loved.*"

I tensed, but she shook her head before I could register a protest.

"It wasn't you," she murmured in a gentle voice. "I know that. I don't even mean love like that. It was *before* all of it. Before Demeter. Before Olympus. Before my memory started fracturing."

Her fingers tightened on mine again.

"I think it must have been before *names.*"

A hush swept over the field, the wind pausing to listen. Somewhere beneath our feet, the land pulsed once. Faint.

Slow. It took me a moment to recognize it for what it was. A heartbeat we'd both missed until now.

Brushing the knuckles of my free hand down her cheek, I said the only words I could. "Then this is where we begin."

The corners of that lush mouth I had already learned to adore, curved upwards before she moved toward the spiral. Hand in hand, she followed a path maybe only she could see, though the grain parted for her on a whisper of welcome.

My feet sank into the earth; the grass teased my flesh, but it didn't irritate. Her footsteps were so light, but I had to wonder if the land kissed at her with each step. The breeze brushed at her robe again, the soft silk wrapped over our joined hands as it bared her legs.

The force of the wind left her naked from the waist down, and as much as I enjoyed the sight, I kept my senses attuned to this space around us. This memory. My task was one I would not fail at.

I would protect and preserve her at all costs.

The air grew heavier with something I hadn't expected. It was a sweetness not marred by decay or divinity. Something older? Though it was hard to imagine anything that was older than us. Even though the Titans came before us and before them had been Gaia and Uranus—and before that?

I had no answer.

The dog rose as we neared the olive tree, giving off one low and soft bark to announce our arrival.

Irina paused at the edge of the spiral. The stones were worn, chipped and pitted by time. The pattern had been set deliberately. There was no mistaking that. It wasn't just a symbol, but some kind of memory encoded geometry.

It reminded me of...

She stepped into the spiral and the moment her foot crossed into the path, the wind shifted. Only slightly, but I definitely felt it and so did she.

Her head snapped up and her tumble of hair blew back from her face. "It's humming."

It was. Not an exact sound, but definitely a vibration. A harp string plucked deep underground. She walked slowly, spiraling inward, and I followed just behind her, my steps shadowing hers.

She passed the same stone three times before she paused, crouched, then brushed her hand over it, revealing a mark. It was nearly faded with age, yet still discernible beneath the dust. It was a sigil. Not Greek. Not any symbol of the divine languages I knew. Not any modern glyph.

Older. Crude. Yet something about it struck me low in the spine. Two crescents, back-to-back, joined by a vertical line. Beneath it, three points etched in a downward arc. A moon. A gate. And—

"She buried her name here," Irina whispered.

I went still.

No fear marked her tone, only awe. She glanced back at me. Her eyes gleamed, not gold or shimmering with the aches of the past, but wet with something half-formed.

"I mean—*I* did," she clarified. "Or, maybe I helped. It wasn't a grave. It was a choice. We buried my name. My *first* name. Before Kore. Before Persephone."

What she didn't add was before the long list of names she'd worn since then.

Turning back to the stone, she traced the sigil again. Her fingers trembled.

"I was someone else here. Before myths. Before

Olympus decided who I was allowed to be." She cast me a quick apology with her eyes. An apology I never needed from her. Her indictment of Olympus was a judgment on them. I'd long avoided aligning myself with them.

She stood then walked the final turns of the spiral. At the center, the earth was darker, richer, like it had been turned in the last season. Above it, nestled into a fold of bark, the olive tree had grown something half-hidden.

A strip of faded cloth, wound around a bone-colored shard, porous, maybe wood, maybe ivory. A keepsake. A token. She closed her fingers around it, removing it, and the tree didn't resist.

"I loved someone here," she said in a soft voice. "But I don't think it was romantic. I think it was deeper. Soul-bound. Someone who taught me how to return. Someone who reminded me that I could be bound to the world and not just fate."

I wanted to speak, but the reverence in her voice kept me silent.

Turning toward me again, she held the token like it might disappear were she to release it. "I think this is the name I gave to myself. Not one someone else placed on me."

Her voice caught and she swallowed hard.

"I don't remember what it was yet. But I remember the feeling of it. The breath held at the top of the hill. A laugh before it breaks. *Home*."

At her feet, the sigils in the stones began to pulse.

One by one, faint blue light flaring like heat lightning beneath the surface, they blazed in recognition.

The dog whined low in his throat and took two steps forward, tail still and ears flat. He looked at the spiral's center and then delicately lay down just beside it. Guarding. Witnessing

The sigil nearest me lit up.

A deeper hue now. Not just blue, but violet edged with gold.

Then I felt it. This wasn't just a memory. This was a piece of her foundation. Memory without language. Name buried among the bones of time.

I moved to her side. "You don't have to rush it."

She didn't answer me immediately. "I'm not," she said finally. "But it's coming back. Like an earworm, I can hear the music but not the lyrics. Not yet. I think—I think it's singing me back to myself."

Her hand clasped mine once more. "I think we're getting close."

I believed her.

She didn't speak again. She didn't need to. The moment she clasped my hand while holding the token she'd taken from the bark, the sigils flared even brighter at our feet. A soft light rose through the stone, a breath exhaled through the veil.

No thunder.

No earthquake.

No sudden, violent explosion.

Just complete stillness.

The vibration shivered over my ribs, into the marrow. The tremor before the lightning strikes. Not terror or warning, only presence.

The dog lifted his head. And gazed at the center of the spiral with a solemn, impossible calm.

Irina—wait. No, *she* stepped into the center of the design as if gravity adjusted for her to make it so. She didn't glow. She *resonated.* The moment she crossed into the exact center, the sigils aligned and finally, I saw it all for what it was.

It wasn't just a path. It was a *lock*.

She was the key.

The violet-gold sigil beneath her flared, the air bent, and memory flooded the space with the density of an unseen sea.

The cloth-wrapped token in her hand crumbled like ash. From its center, a single syllable glittered into being.

I couldn't hear it. It didn't matter. She could. Her breath caught. She swayed, one foot back, her weight shifting and then she spoke.

A name.

It was none of the names I knew, clearly. It was something older, wilder, and composed of syllables that belong to the earth, the wind, the stars, and *choice*.

When she said it, the spiral sank. The whole circle of stone and earth folded inward and descended like a slow-turning helix

Beneath the spiral, a chamber of light opened. Tangible. Warm. Cradling. Something in my chest seized. This wasn't Olympus, the Underworld or even the mortal plane. This wasn't even a place meant for gods. This was *hers*. The in-between place. The liminal.

It was the breath between heartbeats. This was where her soul hid the first version of herself before anyone claimed her. She turned to me once more, and her face wasn't shining. It was whole.

"Do you see it?" Her voice was steady despite the giddiness in her eyes

"I see you." It was my promise. My oath.

Like she couldn't not touch me, she linked our hands again. Then she led us down the steps into the chamber below. The dog and I both followed. As we descended into this soft light, it hit me.

This wasn't the end of the journey.

No, this was not about *endings* at all.

This was the first time she'd been allowed to truly come home.

CHAPTER
TWENTY-TWO

IRINA

It didn't feel like descending. It felt like remembering how to breathe. The chamber unfolded around me not in architecture, but in sensation. Warm air scented with crushed laurel and thyme, something like sun-warmed stones, and the faintest flicker of water in motion.

Yet, there was no stream. No walls. No ceiling. Just presence and *light*. So much light. Soft, diffused, not from above or below, just *here*.

I let go of the token, or at least what remained of it, and it dissolved in midair like it had simply been waiting to be unmade, job complete.

Graven followed in my wake with the dog padding behind us. Though the animal paused at the threshold and settled there to watch. This was my space and he knew it. The flash of insight was just there. A knowing. A truth.

Graven came closer, brushing his fingers against mine. I didn't take them again, not this time. I wanted to. I loved the way he held my hand. At the moment, I needed to feel the air on my skin. I needed to be unmoored from my anchors and standing on my own feet. I needed to feel my own weight and to breathe...

That's when I saw her.

Or rather, *me*.

Maybe she was the first version of what I had been or could have been. She stood at the far side of the chamber, barefoot on stone that glowed faintly beneath her feet. Her hair was long, black as pitch, her skin the color of olive bark and her face... It wasn't like looking in a mirror.

I was Irina now, and I had been so many others before.

This woman, this being, she was the origin. Clothed in a robe of woven green and pale ochre, the earth and the stalk, wrapped together. Around her neck was a simple cord without a pendant.

No crown. No symbols. Nothing *claimed*.

I stared and she canted her head. She didn't smile or offer any threat; she just waited.

"What is this?" I whispered and the words came out rough and a little rusty, like I'd forgotten how to speak for a moment. "Are you me?"

She blinked slowly. "No. You are me."

I staggered back a half-step. Graven's hand was there, pressed against the base of my spine. He didn't grasp or try to control, just steadied me. Grounded me.

The version of me—her—*us*... Yes, us. The version of us stepped forward.

"They called me Melinoë once," she said, and that name rang through me like a bell. Even my brain stuttered.

"I thought that was a myth." That name was associated with different stories and chthonic myths. But how could she...

"Most things are, until we return to them."

My throat tightened in both sadness and awe. "Why now?"

Melinoë knelt, pressing her hand to the center of the chamber's floor. Where her fingers touched, a spiral of light unfurled, smaller than the one above, tighter. A map. A seed. A lock.

"Because you remembered enough to speak the true syllable." Her gaze lifted to mine. "Because you chose. And because he," she continued, her gaze flicking to Graven, "let you."

My chest and throat both ached. So much emotion. Too much. Graven said nothing, yet I felt the shift in him and heard the breath he didn't release.

Melinoë looked back at me.

"Demeter took me first," she said. "Not from anyone. Not from Hades. Not from a father. She took me from *myself*. Gave me a name not mine. Raised me to be hers. Shaped me to need her. When I chose to love someone else and when I chose to leave, she called it betrayal."

A pulse of something electric shimmered around the chamber.

Truth.

"Why didn't anyone tell me?" Yes, I had asked this before, but it was inescapably sad that Melinoë had been locked away, denied her true self to become that which another desired.

"Because it is not her story to release. It is yours."

"But Mnemosyne—"

"Guards memory, yes. Not *access*. You were buried too deep. I hid you. And you consented." She sighed, a sympathetic sound as though she understood my pain. Of course she did, it was *our* pain.

"Then why unlock for me now?" My voice trembled. If the others could only offer me fragments, I needed to know all of it. "Why let me become this again?"

Melinoë moved to me now, close enough that I could feel her actual warmth. She was *real,* not just spirit. She raised a hand and I thought she might touch my face, but she stopped just short and her hand hovered there, close enough I could imagine the contact, the connection.

"Because you finally said *your* name. Not the one given to you. Not the ones written in myth. The one you buried. The one that will set you free"

The pressure behind my eyes increased, and it wasn't just tears. There was a crack—a dam, finally splintering. Not breaking, but opening. Just as suddenly, I knew there were more names. More selves. More truths.

But this one—Melinoë—she was the root. The door we couldn't find because it wasn't built of symbols but of choice. And Graven... creation help me, I looked at him and the ache surged all over again.

As much as I had been Kore and then Persephone, I had always been Melinoë under it all. We hadn't just left this world or fallen in love. We chose. We'd been drawn to Hades even then, before Demeter came.

We loved after because he asked us for nothing. Because he waited and waited and never stopped giving. He hadn't known Melinoë, but we had known him.

The spiral beneath my feet pulsed again, brighter this time, like it knew I was ready to begin—but then, something inside the chamber *tilted.*

Not visibly.

Not structurally.

It was like pressure changed—like the air remembered something *it* didn't want to carry.

I inhaled, then immediately stumbled.

Graven's hand was at my elbow, steadying me. His voice was low. "What is it?"

My vision wavered, like heat rising from stone. I reached up, fingers brushing beneath my nose—

Wet.

Warm.

I stared at the smear on my hand.

Blood.

Just a single drop.

But it shouldn't have been there.

I pressed my wrist to my face. "It's nothing. It's—" A second drop fell.

Melinoë turned her head sharply. Her expression changed. Alert. No longer serene.

"You're being pulled."

"What?" I blinked, dizzy now. "By who?"

"Someone outside this place. One who isn't meant to reach you here." Her voice was clipped now. Grim.

Graven's hand tightened on my arm. "Can it be stopped?"

"I don't know," I whispered. "I don't even know who it is—"

Even as I spoke, a pressure mounted behind my eyes. Not memory this time.

A signal.

A call.

Like a thread being pulled taut from far away.

And then—*a voice*, filtered like it was underwater but *real, immediate*, cutting across the chamber—

"Irina. Can you hear me?"

I gasped. "Mara?"

Graven's head snapped toward me. "Don't answer her."

"I'm not—I didn't—she's not *here*, I don't think—" My words came in the same stutters as my thoughts.

But she was close.

Closer than she should've been.

The dog growled low in his throat—ears pinned back, spine arched.

Melinoë stepped forward, a hand raised as though to shield the space. "You are not *hers* to summon here. This chamber predates her authority."

"She's just trying to check on me," I murmured. But even as I said it, I tasted copper. More blood.

The light in the spiral dimmed slightly. Not fading— *shielding*.

Graven stood between me and the descending light now, his eyes hard, voice even. "I'll sever the tether if I must."

Melinoë didn't disagree.

She moved to the edge of the light and pressed her palm against the curve of the chamber wall. The sigils flared again, this time in red-gold rather than the warm white from before.

"You can't be touched here," she said. "Not unless you *invite* it."

I took a breath.

Steady. Shallow.

The pressure eased.

But the blood didn't stop.

Graven moved to me, hands at either side of my face. His thumbs brushed the edges of my jaw, tender. *Grounding.*

"Look at me," he said, quiet but resolute. "You don't have to go back. Not until you're ready."

"I don't want to go," I whispered. "Not yet. I'm just... not sure how to stay."

The spiral beneath me flickered again.

Melinoë murmured something. It wasn't Greek or Latin. Not in any language I remembered, but my blood responded. It slowed.

The tether frayed.

And somewhere—*far away*—Mara's voice faded like a tide pulling out.

Irina...

I exhaled.

Then looked at Graven again.

"I need to keep going," I said. "But you—"

"I stay," he interrupted. No hesitation.

Even the dog pressed up against my side again, as if to underline it.

The light beneath us brightened once more.

A name reclaimed.

A door opened.

The boundary held—just barely.

The light steadied, the blood stopped. I took another breath, not to ground myself but to let go. Weirdly, Mara reaching out had reminded me of the city, of the Annex, of my work—but also of reality, like this was some kind of fantasy.

I blew out another long breath. *Let go*, I reminded myself. Let go of logic, of resistance, of the instinct to just understand everything. I wasn't a scientist here.

Correction, I didn't *need* to be a scientist here. Graven shifted next to me, moving so he was slightly behind, present but protective. The dog moved up to flank me on my other side, his lanky limbs as awkward as his head was noble.

Melinoë stood in the center, waiting so patiently I imagined she could wait an eternity if I needed it. Had waited.

"Will it hurt?" The quiet question escaped me. The pain wouldn't stop me, but there were all kinds of pain.

"Some of it," she answered in the same soft voice. I'd prefer honesty to lies, right?

Still, I hesitated. "Is it all true?"

"Truth is a prism. Memory is the light that passes through."

"Great," I muttered. "Cryptic me is *so* helpful."

Yet, I still smiled, despite myself—literally. I was still *me* after all, no matter what layers had been peeled back. I wasn't lost.

Extending a hand, Melinoë said, "Come."

No time like the present. Girding myself, I stepped forward and clasped her hand. I fully expected the floor to fall away. For the world to shatter. For everything to just spin wildly. Something.

Nothing broke, though the spiral shifted slightly, bending downward into a sloping stairway. It wasn't just stone or air or dream, but all three at once.

We descended. The light changed as we moved. Amber to violet to the color of dawn before the sun began to stretch his arms upward. Each step was a pulse beneath my feet, a reminder of being touched by me before.

My fingers tightened on hers.

"Why don't I remember being her?" *Why don't I remember being you? Being me?* All three were the same, right?

Melinoë didn't glance back at me. "Because your body wasn't built to hold this essence. Your mind was never meant to carry this many lives at once. That's why the forgetting was sacred. Necessary."

"And now?" *What aren't you telling me?* Even though I hadn't said those words aloud, I suspected she heard them. Or maybe, since we were a "we," she heard them or thought them herself.

Myself.

This was all so confusing.

When she turned to face me, her expression had filled with a gentle sadness. "Now, you're asking to remember not just who you were, but you're becoming."

She continued to guide me down the path to the next chamber. This one was smaller, round, and all stone. An olive tree stood in the center, its roots coiling like veins into the floor, The branches were full and filled with—tokens?

Locks of hair.

Tatter scraps of fabric.

A burned quill.

A broken ring.

A child's ribbon, once green.

I reached for one, acting on pure impulse, but Melinoë caught my wrist. "Not yet. These are echoes. Lives you lived. Choices you made. Regrets you buried. You can't hold them—not until you reclaim the name that bore them."

Of course, I couldn't. I almost muttered an imprecation, a frustration. But Melinoë didn't deserve my irritations.

"How do I do that?"

She glanced down at the base of the tree. Beneath the roots, just barely visible, a single *name* had been carved into the stone.

Not English or Greek, but I *knew* it. Felt it behind my teeth and in the hollow of my ribs.

Kneeling slowly, I reached out. As my fingertips brushed the name, everything *shifted* again. The roots stirred, the tokens swayed, and the lights dimmed, only to return as *sound*. It was a soft hum, a lullaby almost and sung in a voice I had loved once. Maybe as a child or maybe as a mother.

Maybe both. My eyes stung.

"Don't cry," I whispered to myself, to the roots, to the name. The tears came anyway. Melinoë knelt beside me, placing her palm over mine and anchoring us both to the carved letters.

"Say it." The command resonated.

I opened my mouth to protest that I didn't know how, but it came out. The name tasted like rain on clay, harvest smoke, sunlight, and sea salt. It tasted like truth.

When I said it out loud, the tree answered, the tokens rustled, and the roots lifted enough to reveal what had been hidden beneath them.

A silver key. Small. Unadorned.

Even as I reached for it, my hand trembled. I expected it to burn when I closed my fingers around it, but it only pulsed, once, twice, and then stilled again.

"What does it open?"

Melinoë didn't answer until I lifted my gaze to hers. She smiled truly for the first time. "The next door."

I glanced back at Graven. His eyes were focused on me, wide, dark, and soft.

He didn't ask me for what I saw, nor did he try to take the key. All he said was, "I'm still with you."

"I know." That truth was embedded so deeply within me, it seemed to be forming the new bedrock of who I was. I treasured it. I tucked the key into a pocket that formed in the sheer robe as though summoned by my need.

Maybe it had.

The dog wagged his tail. We were all ready to move again.

CHAPTER

TWENTY-THREE

She moved forward like the spiral had always been hers. Like the ground itself remembered her shape.

I should have followed, but I paused. While I didn't doubt her, I did owe someone else a moment—a truth.

Melinoë was already dimming. Her form flickered at the edges, folds of her shadow-blurred robe loosening into the walls of this in-between place. The spiral chamber breathed around her.

"Is it done?" I asked her.

She turned her head slowly. Her face was not beautiful in the way mortals meant, but terrible and sacred in the way old gods were. Eyes like the dark between stars. Mouth soft as the hush before sleep.

"Almost."

"She remembered her name," I said.

Melinoë inclined her head. "The name beneath the names. The truth before the roles."

I studied her for a long moment. "You knew. This whole time."

She didn't smile though her voice held the weight of something gentler than pity. "I knew only what I was allowed to know. Memory is a temple with many locked doors. I hold a torch. I do not hold the keys."

"But you guarded hers."

"Not out of obedience." While she owed me no explanations, I was honored she shared any information with me. "Out of respect. She was more than a maiden. More than a queen. She was never meant to belong to either."

Silence pooled between us. Deeper than thought.

"*Despoina*," I murmured, tasting the name on my tongue. Not a name I expected, yet it didn't surprise me either. "It's not a name the others speak."

"Because they fear it." Her gaze sharpened. "It unravels the stories they built to contain her."

I glanced toward the path Irina had taken. I could still feel her presence, pulse-light in the air. The dog barked softly up ahead, as if guiding her forward.

"You stayed here for her," I said.

Melinoë nodded. "I am the bridge. I do not cross. I do not remain. I hold the passage while others forget, and release it when they remember."

"Then this is goodbye." I swallowed.

For the first time, Melinoë looked... uncertain. Not frightened. But exposed.

"I have not witnessed the key retrieved in many, many lifetimes." Her eyes found mine. "You have no idea what it cost her each time it was denied. What it cost *you*, waiting."

My chest felt suddenly hollow. There was no cost I would not pay for her. "I would have waited forever."

"You nearly did."

Her form shimmered again, flickering along the edges of space like candle smoke. She turned to follow Despoina's trail but did not take a step. Instead, she looked back at me one last time.

"Stay beside her. Even when she forgets again. Even when she doubts the truth of this moment."

The warning lay in her words. *When* not *if.* "I will."

She nodded, soft, solemn. To my surprise, she lifted one hand to my chest, just above my heart. A whisper of cold. A small, bright pressure. Something *settled* there.

"A final gift," she said. "From one who walks the boundary, to one who guards it."

"What is it?"

Her voice was already fading. "A reminder. When she is lost again, you will find her here."

Then, on a breath, she was gone. Not vanished. Just *returned* to the shadowed corridor from which all memory once emerged.

The silence left in her wake was not empty. It was *sacred*.

I turned, the weight of her parting still warm against my chest, and followed the path where Despoina—where *Irina*—was waiting with the key. The key, the dog, and the door.

Once I was with her, she moved ahead with purpose. Barefoot. Robed. Crownless, and yet more sovereign now than I'd ever seen her. The dog padded beside her—long-limbed and almost too large for the space now, ears perked, pace sure. Loyal to the pulse of her. Every moment that passed, he seemed to grow further into his form. A guardian, becoming.

And I—I kept a pace behind. Just enough distance to watch her without intruding.

She didn't turn. Didn't speak. She wasn't trying to leave me behind. Something had changed inside of her and she listened inwardly to that change, to the name she had just reclaimed.

To the ache of lifetimes pressing against the walls of her mind like waves against glass. To the way the chamber trembled slightly with her every step.

I considered the *final gift* Melinoë had given me.

I didn't know what she meant, not fully. Only that something subtle had embedded itself just beneath my skin. I rubbed a hand to that spot, to the echo pressed into place. It hadn't hurt. It hadn't glowed. It had just *settled*, like the feeling of a remembered word that had not yet surfaced.

Was it a marker? A compass? A compass felt right. But it wasn't one attuned to direction so much as devotion.

"When she is lost again, you will find her here."

But where was *here*?

Not a place, I suspected. Not this chamber. Not even this myth. More likely, she had given me some element similar to what she had guarded, a *truth*. A threshold. A state of being that only love could navigate.

Love. I let that emotion swirl through me. Ahead, Irina —*Despoina*—stopped near the next archway. Her shoulders shifted. She was breathing deeper now. Not from exhaustion, but from the slow act of *returning to herself.*

She pressed her hand to the wall. The sigil we had unearthed behind the spiral door was still glowing faintly behind us, like a heartbeat lingering in the stones. But this space was quieter. Thicker. A breath held too long.

She tilted her head slightly. The dog sat, tail thudding once. She turned and her gaze found me. Of course she wasn't surprised to see me; she'd known I was here.

"You're not going to let me do this alone," she said softly.

It wasn't a question. It wasn't even a test for me. She wanted to comfort herself. I stepped to her side, careful not to brush her too suddenly. Her fingers still lingered against the wall, searching.

"I told you," I murmured. "I will always choose you."

She didn't reply, or at least, she didn't with words. She reached for my hand, threading our fingers together. Her grip was strong. Fierce.

The air ahead of us continued to pulse. It was thick with memory and possibility. Whatever waited beyond the next threshold, I knew two things.

She would face it, and I would be right alongside her.

At the door, she squared her shoulders as if she had done it many times before. Maybe she had. Maybe Despoina had stood here a dozen times in a dozen lives, but it had been more than an age since she passed through. The stone knew her, and the threshold trembled with recognition.

She didn't hesitate now.

The key she had found—etched in her memory, revealed through blood and olive-root and spiral song—fit into a groove in the stone that hadn't been there until her hand found it.

There was no click or glow; the stone merely accepted the key and the door shuddered out a breath as it began to open.

It didn't part like something mechanical. It *peeled*, like petals of basalt uncoiling from a flower that hadn't bloomed in ages. Silvery light, soft and lunar spilled out.

A memory soaked in rain washed over me and wrapped

a lullaby from before language around us. Irina didn't flinch.

Her body tensed with recognition and knowing so old it had lived beneath her bones before she had a name.

The dog let out a low, near-whimpering sound and pressed his head gently against the back of her knee. He didn't cross the threshold, but his eyes were wide and solemn, locked on what lay ahead.

I moved beside her. For a moment, one single, solitary moment, I saw what she saw. A wide chamber. Circular. Its walls pulsed with carved veins of glowing stone. The ancient sigils were knotted patterns of grief and grace, with starscapes that shifted and breathed.

In the center of it all: a pool of still, black water.

But the water wasn't empty. It held reflections that didn't match the space around it. Lives flickering past the surface—Thessaloniki, Berlin, Kyoto, Paris. Not memories, exactly. Not visions. But *echoes*. As though each incarnation of her had left behind a single drop of their voice here, preserved in a chamber that had waited for her to reclaim it.

The air was thick with the scent of myrrh and ash. Olive oil. Cold metal. Wildflowers pressed in old books.

Deeper still below it all was the same *truth* that beckoned us on this journey to begin with. The kind that didn't announce itself. The kind you had to *choose to see*.

Irina's fingers trembled in mine.

She stared into the pool, and her reflection rippled, fracturing for just a breath into a dozen different faces. A child. A queen. A singer. A fighter. A girl in a garden who had never been just a daughter.

One by one, the faces smoothed into her own.

Irina. Despoina. Both. All.

She opened her mouth.

Before she could speak, a sound rang through the space like a bell dropped into still water. Low. Pure. Final.

It came from *beneath* the water, from *within* her and from whatever woke in the chamber with her arrival. It was all of them. I didn't ask if she was ready; I didn't need to. My fingers never left hers.

Together, we stepped forward.

The chamber pulsed, softly, almost imperceptibly, as though it were breathing her in and remembering.

Irina stood motionless at the edge of the dark water, the folds of her robe drifting slightly as the air moved. She looked carved from resolve and doubt in equal measure. Her reflection in the pool shimmered, then fragmented again, as though even the surface had to adjust to the fact that she had arrived whole.

She wasn't alone in herself anymore.

The room *felt* that and somehow, it responded to me, too.

Not in the same way. Not in the way it responded to her name or her blood or the thread of divinity braided through her soul. But the chamber didn't resist me. It *acknowledged* me. Dimly. Like a place long-forgotten nodding to a familiar shadow.

The air shifted near the columns, a hand brushed across a harp string, too deep to hear but present enough to feel in my bones. One of the sigils carved into the far wall flared briefly. Had it recognized us, too?

A second later, I felt a soft pressure against my calf.

The dog had circled back. Wordless, silent, he leaned into my leg with a practiced familiarity—as if he'd done this a thousand times in lives I couldn't remember.

A reminder. A tether.

An invitation.

I lowered my hand to his head, fingers brushing his ears. He pushed into the touch for half a heartbeat, then turned again and padded toward her, toward the pool. But he stopped just before the edge. Waiting.

For her. For me. For *all of it*.

Slowly, I wasn't sure what I expected, resistance, maybe. A barrier. An ancient recoil from my presence in this place clearly meant for her. But there was none.

Instead, the floor beneath me gave the faintest glow, like footprints illuminated just behind each step.

Something—*somewhere*—began to hum. A resonance. The matching note of two strings across a great distance. My gaze flicked back to Irina. She had turned slightly and looked at me over her shoulder.

Eyes darker now, rimmed with something ancient, something *hers*. Behind all of it, still her softness. Still her *will*. Still the woman who had pressed her hand to my chest and told me why she chose me.

She didn't need to speak. The squeeze of her hand brought me fully flush to her side. The dog sat again, close enough that our knees nearly brushed his shoulders.

The chamber brightened slightly with presence. Whatever waited here, whatever truth was about to unfold, it had *waited for both of us*.

Not just her, the goddess reborn. Not just me, the death-god lost in devotion. But the *togetherness* of us.

We faced the pool.

It began to change.

The pool's surface broke without a sound.

No splash. No ripple.

The water bent around the rising image, ushering it forth in welcome.

Irina inhaled softly beside me. The dog didn't move.

The memory took form in threads of silver and dusk—light stitched into shape until it became something *real*.

A courtyard. Walled in by wild olive trees. Moonlight so pale it was nearly blue, spilling over stone steps and marble pillars. The scent of sweet grain and tilled earth, green things and gold things, the kind of scent that sticks to your skin when you've walked too long beneath the sun.

A girl knelt by a well. Not a child. Not yet a woman.

Not yet stolen.

She looked up. Her face was Irina's. Not completely, but enough that my heart lurched. In this life, this memory, she was Kore. She bore the flush of springtime across her cheeks, the strength of growing things in her hands.

There was a tension in her. Even then.

She was listening to a *pull*. A calling from the earth. From somewhere deeper.

Just behind her, unseen by that younger self, a shadow moved through the trees. I stiffened at the approach. It wasn't me as I was now or Hades as I had been then or even Aïdes, as I approached her.

Yet *someone* who watched her with ancient eyes.

I felt it before I saw her.

Demeter.

She stepped into the memory like someone walking back into a wound. Beautiful and sharp, cloaked in gold and green, the harvest woven into every step. Her presence hit me like a memory I had no right to feel this sharply.

Irina leaned forward slightly, eyes wide in... conflict. A sharp thread of pain tugged at the corners of her expression.

Then the memory *spoke*.

Demeter's voice filled the chamber, not booming, or even divine, but *personal*. Terrifying only in its precision.

"You don't *need* to know what lies beneath, child. You are *enough* here. With me. This is where you belong. Where you *were planted*. I made this world bloom for you. Isn't that enough?"

The younger Kore did not answer. Though her fingers curled tight around the well's edge, and her gaze *shifted*. Downward. Into the dark.

Toward *me*. Even then, before we had truly met.

The pool shimmered again, the memory flickering, losing clarity. But *not before* I saw Demeter step forward and gently press her hand to Kore's shoulder.

Not before the girl *flinched*.

It wasn't harsh. It wasn't cruel.

Though it wasn't harsh or cruel, it was still a claiming. A quiet, possessive gesture. Gentle fingers that said: "You are mine."

The memory dissolved like smoke into the chamber's breathless hush. I staggered—not with my body, but *inside*.

Because it wasn't the first time I had felt that power. That need. That *grasping fear* dressed as love. Demeter had not wept when Persephone left.

She had *raged*. She had withered fields, split trees, and brought ruin to those who praised spring without her permission. She hadn't *mourned* the loss of her daughter.

She had mourned the loss of *ownership*.

I had seen it once, in another lifetime. Another cycle. Demeter's eyes, hollowed by fury and betrayal. Not of Persephone's disappearance, but her choice.

The memory was clear now. In Paris. After Élise's fire. When I had tried to find the thread of her soul and felt something else tighten around it.

A force not meant to be there.

Demeter.

Not blocking the descent—no.

Reclaiming it.

Like a god refusing to return borrowed time.

The chamber grew cold with the weight of what I'd remembered. I turned to Irina—her face pale, her lips parted, hand tight around mine.

"She took you," I said quietly. "Not once. *Again and again.* Even when you tried to go elsewhere."

Irina swallowed.

Grief and recognition both flickered in her eyes. She had felt it too.

A presence she once trusted, twisting into a cage she couldn't see.

The air had gone sharp and charged, the air before a summer storm, when everything stills in anticipation and you realize the silence itself is *warning you.*

Irina hadn't moved yet. Her fingers were still laced with mine. Still warm. Still here.

Yet there was no escaping this revelation. Demeter would feel it. *Would know.* The memory was a key, and we had just turned it. Not just Irina's reclamation, but her *resistance.*

She had always loved Kore best when she was obedient. Blooming. Rooted. Quiet. The maiden held in sunlit gardens, smiling softly while her soul withered underneath.

But Irina was no longer a spring flower. She had stepped through too many doors. Remembered too many names. I feared what Demeter might do when she realized the girl she once held tight now stood beside *me.*

Not in defiance, but in *freedom.*

I released Irina's hand only long enough to brush two fingers down the curve of her wrist—a quiet signal. *I'm with you.*

Then I moved.

The dog followed at my heel.

I crossed to the far wall of the chamber, where the stones still held the pulse of the memory. Not bright. But ready. I knelt and pressed my hand against one of the still-sleeping sigils—not to open, but to prime.

If she came…

If she forced the path open, in all her harvest fury and love-turned-obsession…

Then I would be ready.

Not with swords. Not with death. But with truth. That was the only thing that could meet her now.

"I'll shield the chamber," I said, glancing over my shoulder at Irina. "If she comes through, I can't stop her entry. But I can slow her reach."

"Then?" Irina's voice was low, steady, but her eyes glinted with something fierce.

"Then we hold our ground," I said. "Together."

Because if Demeter was still holding a piece of her—if she'd twisted the thread of Kore into a chain—then she'd come to reclaim what no longer belonged to her.

But this time, I wouldn't let her walk away with Irina's soul wrapped in vines and silence.

This time, I was *here,* and I had no intention of letting her be taken again.

CHAPTER
TWENTY-FOUR

IRINA

It shouldn't have felt like a decision, not after everything. Not after the memories, the lives, the stolen names, and the shadows pressed around each truth like barbed wire.

At the same time, it *was*. Each breath. Each step. Each word from my mouth that sounded like mine and not mine, hers and not hers—Persephone, Kore, Élise, Leto—*all of them*—I had to *choose* to keep going.

To stay.

To be here, *now*, in this skin and with this truth unraveling around me like vines gone wild.

I wasn't built for this. Not really. I was mortal. Human. My body was bones and blood and memory pressed into a shape barely capable of containing all the lives waking up inside me.

Yet, there was Graven. He said, *I will always choose you.*

He tethered me. That single, resonant truth wrapped

around my ribs and spine like armor. Not chains. Not vines. Not someone else's dream of who I should be. But *a choice.*

Mine.

When I looked at him, at the way he prepared, calm and certain and full of a kind of quiet fury for *me*, I understood something else:

I wasn't alone in this anymore. I never had to be again. Something warm pressed against my leg.

The dog had circled back. His long limbs were a little too big for his body now, tail swishing slowly. His gaze was fixed on me, bright and strangely solemn. Not just a pet. Not just a creature born of instinct and loyalty.

No.

He *knew.*

His eyes held the weight of too many doors. The knowledge of things old and unspoken. He had been waiting for me—not as an accident, but as part of something older than this body, this life.

I knelt in front of him, fingers curling into the soft scruff behind his ears.

"You've been guarding me," I murmured. His nose bumped gently against my chin. "And now you'll help me find the rest of it, won't you?"

He sat straighter. His tail stilled.

Something passed between us—*not words*, not even images. Just understanding.

He was more than a companion. He was a guardian. One of the hounds. One of the gatewalkers.

I didn't know his name.

Not yet.

But he had chosen me, too.

"Okay," I said aloud, and rose again.

The chamber pulsed behind me, something deeper

now. Like the memory had stirred the foundation. A hum that crawled across my skin and into my blood.

I looked at the next door and I felt it before I heard it. The shift in the air.

Anticipation.

Something was coming.

Someone.

For once, I didn't flinch. I rolled my shoulders back, heart steady. "Let her come," I whispered.

Whatever Demeter thought I was still carrying for her, whether it was grief, guilt, or obedience, I would face it. I would face her.

With Graven beside me.

With the hound guarding my path.

With every piece of myself I'd reclaimed *lighting the way forward.*

The silence was too sharp, too vast. If I let it, it would swallow me whole.

So instead, I looked at Graven, took in the way he crouched beside the doorway like some mythic sentinel in a T-shirt and worn jeans, barefoot and glorious, and said, "This is definitely not the outfit I imagined wearing to face a goddess."

He glanced over at me. "You're not a fan of the robe?"

I tugged at the fabric. "It's cozy. It's also aggressively not armor."

His mouth curled. "I find it... dangerous."

"Dangerous?" I arched a brow.

He leaned closer, voice lowering. "Something about bare feet and nothing to lose."

That drew a startled laugh from me. The kind that cracked a little, uncertain and breathless. "You're ridiculous."

"And you love that about me."

"I'm still deciding," I shot back, grinning despite everything.

The dog huffed and flopped against my leg like he was tired of waiting. I reached down to stroke his ears, then looked back up at Graven, more serious now.

"Do you trust me?" I asked.

Graven didn't hesitate. Not for a heartbeat. "With all that I am."

I stretched out for him without thinking, brushing my fingers along the sharp line of his cheekbone, marveling at the warmth there. *God of the dead*, yes—but so *alive* in this moment it made my chest ache.

"Then know I will always find you," I whispered.

His gaze burned steady into mine. "And I will never give up."

We lingered there in the hush between heartbeats— gods and ghosts and past lives held at bay for the smallest, most *eternal* moment.

The light shifted.

The chamber exhaled.

The air thickened, the pressure folding inward like gravity had changed its mind. The dog stood first, alert and tense, fur bristling just slightly.

Graven's hand reached for mine.

Then, she arrived. No door opened. No signal sounded. Demeter simply *was*.

The air grew sweeter. Thick with the scent of crushed wheat, rain-soaked loam, and wildflowers caught at the edge of overgrowth. The room dimmed from the weight of *harvest and ruin* wrapped in skin.

She stood across the stone span of the chamber, wreathed in green gold and shadow, hair like firelight and eyes that had once wept for the child she thought she'd lost.

Her gaze locked on mine and the silence shattered. She looked exactly the way I'd always imagined her, and nothing at all the way I remembered.

Demeter.

The name landed in my chest like a weight and a flare. Recognition and recoil, grief and rage, all folded inside the hollow between heartbeats.

She stood framed by golden light that had no source, the air warping faintly around her with life. With season. With *expectation*. Her presence was so thick I could barely breathe through it.

But I *did*.

I took a breath.

And I didn't bow.

"Hello, Mother," I said, the words scraping my throat like roots tearing through stone.

She flinched.

It might have just been a flicker. But I saw it.

Then her face hardened into the kind of calm only grief can wear. "Irina," she said carefully. "Or is it Persephone again?"

I didn't answer. *She* didn't get to decide which name mattered most.

"I remember," I said instead. "Not everything. Not yet. But enough."

Her expression didn't change. But the ground beneath my bare feet shifted subtly. A slow, warning thrum beneath the stone.

Graven moved slightly beside me. I felt his stillness. Ready. Absolute.

Demeter's gaze flicked to him. "You brought her here."

"She came here," Graven said quietly. "I didn't force her."

"No. You never did, did you?" Her voice twisted around the words like thorns. "You just waited. Watched. Took her when she didn't know enough to say no."

"I *chose* him," I snapped, sharper than I meant. "I *remember* choosing him."

Her eyes darted to mine again. Pain etched around them. "That's what you *think*. But it wasn't your choice. Not then. Not the first time."

"Because you made it first." The words fell out before I could stop them.

Demeter went still.

The dog growled low, deep in his throat.

I stepped forward, chest tight with something ancient and furious. "You took me before anyone else ever could, didn't you? Not Graven. Not even the ones who came before. *You* took me first."

"I *saved* you!" Her voice cracked like thunder over a dry field. "You don't understand what the gods do to those they hunger for. You were a child—*my* child—and I *saved* you!"

"No," I said, shaking. "You *claimed* me. You shaped me. Hid me in mortal skins again and again, tearing me out of the lives I chose because you couldn't stand that I didn't want to stay yours."

Tears sparked in her eyes, but they didn't fall. Demeter's jaw clenched as she flexed her white-knuckled fists.

"You *left me*," she said. "You left me, Kore. Over and over. You chose darkness. Him. *This.*" Her voice broke now, softer. "You chose death."

"No," I said gently, stepping closer. "I chose love."

A pause. Heavy as harvest. Demeter looked at me as if she might break apart and explode all at once.

Then, slowly, the façade of divine serenity erupted—just enough for me to glimpse the grief beneath. The mother. Not the goddess. The one who had carried me before I had a name, and who had never once known how to let go.

I wanted to reach for her, but I didn't.

Some things weren't mine to fix. Some truths had to rot before they could bloom. I was not here to soothe her sorrow.

I was here to reclaim my soul.

"I'm not yours," I said softly. "Not anymore. I was. I will always *love* you. But you can't keep me."

Demeter stared at me for a long time. "Do you remember the olive tree?" Her voice held a ragged note.

I did, so I nodded.

"I planted it for you," Demeter whispered. "So the roots would always find you. Even if I couldn't."

The memory unfolded inside me like a blossom forced open in winter. The spiral. The tree. The buried name. She hadn't just left a piece of herself behind. She had embedded her *claim*.

"I remember," I said, and it hurt.

Demeter took a step forward, expression hardening, that divine storm rising again behind her eyes. "Then you know. If you go further, if you press into what was sealed, you could unmake everything. The balance. The tether. The cycle. *You*."

"And if I don't?" I asked softly. "I stay in your garden forever?"

Her mouth twitched, wounded and furious.

"You can't stop this," I added, steady now. "You can't *keep* me."

Her jaw clenched. "You don't know what you're doing."

"I think that's the first true thing you've said," I replied. "I don't know. Not fully. But I know I'm *done* being broken up and replanted like a damn herb."

The dog growled, low and warning. Demeter's eyes flicked to Graven, and for a breath, the air *fractured*.

He didn't flinch. Didn't step in front of me. He just held his ground. But when he smiled, it was all teeth.

"Please," Graven said, his voice quiet and terrifying. "I *dare* you to try."

Demeter's lips parted, startled.

"She is not alone," he went on. "You are not ambushing her. And I will not hold back. You might be the earth—yes. But I am the devastation that will erase you. The land might recover eventually." A pause. "*You won't.*"

Even I shivered.

But I didn't pull away.

My heart ached for the woman who had once woven garlands for my crib and torn empires apart when I left her.

But the *goddess* in me understood. This cycle of birth and return and captivity cloaked in love, it had never been about protection.

It had been about possession.

I would *not* go back.

"I will be free," I said, locking eyes with Demeter. "Whether we scorch the earth or not is up to you."

The room darkened.

Golden light, thick and alive, gathered around Demeter, wild and vengeful. She looked ready to strike. Desperation pressed her. If she thought punishing me might keep everything from unraveling, she was so violently about to be proven wrong.

A shimmer tore through the chamber like a blade of ice. Wind that wasn't wind. Light that came from no source. A ripple of *Olympian power* descending. Graven's hand flexed on mine and the dog braced.

Voices rose in argument. Shadows and silhouettes in marble and flame. Then they were there.

Athena—cool-eyed and grim.

Hermes—smiling, but not kindly.

Artemis—bow in hand, unreadable.

Apollo—radiant, but tense.

Even Hera, whose silence weighed more than judgment.

Behind them, far quieter stood Mnemosyne, who said nothing but met my eyes, steady and calm.

"No more," Athena said to Demeter, voice as sharp as her spear. "You've done enough."

Demeter reeled. For a moment, I thought she'd strike them all down. Then her shoulders slumped.

Something in her broke. The light around her dimmed.

Hermes stepped forward and, with a gentleness I hadn't expected, touched her shoulder.

She didn't look back at me as they *dragged* her away. She didn't go as a prisoner, but as a goddess who refused to surrender, her power leashed by theirs.

The chamber held its breath after they vanished.

No thunderclap. No earthquake. Just stillness and the slow, deliberate press of the dog's weight against my leg. Grounding me. Holding me.

Graven hadn't moved. Not really. Not since he'd laid down that impossible line in the sand.

His hand hovered near mine. Not reaching—just waiting.

I let myself breathe. Shaky, shallow, real.

Then I turned to him, a wry twist at the edge of my mouth. "Do we dare believe that actually worked?"

He glanced at the space where gods had stood moments

ago, and his shoulders lifted in that graceful, inevitable shrug of his. "Whether she pushes the confrontation to another day... another year... another age—I will do exactly as I said."

He looked at me fully then, eyes steady and unflinching, the storm inside him tempered but no less fierce.

The dog leaned harder into me, as if confirming it all without words.

Graven's voice softened. "We are with you."

He took my hand now. No hesitation.

"So tell me, my love..." A breath. A vow. "Where to next?"

TWENTY-FIVE

GRAVEN

THE SEA-SWEPT CHAMBER

The salt hung in the air like a prophecy. Irina stood knee-deep in black water, the hem of her robe floating like fog, hair tangled from wind that wasn't real but remembered.

A lighthouse pulsed in the distance. A memory—hers, or someone else's. Another lifetime lost to waves and longing. She whispered the name of a drowned brother. A son she had once had. Her mouth trembled, and still, she spoke it.

The dog howled once, low and solemn, and the memory sealed itself inside her chest like a stone. She collapsed against me afterward, breath ragged. But she stood again.

She always did.

THE EMBER GARDEN

Ashes rained like snow in the field where a temple once stood. The ground was scorched. Olive trees burned to the root. And Irina stepped barefoot into flame. No fear. No cry.

Just memory.

She knelt where her altar had been. Kissed the charred soil and named her fire. *Phôs.* Her light. When she stood, her skin smoked. I pressed cool cloth to her wrists, and she let her head rest on my shoulder for five slow heartbeats. Her voice was smaller after that. Not broken. Distant. Like it was echoing through too many walls.

But she moved forward.

THE VAULT OF MIRRORS

She screamed in this one, only once. Her reflection fractured a hundred times over, showing every incarnation of herself: old, young, broken, cruel, divine.

One reached through the mirror and touched her cheek. The mirror shattered. Irina bled.

But she *remembered*.

And I wanted, truly for the first time in this journey, to destroy the world that had demanded she suffer for truth. The dog curled around her as she slept in my lap after, too exhausted to walk. I didn't sleep.

I memorized the shape of her hands instead, in case she forgot how to hold mine.

THE HALL OF ECHOES

The sound shook the bones of the earth.

Ereshkigal.

She was older than time, older than death. Still shaped from obsidian will and endless sky, from void-light and unmaking hunger. Beside her stood *Inanna*, the goddess, embodying love, fertility, and war. Less merciful.

We stepped into that sanctum like breath into the mouth of a sleeping god. I did not let go of her hand.

"I know what I am," Irina said, her voice steady in the presence of their silence. "I know who I am."

Ereshkigal's eyes, black and shoreless, shifted. Inanna only smiled, a crack forming in the veil of reality. "This should be a fool's path," she said, voice like a kiss of spring, bells cheerfully ringing.

"Should?" I asked, stepping forward, feeling some of the dread fall away.

"Yes," Ereshkigal answered in a voice like a grinding mountain, ancient and fresh all at once. "But it's merely the end of a journey—and the beginning of another."

The end of *theirs*. The women both gazed at Irina with what I suspected might be affection, but also acceptance. They were ready and had been. The light bloomed behind Irina—not borrowed, not given. Born. Not from them. *From her.* For the first time in ten thousand forgotten ages, Irina became more of who she always was. Not prey. Not a child. But a reckoning.

A QUIET BETWEEN STORMS

She slept again after.

On her side, curled like a fallen crescent, the dog pressed against her back, guarding even in dreams. I held fast to the last gift Melinoë had given me. She called it an anchor, so I kept it safe, nurtured in the cradle of my power.

If a time came during this journey she could no longer

remember herself, I would hold it for her. My hands shook, but my resolve never did. Should the time come that she needed my heart carved out, offered on the altar of her rebirth, I would give it.

Gladly.

THE GARDEN OF SILK AND STONE

We found her name carved into a slab of marble under the roots of a white cypress. A new one, not Irina, Persephone, or Kore.

Olwen.

Irina traced it with her fingertips, and something inside her *shuddered.* Like a fault line cracking wide open. She remembered the woman who had journeyed with her lover, desperate to complete every single task that would allow them to be together. Endless tasks, tasks no one thought they would complete.

"She never wanted to go back," she said softly, voice tight with grief and wonder.

"You don't have to," I promised even as I accepted the knowledge that she would. Because Olwen had left for love —and Irina was the part of her still brave enough to return for it.

HELIOPOLIS

Isis didn't look at me. She never had to. Her disdain was a blade honed over centuries, but I wasn't worried about her approval or lack thereof.

"So, you are back," she murmured. "Finally."

The words puzzled me. This being was not Irina nor any of the others, but she knew her. "Yes," Irina answered.

"What do you want?"

"My name." So much power wound through a name. Her challenge to such a primordial power was neither an entreaty nor a demand. It was an expectation.

With a long sigh, Isis lifted her gaze to the distance. I didn't make the mistake of looking away from her. She was a goddess of life *and* death. A being that straddled the in between. It made sense that she would have a piece.

"Do you think you are *ready?*" The coldness in her voice surprised me, but Irina merely shrugged.

"I think I am real and I think the name is *mine.*" She did not bend, her frail mortal frame stood even straighter as the goddess finally met her gaze. "I bled for it. I broke for it. I remember all of it."

"And after you have it?" Isis tipped her head. "You expect justice?"

"No," Irina said quietly. "I expect *freedom.*"

The silence after was taut as wire. I watched Isis measure Irina like a rival, not a daughter of the court. She flicked a glance to the dog, then to me before returning that speculative look to Irina. "*Nepthys.*"

With that utterance, she vanished.

Irina swayed.

I caught her before her knees hit the ground.

THE CHAMBER OF ECHOES

Her past selves spoke here. Too many voices, layered over one another. Laughing. Weeping. Cursing.

"*You were a healer.*"

"*You were a daughter.*"

"*You were a weapon.*"

Irina stood in the center of the storm and refused to flinch.

She looked at all of them—herself in warrior's armor, in temple robes, in bloodstained linen and bridal silks—and said:

"I remember all of you."

And then:

"But I am not *just* you."

The chamber fell still. Her nose began to bleed again. A thin line of red across her lip, sacred and raw. I wiped it away with my thumb, gently.

AT THE RIVER'S EDGE

The dog ran ahead, barking once into the mist. Irina followed, barefoot, robes trailing through reeds and damp soil.

I followed her, always.

The river looked like Lethe. But it wasn't. It shimmered with *choice*.

One step forward, and she could forget.

One step back, and she would remain mortal.

"I'm not giving it up," she said to no one in particular.

"Not your humanity?"

"Not anything."

I said nothing. Just stood beside her as she dipped her hand into the water—and came away with a flame, not wetness. Her eyes—her eyes burned with every life she had lived.

THE FINAL DOOR

It stood beneath roots and sky, silver-veined and waiting. The sigils thrummed, reacting to her touch before it even made contact. She staggered. Her breath came thin, but she smiled at me. Pale, trembling, beautiful in her stubbornness.

"If I fall," she whispered, "promise me you won't stop."

I cupped her face in both hands, pressing my forehead to hers. "I won't let you fall."

"You can't stop it."

"I *don't care.* I'll follow you into memory, into madness—whatever this is. I will not leave you alone in it."

She kissed me once. A whisper of a kiss.

Then turned and opened the door.

The wind changed. There was no warning. Just a weight in the air that pressed down like the hand of some vast, indifferent god—and then the sky itself split.

One flash of lightning, and Zeus stepped through. The ground he stood on cracked beneath his feet. Poseidon followed a breath behind, trailing seawater and arrogance, his trident humming with latent threat.

Irina didn't flinch.

I did not step in front of her—not yet.

But I *was ready.*

They had come in full form. Not avatars. Not projections. No polite illusions for the sake of mortal eyes. This was the pantheon as they had been in the old wars—divine, terrible, and unyielding. A violent punishment for her remaining mortality.

I would break both of them if I had to.

"Step aside, brother," Zeus said without preamble. His voice was thunder contained in bone.

"No," I said.

"This isn't yours to guard."

"She isn't yours to *command*," I returned. "She never was."

Poseidon's sneer was slick and cold. "Then you admit it. You claim her."

"I *stand* with her."

Zeus raised a hand, sparks crackling along his knuckles.

Irina stepped forward. Barefoot. Robes stained with dust and memory. Her breath shallow, her body visibly faltering. But her spine? Unbending. She looked at the King of Olympus and said, quietly: "You are not my father."

That stopped even the sky for a moment.

"You *dare*—" Zeus began, but Poseidon raised his trident in warning.

"She *remembers*," he murmured. He wasn't mocking. He was... wary.

Zeus's brow furrowed. "What does she remember?"

"Everything," Irina said. Her voice trembled—but not with fear. With exhaustion. With pain. And still, with defiance.

The dog pressed against her leg. A guardian, a friend, a sentinel of souls.

"I know what you did," she said to them both. "To me. To her. To all of us."

She swayed slightly. I reached for her, but her hand lifted—not to stop me, but to squeeze my fingers once. A silent *I'm still here.* Not for much longer. Not like this.

Her mortal shell, this body, this borrowed flesh, was almost done. It had carried too many truths, held too many burdens. The cost was etched in her skin, her bones, her breath. But her soul—

Her soul was radiant. Complete. And *theirs no longer.*

"I am not your vessel," she whispered. "I am not your pawn. And I will not kneel."

The dog growled. The earth responded. The very air shimmered.

When Zeus raised his hand again, I stepped between them. Power burned through me like molten silver. "Try it," I said, low and dark and final. "I *dare* you to try."

Poseidon tilted his head. "You'd go to war over her?"

"I'd go to *ruin*," I said. "And take you with me."

For a moment, everything balanced on a blade's edge. The old gods were far from sentimental, but most of the time they were not unforgivably stupid.

She stood behind me, shaking. Her heart barely held in her chest. But she was whole. She was *herself*. The whole of the universe, Olympus included, needed to understand I would *burn the sky* to keep her.

My brothers stared at me. Never had we been unified, not even when Zeus freed us from Cronus. Then he had declared himself king of heavens and Poseiden claimed the seas. I had no interest in battling either of them nor bowing to them.

None saw the value in the Underworld, save for me. Maybe they still didn't. I didn't care. But I had never offered to battle them before and they must have finally understood I meant exactly what I said. I would set fire to Olympus and cast it down and boil the seas until their kingdoms were barren. For while their power diminished, *everything* died. Even gods.

Zeus lowered his hand. Poseidon exhaled. "This will not end here."

"No," I agreed. "But it ends *with her*. Not you."

They vanished with a crack of thunder and salt and fury. Silence rushed in behind them. I turned. She was already falling. I caught her—light as breath, radiant as the sunrise—and she looked up at me with tears spilling down her face.

"I can't hold it," she whispered.

"You don't have to," I said. "I've got you."

Her body shivered once—then stilled, but her light didn't go out.

It *flared.*

The mortal shell fractured, and the god-soul rose. She was Persephone now. And more. Not a title. Not a myth. A *truth,* fully formed. The rebirth had come. She chose her shape, her form, and her name. She *became* what she should have always been.

I kept my promise. I stayed with her. I held her through it. I was the god who waited no more, because we were together.

TWENTY-SIX

PERSEPHONE

It was not the end. Not death. Not undoing. Not even silence. The pain as soul-fire burned away the mortal shell, and it cracked open to let me emerge, a seed given life finally.

When I opened my eyes, I was standing at the Gates. Not the cold steel security door of Thanatek's simulation rooms. Not the hall of data. This was the real place. The First Threshold.

Ancient stone. Skyless black above. An arch chiseled from obsidian and veined with silver memory. Symbols shimmered in the air—some I remembered, some I *had written.*

The Gates of the Underworld had always recognized me. This time, however, they bowed. The air vibrated. Then, he was there.

Graven was gone—no, *shed.* Unmasked. The illusion peeled away like twilight fading into dusk.

Aïdes. Lord of the Dead. My once-husband. My only constant.

His shadow-cloak rippled behind him like smoke caught in slow wind. His hair longer, black threaded with gold, his eyes molten obsidian rimmed in pale fire. A god returned to form, but so much more than that. *The one who waited.* The soul who chose.

With him, the dog. No longer soft-pawed and gangly. No longer "puppy."

Kerberos surged forward—three heads now, each different, each remembering me. One barked with joy. One whined, low and protective. One simply *watched*, tail sweeping a slow, thunderous rhythm against the stone.

I fell to my knees.

Not from weakness.

From awe. From gravity. From *recognition.*

Aïdes crossed to me without hesitation, the storm of his form gentling as he reached out. He knelt with me, his hand pressing against my back, warm through the thin folds of my robe.

"You're home," he said.

My hands trembled. The words trembled with me. "Then why does it still hurt?"

He exhaled, forehead touching mine. "Because you remember *everything.*"

I did.

The field. The tree. The first name. The stolen years. The gentle lies. The angry ones. The mothers who refused to let go. The brothers who tried to own me. And him—*always him.* Who *never* forced. Who *never* took.

"You waited so long," I whispered.

He nodded. "I would've waited eternally."

Kerberos leaned in, pressing all three heads close—

earth and ash and stars rising in his breath. He was larger than I remembered. All things in this place were.

"I didn't think I'd make it," I admitted.

"You did," Aïdes said. "Even when it broke you. Even when we all thought it might unmake you."

"Did it?" I asked, uncertain.

He tilted his head. "No," he said softly. "You *remade* you."

The Gates pulsed once. Welcoming. They opened. Not to let me *in*. To let me *through*. Because this was never the final stop. This was only the place I'd always had to pass through to become what I was meant to be.

Longing filled me as I stared into his eyes. "Remind me later that I have a gift for you."

Kerberos barked once, low, resonant, like a bell in the bones.

"You have my word." Aïdes rose and offered me his hand. "Come with me," he said. "There's more to remember. And still more to build."

I took it, coming home *finally* and from here, we could walk forward, together.

THERE WAS a silence that was not empty. It was ancient. Sacred. Alive.

The Underworld was never a prison, never meant to be a prison. It was a boundary for mortal and immortal alike. A place in between, and the root from which everything could grow. Now, it breathed again.

My hand still curled in Aïdes', the stone beneath our feet no longer cold but warm with the echo of memory. Lights shimmered along the ceiling, not torches, not stars

—but souls. Tiny glimmers of past lives, each one luminous with the weight of their own truths.

Kerberos stalked ahead of us, his three heads alert, calm. Triumphant. The halls opened as we walked, welcoming me with reverence, not fear.

Queen. The title wasn't one I sought, but I accepted because I was needed. Just as Aïdes had chosen the Underworld and loved me, he found me again and I loved him. We chose each other.

Then—they came. Not mortals. Not ghosts. The gods. One by one. Not with thunder or titles. So many came, some I had always known while others were just acquaintances. Still more had been born during my absence. They came with offerings.

Hermes was the first. Always first. A friend for so many lifetimes, always offering assistance when he could, and it often came with a twinkle in his eyes and mischief on his mind.

He stepped through the Veil with his usual grin, but it faltered the moment our eyes met. He wore no winged helmet today, only his traveling cloak, soft and weather-worn. From his bag, he pulled a bundle wrapped in silk and tied with a simple knot.

"For the roads you walked," he said, voice gentler than I remembered. "And those you still must." Inside were my sandals from an ancient life, woven with moon thread and ash bark.

I smiled and kissed his cheek. "You remembered." He bowed low, and *left the same way he always had—between one breath and the next.*

Hephaestus came next, massive and quiet, his hammer slung at his back. No words passed between us for a long moment. Then he offered a simple, strange object: a key, forged from obsidian and wrapped in molten gold filigree. On the head of it, my sigil burned softly.

"It's for you," he said. "Only you."

I touched the key. "What does it unlock?"

He glanced around. "Whatever was once denied." *Whatever you need.*

Aphrodite arrived in a gust of rose-scented light. Not adorned as the world paints her, but wild-haired, barefoot, and radiant with joy. "My love," she said, folding me into her arms. "We missed you."

I held her in return, stunned by how deeply I'd longed for this. When she stepped back, she brushed a hand against my brow. "We tried to love you in the way we understood love. You left, and we did not know how to grieve. We only knew how to *claim.* I'm sorry."

I nodded. "You've learned."

She laughed. "From you."

Others came.

Artemis, silent and fierce, pressed a crescent-bladed knife into my palm.

Athena, who lingered longest, said only, "I see now. We were wrong."

Dionysus, chaotic and bright-eyed, brought wine older than even this realm. "To freedom," he said, "and to the queen who earned it."

Even Poseidon arrived. He did not bow. But he did *kneel.* His trident laid at my feet, his head dipped low. "I was cruel," he said. "And you did not deserve it."

"I know," I replied. "But now—do better."

It wasn't forgiveness, only acceptance. He rose and vanished without fanfare.

Even Apollo and Ares made their own overtures, their gifts to curry favor, and the offering of an olive branch that I neither needed nor wanted. Still, I accepted, because I would have this time for us.

And yet—two did not come.

Not Demeter.

Not Zeus.

Their absence echoed louder than all the others' who came, but the Underworld did not mourn their lack. Because *I* did not mourn them.

Aïdes stood at my side, his gaze never wavering, his presence the anchor I had long forgotten I needed. I could feel the rage still simmering in him, what it cost him to let the others speak without striking, but he did it. For me.

Kerberos laid his body across the steps of the throne dais. Watchful. Loyal.

I looked at them both, and for the first time in all my lives, I did not feel torn.

I was whole. This was not a war. This was a *reclamation*. The gods had seen it. They had come to honor it. Not with chains. But with *respect*.

She came at the last, but I should have expected as much. Hecate was not known for needing the show any more than I was. We just wanted to exist. In her eyes were a myriad of mysteries and her smile held fast to her secrets. When I hugged her silently, she returned the embrace and held me tight.

"Good," she whispered finally as she drew back. "Now... *live*." Then she too was gone.

We'd never needed words.

THE AIR in the Underworld garden was thick with jasmine. Petals drifted on unseen currents, weightless as breath.

Somewhere nearby, a spring bubbled up through ancient stone, feeding the roots of trees that should not have grown in this place. Olive. Pomegranate. Cypress. Laurel. All living together in quiet contradiction.

We walked side by side, barefoot. He had slipped off his armor, though I knew he would don it again if I so much as faltered.

Aïdes. Graven. My shadow-twin. My keeper and beloved. My mirror. "You've made it beautiful again," I murmured, brushing my fingers along a low-hanging bough.

He gave a half-smile. "It was always yours to shape. I just kept the path clear."

A gentle breeze stirred the hem of my robe. Kerberos followed behind us, quieter now, just one head visible, panting contentedly like any oversized mutt, though his eyes tracked the far edges of the grove. Still guarding. Still vigilant.

"You said earlier," he murmured after a time, "that you had a gift."

Had I? Oh yes, the words had come to me before the others arrived. I stopped beside the olive tree. The one that always found me, even when I had forgotten how to find myself.

"I do."

He looked down at me, eyes darker than shadow and deeper than time. "You don't have to give me anything," he said softly. "I have *all* I need."

I reached up and brushed a curl away from his brow. My fingers lingered on his skin—warm now, alive with divine pulse. "This isn't something new," I said. "It's something old. Something that was *stolen* before it could be spoken."

He frowned, uncertain—but not afraid. Never afraid of me.

I pressed my hand gently over his heart.

Right where Melinoë had given him her parting gift. A thread, woven in silence. A spark he didn't yet understand.

Until now.

His eyes widened.

"You kept it," he whispered. "All this time..."

"I had to hide it," I said. "When I was taken, before *Demeter,* before the names, before all of it, I had to tear away this one truth. To keep it safe. Until I could return."

"And it's..." He trailed off, voice breaking with something he couldn't quite hold.

"Our child," I whispered. "The one we made before the gods fractured us."

He dropped to his knees.

Not in worship.

In awe.

His arms came around my waist and his forehead pressed to my stomach, reverent and silent. Kerberos curled close beside us with a whine, sensing the sacredness of the moment.

"They have been waiting," I said, voice raw with wonder. "Waiting to be called forward again. And now... I remember where I placed the spark. Melinoë carried it. So you could gift them to me again. So we could return whole."

He looked up at me, his eyes wet, luminous with the weight of a thousand years of devotion. "I will protect you both," he said. "I will raze the world then *rebuild* it if that's what it takes."

I knelt beside him, pressing our foreheads together.

"You already have," I whispered. "You found me, Graven. You waited, Aïdes. You *never stopped.*"

The garden rustled around us, alive with more than just wind. The Underworld pulsed beneath us—not as tomb, but as *womb*. A place where all beginnings were once endings, and all endings could begin again.

THE UNDERWORLD HAD CHANGED.

Or perhaps it would be better said that the Underworld merely *remembered* itself.

The throne was not made of iron, nor obsidian, nor gold. It was a living thing now—grown from the roots of the olive tree whose branches still curved above us, canopying the chamber in a soft, silver-green halo.

The light here came from nowhere, and everywhere, and in my arms, the twins stirred.

One was flame and hunger, gaze too ancient for the softness of his skin. The other was twilight itself, a silence that moved like thought, fingers curled tightly around my thumb.

"They are perfect," Aïdes whispered from beside me.

He stood watch, one hand resting lightly on the back of the throne. Constant. Eternal. Kerberos lay sprawled beside the dais, all three heads drowsing, though one eye always watched. The others returned to offer gifts and blessings of their own.

Hermes had left them a gift: a map that folded and refolded itself in infinite shapes—always changing, always guiding. Aphrodite had whispered blessings of devotion and strength. Even Hephaestus had left behind an unbreakable circlet: not for ruling, but for *remembering*.

Poseidon's gift had come in the form of still water, a

mirror that revealed only truth. He had bowed low. He had meant it.

Only two had not come.

Demeter had never returned or reached out. Neither had Zeus. But their silence did not undo the moment. Could not unravel what had been hard-earned, soul-bound, and forged in fire, grief, and devotion.

I looked down at my children, my *second bloom,* the seed I once hid in fear and returned to in full knowing—and smiled.

Aïdes moved beside me, and knelt. He kissed each child's forehead, then mine. When he met my eyes again, I saw not the Lord of the Dead, not the lost man from Thanatek, not the god forged from ashes and waiting—

I saw my beginning.

My equal.

My chosen.

"They will have their own stories," I said softly. "But this one… this one is ours."

He nodded. "And I will tell it for as long as stories are remembered."

Outside, the laurel moon rose—silver, steady, and soft as a lullaby.

Deep in the heart of the Underworld, where death no longer meant forgetting, I held both life and memory in my arms. We were the end and the beginning, and what we created together was life.

We were loved and we loved.

THE END

—or rather, the beginning again.

THE LETTER

My lord of silence, I remember you again.

The days are long in Siena now, but the nights longer still. I sit by the well behind my father's house, the one with the stone lip worn smooth by generations of hands—hands like mine, restless with remembering. I look into the water there, still as glass, and there you are again. Not as you were, perhaps, but as you became in me.

You must know, wherever you are, that I still think of you. Or perhaps you knew I always would. Everyone always says I am brilliant—too brilliant, as though a woman's mind is a dangerous thing to carry unguarded through the world. But with you... I never needed to quiet myself, never needed to dim or soften. You listened. I know this as I know you.

Now, in that silent pool, I see not only you, but the woman I was with you. Not a girl scribbling translations by candlelight, not the scholar's daughter in her father's shadow. I was the woman who laughed, who dared, and who loved.

I miss her almost as much as I miss you.

They still call me bold. They still say I am sharp, dazzling, impossible. But they do not know the hollow space beneath it, the place where your voice echoes—not in words, no, but in that silence we shared so well. You taught me silence was not emptiness. With you, it was presence.

I have no way to send this letter, this prayer to the one I know in my soul but cannot find. Yet, I must write this and hope that this prayer finds you.

Until we find each other again,
Livia

AFTERWORD

Thank you for reading. Truly.

Thank you for walking with me through the underworld and back. For stepping into this retelling with open eyes and an open heart, and for staying until the last page.

This story has lived inside me for so long—it has grown and shifted, whispered and roared—and now, having shared it with you, I feel both full and undone in the best possible way. These characters, this myth, this love story... it means more to me than I can say. I hope, in some small way, it found a place in you too.

Retelling myths isn't about rewriting history. It's about listening for the echoes that still speak to us now—the tenderness, the rage, the longing, the hope—and answering back in our own voice. It's about finding ourselves in the spaces between the lines.

I'm so grateful you chose to spend time in this world with me.

Until our next story—

xoxo

Heather

Website:
heatherlong.net
Reader group:
facebook.com/groups/heatherspack

About Heather Long

I *love* books. Not just a little bit, but a lot. Books were my best friends when I was growing up. Books didn't care if I was new to a town or to a class. They were always there, my trustiest of companions. Until they turned on me and said I had to write them.

I can tell you that my own personal happily ever after included writing books. I've always said that an HEA is a work in progress. It's true in my marriage, my friendships, and in my career. I am constantly nurturing my muse as we dive into new tales, new tropes, new characters and more.

After seventeen years in Texas, we relocated to the Pacific Northwest in search of seasons, new experiences, and new geography. I can't wait to discover what life (and my muse) have in store for me.

Maybe writing was always my destiny and romance my fate. After all, my grandmother wasn't a fan of picture books and used to read me her Harlequin Romance novels.

Follow Heather & Sign up for her newsletter:
www.heatherlong.net
TikTok

ALSO BY HEATHER LONG

82nd Street Vandals

Savage Vandal

Vicious Rebel

Ruthless Traitor

Dirty Devil

Shamelessly Loyal (Novella)

Brutal Fighter

Dangerous Renegade

Merciless Spy

Reckless Thief

Fierce Dancer

Dirty Dancer

Bay Ridge Royals

Shamelessly Loyal (Novella)

Battle Lines

Deceptive Truce

Wicked Surrender

Violent Chaos

Desperate Victory

BLOOD Brothers

Burn

Lure

Blue Ivy Prep

Problem Child

Mad Boys

Party Crashers

Money Shot

Bravo Team Wolf

When Danger Bites

Bitten Under Fire

Cardinal Sins

Kill Song

First Chorus

High Note

Last Word

Chance Monroe

Earth Witches Aren't Easy

Plan Witch from Out of Town

Bad Witch Rising

Fevered Hearts

Marshal of Hel Dorado

Brave are the Lonely

Micah & Mrs. Miller

A Fistful of Dreams

Raising Kane

Wanted: Fevered or Alive

Wild and Fevered

The Quick & The Fevered

A Man Called Wyatt

Going Royal

Some Like it Royal

Some Like it Scandalous

Some Like it Deadly

Some Like it Secret

Some Like it Easy

Heart of the Nebula

Queenmaker

Deal Breaker

Throne Taker

Lone Star Leathernecks

Semper Fi Cowboy

As You Were, Cowboy

Shackled Souls

Succubus Chained

Succubus Unchained

Succubus Blessed

Shackled Souls (Omnibus)

STANDALONES

Kiss of Fate (w/Blake Blessing)

Taste of Karma (w/Blake Blessing)

I'll Be Home... (w/Tate James)

Overexposed (w/ Tate James)

Switchboard Duet

Talk to Me

Don't Let Go

Untouchable

Rules and Roses

Changes and Chocolates

Keys and Kisses

Whispers and Wishes

Hangovers and Holidays

Brazen and Breathless

Trials and Tiaras

Graduation and Gifts

Defiance and Dedication

Songs and Sweethearts

Legacy and Lovers

Farewells and Forever

Hellos and Happily Ever Afters

Wolves of Willow Bend

Wolf at Law

Wolf Bite

Caged Wolf

Wolf Claim

Wolf Next Door

Rogue Wolf

Bayou Wolf

Untamed Wolf

Wolf with Benefits

River Wolf

Single Wicked Wolf

Desert Wolf

Snow Wolf

Wolf on Board

Holly Jolly Wolf

Shadow Wolf

His Moonstruck Wolf

Thunder Wolf

Ghost Wolf

Outlaw Wolves

Wolf Unleashed